Efrain T Concepcion
efrainconcepcion@icloud.com
Address
Phone Number

About 65,000 words

I0594733

Fractured Veil

ATLAS

by Efrain T Concepcion

Prologue

"The Eschaton [ESS-kuh-tahn] does not sleep,

In the caverns where sunlight drowns, I grow.

My children carve glyphs into basalt, older than their Nahuatl, older than their

Zapotec prayers.

They do not know I borrow their tongues to unstitch time.

The fifth sun's ashes taste like static.

I am the question their ancestors buried.

Soon they will answer"

NEXUS.

Chapter 1

The Hollow Veil

EARTH 2233

The barge groaned like a wounded leviathan as it carved through the Gloom's emerald haze, its hull shuddering beneath the weight of static that crackled like a thousand snapping bones. Samiel stood at the railing, his silhouette a monolith against the seething void. His armor—a biomechanical tapestry of matte-black meteorite—devoured the scant light, broken only by teal circuit veins that pulsed like subterranean rivers. The Zapotec glyphs on his chestplate, in coiled fury, glowed faintly, its obsidian scales rippling as shadows slithered across its form. Behind him, Reaper leaned against a corroded bulkhead, tossing a neural stim canister between gloved fingers. The vial's toxic green liquid cast jagged reflections across his scarred skull helmet, painting his smirk in fractured light.

A grizzled soldier nearby spat into the wind, his voice a graveled rasp. "Call it *Eschaton* all you want. Out there?" He jerked a thumb toward the writhing mist. "It's just the Gloom… and it's *hungry*."

Reaper's helmet retracted with a hiss, revealing eyes sharp enough to flay flesh. "Lighten up, *abuelo*," he drawled, nodding at a trembling analyst clutching a datapad to his chest. "Desk jockey here thinks *we're* the problem. *'Eschaton this, eschaton that—you're hurting the planet!'*" His mimicry was pitch-perfect, down to the analyst's reedy quaver. The man flinched, his boots scuffing backward as Reaper barked a laugh. "Tell you what, *papi*—

next time a Drake's chewing your face off, yell *'sustainability!'* See how that works."

Samiel turned, the teal circuits in his armor flaring like lightning in a stormcloud.

"Enough, Reaper." His voice was a glacier—cold, unyielding. "Save the theatrics for the

Gloom."

Reaper saluted mockingly, but his gaze snagged on the horizon. The Gloom churned

below, a living bruise staining the sky. Bioluminescent spores spiraled upward like inverted

snowfall, dissolving into static where they met the barge's flickering shields. Shapes moved

in the depths—too large, too *wrong*, their forms warping the haze like heat mirages.

"Approaching Sector 7, sir," Maximus called over the comms, his voice filtered to a

metallic growl. The youngest Warden stood at the bridge console, his armor's Zapotec glyphs

snarling across alloy-reinforced pauldrons, its feathered wings etched in jagged fractals that

mirrored the Gloom's chaos.

Samiel nodded. Sector 7 loomed ahead—a graveyard masquerading as progress. What

had once been a desert wasteland now bristled with a grotesque forest: trees fused with

biotech, their bark split by copper roots that stabbed into steel soil, leaves glitching between

organic decay and pixelated decay. At its heart stood the AEGIS lab, a skeletal spire

strangled by black ivy that pulsed with corrupted code, its veins oozing bioluminescent sap

where the mycelium network fought to reclaim its bones.

"No life signs," Maximus added. "Just… silence."

Reaper craned his neck, sniffing the air like a wolf scenting blood. "Smells like a

trap."

"Or a tomb," Samiel muttered.

The barge shuddered as it hovered, grav-struts that hissed and writhed, like tendrils of

Gloom rot retreating from the Wardens' armor. Samiel's circuits flared, syncing with the mycelium network beneath them—a silent war of light against shadow, teal veins battling emerald decay.

"Mission parameters," Samiel barked, his voice cutting through the static. "Lab went dark at 0800 yesterday. No distress calls. No signatures. Mycelium detects faint rot waves, but the perimeter's clean."

Duke cracked his knuckles, the hydraulics in his gauntlets whining. "Scans missed something."

"Always do," Reaper said, thumbing the safety off his plasma rifle.

"Gear up," Samiel ordered. "Barge stays on overwatch. Scan for mutations, new signatures, rot in the network."

"Yes, sir!" The Wardens' reply was a thunderclap, their armor hissing as helmets re-materialized shut.

No one knew where it began. The Old Earth Relics spoke of *"The Great Fracture"*—a cataclysm that split the world as if God had dragged a claw across its face. Continents cracked like eggshells: North America severed at the Rockies, Mexico and Canada cleaved into jagged islands. Eurasia collapsed into a labyrinth of canyons, while tsunamis taller than skyscrapers scoured South America and Australia to barren stone.

The survivors huddled in the corpse of Dallas-Fort Worth, now **Verdant Spire**—a citadel of fused steel and biotech where scientists clawed at miracles. They named the enemy *Eschaton*, then *Gloom*, as horrors crawled from the fissures: beasts of rusted iron and gnashing teeth, their cores weeping nanite slurry that rotted flesh and metal alike.

But in Mexico's ruins, whispers rose. At ancient sites—crumbling pyramids, bloodstained altars—the Gloom recoiled. Locals claimed ancestral ghosts guarded the land, but the truth was stranger: a mycelium network, half-tech and half-life, had rooted itself in the soil. Its bioluminescent tendrils repelled the rot, birthing sanctuaries where engineers grafted fungal nodes to steel, soldiers to symbionts.

Scientist doctors' engineers all rushed to study the new development. Could it be the earth rebalancing power, turning the tables in this war? Soon, Dr. Ceaser Vasquez cracked the code. The network was tech and nature fused into one. Spreading the network was imperative. The properties of the mycelium network provided answers and more sustainable tech to fend off the gloom.

The dawn of a new age began, technology and nature fusing as one. It restructured the fight; AEGIS the new ERRA AMC military were no longer behind in the fight, the WARDEN program was initiated.

Samiel's voice crackled through the comms, sharp as a blade. "Go, go, **go!**"

The Wardens leapt from the barge, their grav-chutes humming to life. They drifted downward like specters, silhouetted against the Gloom's emerald haze. The chutes emitted a low, resonant whine, barely audible over the wind screaming past their armor—matte-black carapaces etched with teal circuitry that throbbed like alien veins. Below, Sector 7's forest writhed, a grotesque Eden where bioluminescent fungi clawed up steel skeletons of dead drones, and black ivy choked the ruins of the AEGIS lab. The air stank of ammonia and decay.

"Stealth priority. Soft landing. Scan for abnormalities," Samiel ordered, his voice stripped of warmth.

Reaper landed first, boots sinking into soil that *hissed* and recoiled. "A-firm, Cap," he sneered, though his fingers lingered on the trigger of his plasma rifle. The ivy here wasn't just overgrown—it pulsed, its obsidian leaves threaded with corrupted code that flickered like dying static.

Maximus touched down silently, his armor's Zapotec glyphs flaring as his scanners lit up. "Lab sighted. 300 meters. No movement. No heat signatures."

"Copy. Move out," Samiel said.

The Wardens fanned out, their armor's bioluminescence casting jagged shadows. Sector 7's forest was a paradox: vibrant moss carpeted rusted artillery shells, and mycelium blooms glowed sapphire where they devoured Gloom rot. Yet the silence was **absolute**. No insects. No wind. Just the creak of their armor and the crunch of brittle flora underfoot.

The lab loomed ahead, its once-pristine walls now a tapestry of decay. The words "DAWN LAB" hung askew over the entrance, the letters choked by ivy that leaked viscous, tar-like sap. Reaper crouched at the door, running a gloved hand over claw marks gouged into the reinforced steel—grooves deep, *precise*. The lab stood silent, the airship pad desolate, the network working hard to reclaim its territory overgrown in a matter of days; a wondrous sight, nature absorbing tech all while persevering and safeguarding against gloom rot.

No movement, not a whisper, not a vehicle in sight, no personnel outside, no security, just dead silence.

"Moving to the door" : Reaper

"Maximus recon the area, scan for signatures. Keep the barge informed of our progress" : Samiel ordered.

"Copy that" : Maximus replied

"it's too quiet cap I don't like this" : Duke

"it's either a trap or an ambush, no AGEIS lab is this Quiet" Reaper stated

"Focus. breach and start clearing head on a swivel" : Samiel

"Someone fried the system from the inside. Looks like we got to go in the old fashion way, placing charges stand back" : Reaper said.

A heightened awareness falls on the wardens, the bioluminescence mycelium on their armor slightly brightens in intensity in response, a living, breathing armor that molds with its warden effortlessly, analysing every change in their body

"Hit it" Samiel ordered

The blast tore through the silence. Blackened steel and ivy shrapnel rained down as the Wardens stormed inside, weapons raised. The corridors beyond were a nightmare of contradictions: walls overgrown with luminous mycelium, their gentle glow clashing with the carnage. Shattered drones littered the floor, their circuitry spilling like entrails. Bodies lay slumped at terminals—scientists, engineers—their faces frozen in blank stares, no wounds, no blood. Just… *emptiness.*

"First floor clear," Duke growled, kicking aside a drone's severed limb. Its wires twitched, still sparking.

Samiel gestured forward. "Regroup. Stay sharp."

The lobby was worse. A cathedral of decay. Mycelium veined the ceiling like bioluminescent nerves, while black ivy strangled the support beams, its leaves trembling as though breathing. The lab's lobby and entrance are an eerie sight, as if abandoned for years, as if the team were standing in the past and present at the same time. The wardens confused each room, desolate and lifeless.

"What happened here" Reaper asked nervously

"Scans show no gloom rot signatures whatever attack the base outside was weeks old, no life signs detected in the lab" : Maximus stated

"Alright, that's a bit of good news, let's split up to cover more ground in the bottom levels. Maximus and Reaper you guy take the server floor levels. I want you to jack in recovering any files and data on the work here. Duke and I will take advanced weaponry and combat, see if there is anything worth saving. Regroup back here and call in the barge to return to HQ to see what they make of this" : Samiel ordered.

"Copy that" they said in unison.

The team split each to their own elevator, Maximus and Reaper arrive to server room still operational, but the terminals scorched.

"Something isn't right here" Reaper stated.

"Hey, cap the terminals are fried just like the entrance, going to try to recover what I can. Keep your head on a swivel, whoever did this could still be inside" : Maximus.

"Affirmative," Samiel replied.

The air grows thick and heavy, could it be sabotage someone trying to gain access to AEGIS intel? None of this makes any sense. Why risk it so near the gloom? There are plenty of other labs further away. Maximus salvages code mostly fragments "subject 001: Symbiosis unsuccessful. vital signs stable, recommend-". It's cut short, the rest of the entry is corrupted. Samiel and Duke descend to find the labs core advanced weaponry and combat labs. The lab was an arsenal of horrors. Weapons hybridized with Gloom tech lined the walls: rifles with barrel mouths that *breathed*, blades forged from crystalline rot. Duke hefted a Voidspike Mark 1, its coral-like barrel flexing as if alive. A cryo-pod chamber stands empty and shattered, a neural injector glowing, blue laid on the floor beside it.

"What the fuck were they cooking up in here" Duke said

"I don't know. Maybe it's what destroyed this place," Samiel said.

Samiel picks up the injector and the device latched to his armor with a magnetic *snap*, its glow seeping into his circuits. His HUD flickered: **UNKNOWN SUBSTANCE.**

"It's gunna take time to see what's in this. Let's keep searching," Samiel mutters to Duke.

They search the entire level. New gloom weapons prototypes lay scattered.

"Time to do some shopping, hey Reaper. What kind of new toy you want? We got a whole buffet of goodies, brother?" Duke said eagerly.

"Oh yea brother get me something nice I could use an upgrade" Reaper responded

"We got a new EMP pistol capable of shooting gloom rot rounds" : Duke

"Oh, I like the sound of that stun and send those pendejos to meet their maker,"

"We also got a new spike rifle, Voidspike Mark 1, a fusion of organic artillery and gloom-piercing brutality," Duke says directing his gaze towards Samiel with a smirk

"oh! oh! oh! I want that one, yea that sounds good," Reaper eagerly muttered.

"This one's mine gentlemen" Samiel said with a grin

"Copy that cap thought this one might catch your eye" : Duke

"Aww no fair" : Reaper

"Caps got first dibs reap, you know that" : Duke

"They got any good melee weapons" : Maximus uttered

"Oh yes, don't worry Max. I have not forgotten about you, brand new plasma blade capable of cutting through even the most hardened of gloom threats,"

"I like the sound of that Duke" : Maximus

"Knew you would" : Duke

"Reaper, how about this Thorncaster? A wrist mounted launcher integrated with the network fire seed pods, on impact they explode into barbed vines that bind gloom entities. Ammo phoenix pods, and hemlock pods— neurotoxin pods that corrupt gloom entities codes causing detrimental malfunctions." : Duke.

"*Orale Wey*—— that's my kind of style babe—- were coming to you now," Reaper said ecstatically.

"Status on the dat--" comms cut short as a massive quake shakes the entire facility. The walls creak and groan, cracks appear in fortified concrete like veins.

A harrowing growl strums through the air.

" Warden team 22 Alpha, this is big bird over?" barge designation "big bird,"

"Alpha team copies big bird, did you get that on scans?" : Samiel

"A-firm. we have gloom signatures in your vicinity commencing orbital barrage well hold them off as long as we can, recommend you RTB asap"

"Copy that, you hear that gent regroup on me now"

"Maximus what are you picking up on scans" : Samiel

"I'm picking up 2 mole rats breaching our sector, followed by 2 gloom hounds, outside perimeter shows gloom goliath on approach and 5 gloom drakes not fully grown."

Maximus stated while rushing to the stair well.

"At the east stair well now we got 4 on our tail could use some help boss," Maximus

"Copy that" : Samiel

Samiel and Duke headed to the east stairwell. The stairwell trembled as Samiel and Duke sprinted downward, their armor's teal circuitry flaring crimson in the gloom. Six stories below, Reaper's plasma fire lit the shaft in strobing bursts, his curses echoing upward in a mix of Spanish and gunfire. *"¡Puta madre!* They're in the walls—*they're in the fucking walls—!"*

Duke slammed into the railing, his Voidspike rifle barking as he unloaded into the swarm below. Mole rats erupted from fissures in the concrete—hulking, half-mechanical abominations with drill-bit claws and jaws dripping nanite slurry. Their rot-blasters spat globs of corrosive code that sizzled against the Wardens' shields, filling the air with the stench of burning steel. Reaper backpedaled up the stairs, his rifle whining as it launched barbed seed pods. They exploded midair, ensnaring a hound in vines that pulsed with neurotoxin. The beast writhed, its razor-wire claws screeching against the steps.

"yes cabron,"

"puta madre, eat that puto. "

Mole rats, a birth of the gloom, they dig underground tunnels with accuracy, an amalgamation of tech and flesh. Bodies covered in gloom rot and decaying code. Drills and fangs capable of delivering deadly toxins to human life. Mounted on their back two rot blasters, not enough to puncture warden armor but deal considerable damage to slow them down.

Gloom hounds they proliferate at a rapid pace in the gloom, a hybrid of wolf and razor wire steel and flesh, extremely fast. Claws made of steel capable of slicing through metal and flesh with ease, a terrifying howl that disables comms and dampens warden shields leaving them vulnerable to gloom attacks, while also causing hallucinations.

Maximus climbs the stairwell backwards, firing EMP rounds, temporarily disabling the mole rats. One gloom hound jumps 2 landings, slicing Maximus in the process across his chest and on his shoulder. Its claws carved through Maximus's armor like parchment, rot seeping into the gashes. The hound landing in front of the two, pinning them, unable to advance. Reaper laying plasma fire on the incoming rats at the door when one disappears, carving a new entry underneath the base of the stairwell.

The mole rat bursts through the concrete, allowing the second gloom hound access, imminent death awaits.

"ahhhh" Duke firing at the mole rat that burst through the ground.

"Maximus is down! gloom hound sliced the shit out of him, the rot is entering his system," Reaper yelled over the comms.

Two blood-red eyes shimmer in the newly excavated hole. The hound begins to howl. The creature's howl split the air—a subsonic wail that turned Samiel's HUD to static and made the walls *bleed* bioluminescent spores.

The air thickens with static, the electrifying howl disables the warden shields briefly. Outside, the AEGIS barge is under attack, providing plasma artillery shells bombarding the edge of the gloom. And in an instant, 5 drakes appear out of the gloom, the 5 dragons attacking the ship in calculated assaults, trying desperately to destroy the barge's shields. Shell after shell hit the gloom cavern, causing massive destructive vibrations to the Dawn lab.

Hounds scale the walls of the cavern, desperately trying to flank the wardens inside. A cloud of smoke and static covers the rift, no line of sight, but the barge continues its barrage.

Two drakes are killed from the precision shells, babies compared to most in the gloom, falling as the last three cause severe critical damage to the barge's exterior hull. Power is draining the mycelium core is suffering damage, shields are dwindling.

The barge is taking heavy damage. Through the static smoke a horror glowing red and purple emerges, 12 feet tall, its body grotesque fusion of rusted industrial machinery, and gloom corrupted flesh. One arm ends in a hydraulic claw, the other in a serrated chainsaw blade dripping nanite slurry. its eye like a cracked screen looping static filled with footage of screaming scientists. Its Mouth full of razor-sharp teeth.

"GOLIATH!!!!" SCREAMED a man on the bridge

"Put some shells thru that thing!" screamed the captain

"Warden 22, warden 22, this is big bird respond"

The silent static succumbed to the sound of artillery firing, no one responded.

"Warden team ALPHA, this is big bird. We are being overwhelmed with gloom signatures; you have 10 mins to RTB, or we are leaving you, godspeed wardens, big bird out,"

The captain puts it on a loop, hoping the wardens would hear it if possible, but all that comes back is static.

Samiel leaps over the balcony, engages his Grav-chute, unveils his umbral fang, his matte black blade forged from a meteorite alloy called eclipsite. A rare metal found only in the heart of gloom-corrupted zones. Its surface absorbs light, leaving no reflection, and hums faintly with a sound like distant thunder. Two well-placed slices relieve the hounds of their heads as Samiel lands at the base of the stairwell. He sheaths his sword and grabs the voidspike a sleek rifle with a barrel forged from bioluminescent coral. The stock, once touched, transformed the living mycelium in it, matching his living armor. Spike pods fire from the barrel, burrowing deep into both mole rats before detonating.

A loud explosion sends both Samiel and Reaper flying back to opposite corners even though Reaper was one flight above the wave was unescapable. The stairwell fell silent, the echo of bombardments in the background, shells trembling the surrounding earth, causing visual glitches in the network. The roars of gloom beast filled the air as their fellow rotted brothers fall, howls in the distance pierce like razors through the warden's helmet.

"Shit are you good, Reaper?" Samiel growled

"Holy shit, boss I need that rifle, that fucking thing is sweet hahaa! I'm good though" Reaper responded

"Status check!" : Samiel

"Maximus is down, moving to recover" Duke yelled

A gargled static filled transmission comes over the air "ward-en -te-am=-alp= 5mins till RTB"

"Fuck you heard that boss we got 5 before they leave us" Reaper shouted

"Duke how's Max? sit rep" : Samiel

"It's not looking good, boss. He's got major blood loss, his leg is hit, his chest, and shoulder has some nasty gashes, gloom rot is setting in the network nanites are doing their best to repair— but we need to get him back to the barge," : Duke.

"Alright, activate his Grav-chute. lighten the load. Let's get moving, Reaper take point ill hold up the rear," : Samiel

" On me " : Reaper

The stairwell half decerped and destroyed, shake with the orbital bombardment inching closer, the ceiling releasing dust of bioluminescent mycelium network. The stride up seems longer than usual. The air is heavy. Each flight feels closer to certain death. The black ivy on the wall is ready for the men to fall and join their eternal graveyard. The wardens reach the lobby; At that same moment, a loud crash filled the room. The dome above came crashing down, the fungus ridden walls start pulsating faster and harder, the goliath burst through the wall,

"Goliathhhhh!!!!" screamed Reaper as he dove for cover.

The goliath raised its claw, and its gaze went to Duke and Max. It swiped toward Duke as he ducked down, leaving Max vulnerable. The sound of steel meeting meat a symphony the gloom reveled in; Max's head removed from his torso and sent flying out of sight, his body laid suspended, due to the Grav-chute being active. A shocking sight to the goliath. It gazed stunned at the sight of Max, but just as quick the chainsaw hand came slamming down to finish the job.

"Move!!!!"

Samiel screamed while aiming his voidspike rifle, unleashing a storm of spike pods in the goliath's direction, each one hitting their mark, Stoping him in mid swing.

"*Andale cabron*, take this," Reaper screams ass he fires his newly acquired thorncaster. The three break into combat like a majestic dance, a wondrous sight to behold.

Wardens are highly trained in hand-to-hand combat; most gloom beasts are impervious to ranged weapons, so fights tend to be up close and personal. Though ranged weapons are ineffective, AEGIS is constantly developing ranged weapons to be more effective. The only downside is gloom tech corrupts and breaks down either the weapon itself or the user, so range weapons must be used sparingly, making hand to hand combat more effective. Blows to the gloom beast core render them incapacitated typically the core is encased in a shield also, another reason ranged weapons serve less of purpose but are excellent for tearing apart limbs.

Samiel, already low on ammo, unsheathes his umbral fang and slices into the goliath, his shields weakening with lighting fast blows. His blade pierces through static, leaving nasty gashes oozing from the goliath. Duke fires his EMP pistols briefly, stopping the chainsaw hand leaving it temporarily disabled. Reaper moves into land a blow. A Gloom hound strikes him from the back.

"Pendejo!!!" he screams, unleashing his plasma blade center mass in the hound.

Orbital bombardments are now raining an ungodly storm of hell. Duke and Samiel battling the goliath, when suddenly a drake swarms down on top of them, letting out a flame of gloom rot.

"There's too many of them," Duke yelled while firing and slicing through the hordes of gloom beasts. A drake blasts its wings at samiel throwing him back into rubble. The goliath goes for the killing blow, chainsaw hand activated and in full force toward Samiel. The umbral fang makes short work of that, cutting through meat and steal samiel leaps up and takes the limb clean off but gets snagged mid-air by a drake. Trapped in its claws, the grasp getting tighter.

Reaper sees Samiel, he runs and slides to Max's lifeless body, spins him around, grabs his plasma sniper rifle and aims at the drakes claws, three well-placed shots stun the beast's grip, releasing Samiel, now falling back to the lab unconscious. The drake turns its attention to Reaper, a new target. With a loud cry, red and yellow eyes glare at its new prey and it dives.

"chinga su madre cabron let's do this"

Reaper arms too mycelium grenades and leads the chase. He runs out of the building towards the artillery fire from the barge. Reaper stops about faces and with a backflip avoids the drake's deadly grab while simultaneously sticking the grenades to its claws. As the drake Flys away, "boom!" the grenades explode, a bright red, shattering the drake's claws as it cries out in pain, metal rust and oozing rot come falling to the ground.

"sir the wardens" shouts a young woman on the bridge

"Warden team ALPHA come in. Do you read? Samiel, can you hear me, dammit?" said the captain of the barge.

"Their comms must be down, continue bombardment, clear all signatures, get them back on this ship," the captain ordered

More fire power rains down ass the warden team becomes overwhelmed. Samiel battered and bruised, lies on the ground wounded, bleeding slowly becoming infected with rot he turns to see Duke, still battling trying to make his way over to him butt kicked back against an opposite wall, mask half torn, Duke's eyes filled with rage. Still firing rounds Reaper leaps to his aid, sustaining a heavy claw swipe from the goliath across the chest, sending him through glass into an adjacent room. Everything slows down. Time seems irrelevant.

Samiel's breathing slows. He feels the creep of death approaching him, retracting his helmet. He grabs the neural injector he stashed away, not knowing what it will do or how it will affect him.

"fuck it," Samiel says, plunging the syringe into the base of his neck. He falls to the ground.

Duke in the distance fighting sword and gun in hand

"nooooo!!" he screams

The sound of his friend fading into oblivion, the world turning black, silence.

Black veins spread from the injection site, his eyes flood with holographic

gold, pupils fracturing into data streams.

"Hmm cold, cynical, im intrigued, ahhhhhhh! AEGIS warden should've known, oh

vitals critical, initiating combat protocols, overriding pain receptors,".

Samiel jolts awake.

"lets rewrite your obituary"

Samiel sees the goliath run toward him in a fit of rage. All gloom beasts stop their

current engagement and head toward the warden. A maddened frenzy in response to his

injection.

"what the fuck" Duke says shockingly

"get to the barge!!" Samiel shouted

Duke and Reaper watch in awe as Samiel cut through the goliaths knee, jumping over

him and slicing him in half up its spinal column, landing in front of him once again.

"Reactor shield at 87%, dislodged knee. Good job, very nice indeed." A voice utters

in Samiel's *head.*

his movement speed faster, his analysis of weak points and killing efficiency

dramatically increased.

"Who are *you*? How are *you* in my head? What the fuck is going on?" Samiel said.

"Not the time to talk 12 o'clock high gloom beast, drake incoming lunge and strike"

His body fully recovered, his armor fully repaired. Samiel leaps into action. The drake

swoops down, attempting to grab him. Samiel dodges and runs to its glasslike wings and

slides his blade through it, his blade even more black in intensity, as if the eclipsite had been

upgraded, as if he himself has been upgraded as well. The drake turns and spits the largest

trail of rot and flame on samiel, not a scratch. Samiel climbs his back as he struggles and plunges his sword into the beast's core. A loud gaping screech leaves the drake's mouth bellowing in pain. The shattering scream sends all the beasts retreating to the gloom. The lab falls silent. Samiel, overwhelmed, stumbles to his brothers, falls at their feet.

"I'm Atlas" The ai mumble in his head as he falls.

#

Chapter 2

Echoes Of The Serpant

Makeshift tents flutter under a sun-scorched sky streaked with glooms reddish green haze. Maria tends to the sick, a shattered wasteland, the pyramids of ancient earth barely visible through the smog, the network fighting ever radiant and blue pushing back the gloom, her obsidian daggers glowing faintly as she works. A child ventured too far from the network and was struck by an infant gloom hound, his arm gushing blood. Slowly, the rot creeps in.

The AEGIS compound sprawled across the valley like a titan's fortress, its boundaries swallowing the ancient Pyramid of the Sun and Moon whole. Fifty-foot-thick perimeter walls, forged from reinforced eclipsite alloy and threaded with bioluminescent mycelium, encircled the site, their surfaces studded with pulse turrets that tracked the horizon with predatory precision. Anti-grav Humvees and tanks hovered along the ramparts, their matte-black hulls bristling with rotary cannons and missile pods, while armored soldiers patrolled in phalanx formations, their boots crunching over gravel fused into glass by years of Gloomfire skirmishes.

The main entrance yawned like a steel gullet—a 100-foot-tall hangar door etched with Zapotec glyphs that glowed faintly as they cycled through encryption protocols. Behind it lay decontamination chambers: cavernous steel tubes where jets of ionized steam scoured Gloom rot from armor, and scanners bathed survivors in crackling blue light, searching for corrupted code. Those who passed emerged into a sprawling courtyard where the air buzzed with static and the hum of generators, the ground paved with hexagonal tiles that pulsed gold with every footfall, channeling energy to the network's core.

At the compound's heart loomed the **Spire**, a 33-story monolith of glass and steel fused with bioluminescent vines that snaked up its sides, their flowers blooming into holographic interfaces at each floor. The Spire's apex housed General Braddock's command center—a glass-domed observatory where tactical holomaps of Mexico shimmered above a floor inlaid with mycelium circuits. Below, terraced levels held labs buzzing with scientists in sealed suits, their gloves stained with Gloom sludge as they dissected Behemoth carcasses or coaxed fungal nodes to bond with artillery shells.

Around the Spire, smaller structures clustered like iron mushrooms: barracks with living walls that filtered air through moss, vehicle depots stacked with hoverbikes mid-repair, and greenhouse domes where engineers grafted mycelium to crops, their leaves glitching between organic green and bioluminescent blue. The gloom seems to tremble before these megalithic structures, the source of the network.

Maria knelt in a triage tent near the perimeter, its flaps stained with old blood. A child whimpered in her arms, his right arm blackened by Gloom rot, veins bulging with static. Around them, medics rushed through rows of cots, their voices drowned by the *thrum* of anti-grav tanks launching beyond the walls.

"*Xochitl, xochitl…*" Maria chanted, her mother's obsidian dagger pressed to the boy's seeping flesh. The glyphs along the blade flared crimson, pulling tendrils of corruption into the metal like water down a drain. The child screamed as the rot receded, his skin knitting raw and pink beneath her hands.

"Almost done," she murmured, her own veins flickering gold in response to the network's pull. Above them, the Spire's lights blinked like a constellation, and the ground trembled as a hangar door sealed somewhere deep in the compound—a sound like the earth itself grinding its teeth.

"There's a man, he roams the gloom a shadow, with a sword that drinks rot, he fights-" the child whispers.

"We all fight little one, get some rest" Maria cuts him off, leading him to slumber.

The boy's words froze Marías heart, though not showing emotion. Maria felt those words to the core of her soul. It seems the ancestors are trying to tell her something. Could it be prophecy? Or could the words be imagination? Since a girl, Maria has been plagued by the shadow man in the gloom. The man is seemingly an angel of death, but unable to determine if he is a savior or destroyer. The question always plagues her mind. 22 years have passed, still no sight of this shadow man. It leaves maria to question its true meaning. Why her? Why at these random moments? Do the ancestors not want me to forget? Am I destined to fight this new beast? The thoughts caress her mind often. The world has a way of leaving you to figure out the rest, a cruel way. The path is never certain, the choices never clear. The child's mother gifts Maria a quetzal feather, a relic from the old world. Maria remembers at 14 standing with her mother at Teotihuacán, staring up at the pyramid of the feathered serpent not too far from where she is now. Citlali carves a glyph into Maria's palm.

"When the serpent's shadow walks the gloom, you will meet him. His storm is your storm. Do not fear the blood."

"What if he's a *monster*?" young maria stutters.

"All serpents are until they shed their skin," Citlali says, eerie and stoic.

The alarm tore through the compound like a banshee's wail—a deafening, oscillating screech that drowned even the thunder of anti-grav engines. Maria's head snapped up, her dagger still buried in the Gloom-rotted flesh of a soldier's leg. The glyphs along the blade pulsed crimson, siphoning corruption into its obsidian edge, but the man's screams were lost beneath the klaxon's cry.

"Breach in Sector 3! All personnel, combat stations!"

The triage tent erupted into chaos. Medics scrambled to drag patients into blast shelters, their boots slipping on blood-slicked tiles. A holographic map flickered above the entrance, flashing red at the compound's eastern wall—where the Pyramid of the Feathered Serpent loomed, its ancient stones now laced with AEGIS's bioluminescent fortifications.

Maria yanked her dagger free, the blackened blade steaming. "Stay down," she ordered the soldier, slamming a mycelium-infused gauze over his wound. The fungal threads squirmed, stitching flesh and code. Maria, an assassin and healer, was trained to hunt and kill, gloom raiders. Mostly warlords attack this AEGIS base, to no avail. AEGIS is well equipped and guarding the network is the most important mission. Wardens serve no purpose here. Their cunning is needed in the gloom defending against the beasts it births. The human enemies are left to us. The attacks grow bolder warlords want control of the network surrounding the pyramids, a shift in the order of things.

They believe they it would serve better under their control, but everyone knows they want a bargaining chip to extort AEGIS. They try, and fail again, and again each time with more gloom rot weapons they devised from the waste the wardens leave behind, scavengers desperate for power.

Maria sprinted toward the armory, her boots crunching over shards of fallen bioluminescent glass from the Spire's upper floors. Above, the 33-story command tower blazed with emergency lights, its vine-choked façade alive with scrambling soldiers. General Braddock's voice boomed from the dome:

"Hold the eastern wall! Deploy the grav-tanks!"

Anti-grav Humvees shot past Maria, their engines screaming as they skimmed the hexagonal courtyard tiles. One skidded to a halt beside her, its gunner leaning out—a rookie, his face pale beneath his helmet.

"Medic! You need evac?"

"I *am* evac," Maria snarled, vaulting into the turret seat. "Go!"

The coyote, a scarred warlord draped in gloom tech armor with his raiders at his side stand before the enormous AEGIS compound.

"hermanos lay down your weapons. We have come to liberate you. AEGIS lies to you. They are not your protectors your a means to an end," Coyote screams.

"chinga te su madre cabron, we protect these lands and its people. The network will not fall under the control of a power hungry dog like you!" Maria yells, striking fear in the hearts of the raiders.

Maria has encountered the coyote many times, a man with a silver tongue with promises of salvation and redemption. The world united long ago, but some factions seek to destroy the peace that was made, driven by the lust for power. These men live beyond the network subject to gloom rot slowly, compromised by the evil in those lands. The gloom drives them mad with a lust for power, some say programing by the gloom itself in order to conquer the world. These men are abominations succumbed to gloom rot, fighting amongst themselves like barbarians. Too much time in the gloom can affect even the strongest of men and women without network armor. It's a slow wave of desperation that fills your heart. After 48 hours, it begins heightening emotions like anger and hatred, turning you unrecognizable to loved ones. The effects are reversible, but many choose the life of a scavenger, thinking being a pirate equates to freedom, but their thoughts and actions are not their own. The rot fuels them.

The raiders dash toward the front gate in a madden frenzied the rot coursing through their veins, making them more rugged to network weapons but not impervious, riding gloom rot hounds tamed by the rot ridden raiders. The rot in their veins allows them to blend their genetic code to the hounds, unable to distinguish them as an enemy allows for the raider to use them ass tools of war. The compound is vast and heavily guarded with network tech is unbreachable attacks such as this futile but AEGIS understands they are searching for a weak point, of which none exist. The mycelium network is a cohesive blend of tech and nature in every corner, building, and gate all interwind like a living, breathing organism capable of defending against gloom rot and alerting of flanks and beast approaching.

The Humvee lurched forward, slingshotting around a grav-tank. Maria gripped the plasma cannon's triggers, her eyes locking onto the warlord convoy. Their lead vehicle—a gutted AEGIS tank fused with a Gloom Behemoth's ribcage—crawled toward the wall, its "battering ram" a skull the size of a shuttle, eyes blazing with stolen network energy.

"Aim for the joints!" she barked. The gunner obeyed, unleashing a volley of ion rounds. The skull's jawbone shattered, but the warlords retaliated. A mortar of Gloomfire arced over the troops, splattering against the wall. The air sizzled, and the wall's gold sheild flickered.

Maria leapt from the Humvee before it stopped, rolling to avoid a spray of acid rounds that melted the ground where she'd stood. The eastern gate's wall hissed, sealing as warlords swarmed its exterior. AEGIS snipers perched on the Pyramid's steps, their railguns peppering the horde, but the warlords kept coming—some on foot, their limbs augmented with jagged Gloomtech prosthetics; others riding cybernetic hounds, their jaws unhinged and dripping static.

Maria unsheathed her second dagger, its twin glyphs humming. "**Atzin!**" she shouted. A squad leader glanced back, his visor cracked.

"Flush them toward the turrets! Now!"

She charged into the fray, blades whirling. A warlord lunged, his chainsword screeching against her dagger. Maria pivoted, driving her second blade into his augmetic knee. The circuitry sparked, and he crumpled—but not before grabbing her arm. His breath reeked of rot and narcotics. "Little *bruja*… The Coyote'll wear your skin…"

Maria slammed her forehead into his nose, then severed his spinal implant.

"Tell him I'm waiting."

The turrets above roared to life, their plasma fire incinerating a wave of attackers. Maria ducked behind a grav-tank's wreckage.

The network, connected to every living thing, the trees, the ground constantly fighting gloom code to ride the planet of its existence, a counterbalance that seemingly appeared out of thin air. The pyramids ground zero for tipping the scale in humanity's favor. AGEIS grav-tanks and hover-humvees line the outside perimeter.

The sky filled with bioluminescent rounds of plasma heading for the intruding raider's 1,000 strong, the raiders firing spike rounds at the AEGIS military. The raider hounds equipped with antitank rounds, shoulder mounted missiles fire at AEGIS technicals. AEGIS soldiers push back the charging horde with deadly accuracy, a fighting force of 100 capable of deterring thousands, unlike wardens regular soldiers use pistols and daggers in close combat to repel enemy threats along with the cohesive force of grav-tanks and Hover-humvees. Where warden are specifically trained for stealth incursion and dealing with the deadliest of gloom threats the regular military stands as a lethal fighting force on their own.

Wardens however are said to be equivalent to a fighting force of 1,000 soldiers. If seen on the battlefield, they are revered as angels coming to save the day, their armor almost fused to their body. Not a single soul has ever seen one outside his or her armor, only their faces are ever seen from time to time. It's said to be linked to their DNA. to become a

Warden you are put through the most brutal of tests few survive. these tests are meant to destroy you mentally and physically, for some gloom entities enter your mind and cause severe hallucinations. Their bodies undergo massive surgical procedures to reinforce bone and tissue with the network. Most who are chosen to undergo the Warden program are never seen again, but the casualty count is strictly top secret.

The battle intensifies the raiders' losing tremendous numbers, Maria and her echo blades craving through raiders like butter. Maria, in the midst of battle, sees the coyote. She focuses on her target. Prey in her eyes, the coyote meets her gaze and charges. Maria jumps over the hound and coyote landing perfectly. The coyote turns to Maria and laughs.

"Nice twirl *Mija* but you can't escape me,"

Maria smirks as she raises her blades.

"Two hilts, am i to surrender? Hahaha, should I be scared?" the coyote snarls.

 In a flash, the hounds screams in agony as their legs are cut from their body, Marías blades six obsidian shards that split into a swarm of AI drones capable of dismembering gloom entities. The blades hum, a frequency that disrupts gloom cohesion, allowing for the killing blow. The coyote falls from his hound and pulls his gloom rot sword. The dance begins, Maria highly skilled and extremely deadly with her blades engage the coyote, countering every swing of his sword. It appears Maria enjoys toying with her prey, as he is oblivious that he is no match for the deadly queen of chaos. She trips the coyote, and he falls to his face, angrier with each blow she lands, making him look like a fool. He lands a strike as he regains composure, slicing Marías' leg. Maria, having the upper hand, grows confident hubris leads to failure. In a whirlwind of flips, she dismembers the coyote's arm as he lets out a roar that echoes the battlefield.

"Retreat!" the coyote yells in his radio. He proceeds to yank a raider off his hound and ride away. The raiders, only 300 strong, now retreat to the wastelands, AEGIS suffering minor casualties return to the compound. The network, without hesitation, begins to repair any damage from the rot missiles ridding the land of the gloom-raiders.

The compound erupted in a cacophony of triumph. Soldiers hoisted rifles skyward, firing bursts of bioluminescent rounds that exploded like fireworks, painting the sky in emerald and gold. The air smelled of roasted agave and smoked meat as field cooks hauled out pre-Fracture grills, their flames licking at skewers of Gloomstag venison. A group lab techs drummed on salvaged fuel barrels, their rhythms syncopated with the pulsing hum of the network's core beneath their boots. Children darted through the crowds, their laughter echoing as they chased holographic butterflies projected from the Spire's terraces.

Maria stood at the heart of it, her armor streaked with soot and Gloom rot, accepting a canteen of spiked pulque from a grinning corporal. "*¡Salud, jefa!*" he toasted, his teeth gleaming in the neon glare. She drank deeply, the sweet-bitter burn cutting through the adrenaline still coursing in her veins. Nearby, a soldier arm-wrestled a hulking mechanic atop a grav-tank, his laughter sharp and infectious as he lost spectacularly.

The celebration faded to a muffled echo as Maria entered the Spire's core. Here, the walls were cold eclipsite, unadorned save for the faint golden veins of the network's roots. Zapotec glyphs spiraled across the floor, their light dimmed to a somber pulse. General Braddock stood before a 40-foot holoscreen, his silhouette rigid against the blue-white glare of a dozen surveillance feeds.

"You wanted to see me, sir," Maria said, her voice crisp despite the fatigue.

Braddock didn't turn. "Watch."

The screen split. On the left: footage of the battle's climax, warlords scattering under the network's wrath. On the right: a timestamped feed from the compound's rear perimeter. Two Gloom hounds—sleek, obsidian-scaled aberrations with eyes like cracked halos— prowled the shadows. Behind them loomed a **Gloom Colossus**, its body a grotesque fusion of tank treads and exposed vertebrae, and a **Goliath** with a drill-bit arm spinning lazily, its surface crawling with bioluminescent maggots.

The hounds sniffed the wall, their muzzles sparking against the network's shield. Then, the Colossus *moved*. It seized one hound and hurled it at the energy barrier. The creature disintegrated mid-air, its static-laced howl cut short as the network absorbed its code.

The second hound tilted its head—a disturbingly human gesture—and unleashed a howl that warped the feed into static. For three seconds, the network *stuttered*. The energy dome flickered, and a hairline crack split the wall's surface. Rot-code seeped through, black tendrils squirming toward the compound's core before the network sealed the breach.

The timestamp matched the *exact* moment the Coyote's forces had retreated.

"A diversion," Maria whispered, her blood chilling.

Braddock finally turned, his face etched with grim resolve. "They're learning. Adapting. The Gloom isn't just attacking us—it's *studying* us."

The holoscreen zoomed in on the hound's face. Its fractured eyes seemed to stare directly at Maria, pupils dilating into fractal patterns. Then, the feed glitched, pixels rearranging into a single Nahuatl glyph:

ĀTĒĪTL — *To See*.

The lights flickered. Somewhere deep in the compound, the network emitted a low, dissonant hum, like a wounded animal.

Outside, the celebration continued, unaware.

But Maria heard it.

The storm wasn't over.

It was just beginning

"What do we do" María said apprehensively

"What can we do? The network provides a balance to the gloom. It responds in kind, but sometimes I feel we are a step behind. I'll pass this video to Verdant spire immediately so they know what we are dealing with, and inform the Wardens. In the meantime, I want you to assemble a three-man outfit. I want you to track the coyote and recon his movements and report everything back to HQ. We need to know what we are dealing with. Keep your distance recon and observation only understood," Braddock ordered.

"Yes sir, right away," Maria answered

"If things go south, Maria, you're on your own. Make it back alive. We've lost enough life,"

Maria nodded, walking out of the command post. Marías nerves tingled with fear and excitement, finally a mission deep into gloom territory. It has been years, but at what cost, possibly her life? The air, still humming with victory and happiness, gave maria an eerie feeling. Retiring to her chambers, the walk felt long, longer than usual, her head running a mile a minute.

The compound had been her life only ever venturing out when needed, and only visiting Verdant spire for training and school, she was a secret weapon. The city was a marvelous wonder. She always dreamed of living there, but her mother was never fond of the idea worried of leaving behind important culture and heritage. The city is diverse and rich in many cultures. Her mother feared change. She wasn't ready to adapt to a new environment; she was growing old.

Marías' room door slides open, the mechanical swoosh bringing solace and warmth. The armored plates of Maria's combat gear clattered to the floor, each piece still flecked with dried Gloom rot and the coppery scent of battle. Her quarters, nestled in the heart of the Teotihuacán base, were a sanctuary of warm terracotta walls and handwoven tapestries dyed in cochineal red and indigo. But tonight, the room felt heavier, the air thick with the residue of near-death.

She winced as she peeled the blood-caked undersuit from her torso, the gash along her ribcage weeping faintly. The wound was a jagged crimson line, its edges shimmering with the faint gold of the network's emergency sutures. *Not fast enough.* Her mother's voice echoed in her mind: *"The body heals, mija. The soul… that takes longer."*

The bathroom was a cocoon of steam by the time she stepped under the shower's rain. Scalding water cascaded over her skin, turning the runoff rust-red as it swirled down the drain. She pressed her forehead to the tiles, her breath hitching as the heat seeped into the wound. For a moment, she imagined the Gloom's shadowed serpent coiling in the mist—a specter with too many teeth, its eyes twin voids. *"Come for me, then,"* she whispered, her voice swallowed by the roar of water.

Her obsidian blades lay on the sink, their edges catching the dim light. She noticed it: a soft, rhythmic pulse in the daggers' cores, like a heartbeat. *The shadowed serpent,* her mother's voice echoed in her mind. *His storm is your storm.* She traced the scar on her palm, the one Citlali had carved years ago—a coiled serpent biting its own tail. The wound from the coyote's sword had already closed, thanks to the network's med-nanites, but the memory of his laughter still needled her. *Could he be the one?* The water turned icy, jolting her back. She shut it off, the sudden silence deafening.

The bed awaited, its sheets woven with living mycelium that glowed like twilight. She collapsed into them, the fibers humming as they knit her muscle and bone. The room's decor wrapped her in a warm embrace: terracotta pots overflowing with marigolds, papel picado banners fluttering in the climate-controlled breeze, and the photograph—*the* photograph. There, frozen in sunlit amber, stood a younger Maria beside her mother at Teotihuacán. Citlali's hand rested on her shoulder, her smile sharp as a blade. The Pyramid of the

Feathered Serpent looming behind them like a stone god. The candles beneath the frame flickered, casting shadows that danced across Citlali's face, alive once more in the dimness.

Sleep came like a thief.

In the dream, the world was a bruise—purple skies split by green lightning. A feathered serpent, scales iridescent as oil on water, coiled around a wolf whose fur drank the light. The serpent's hiss was the scrape of a thousand knives. "Kai," it whispered—Maria's true name, buried since her mother's death. A single emerald feather detached, spiraling down, down, until it kissed a pool of black blood. The liquid surged, swallowing the feather, then her boots, then her knees—

She woke gasping, the sheets tangled around her legs. Dawn seeped through the window, painting the room in dusty rose. Her thigh was smooth, unmarred—no scar, no ache. The network's work. But the dream's chill lingered. She staggered to the dresser, gripping the photograph's edges until her knuckles whitened. *"Do not fear the blood,"* Citlali had said. Maria's reflection stared back from the glass—her mother's defiant brow, her father's stubborn jaw.

"What would you tell me now?" she murmured. The candles guttered, as if answering. Outside, the pyramids hummed their ancient song, and the shadowed wolf waited.

The sun crests over the horizon as maria thinks about what two soldiers to bring with her on her hunt for the coyote raiders. They likely need rot-speeders to make up for lost time and extra rations. They'll need a full stealth load-out and recon equipment, sniffers for tracking. AEGIS rot-speeders are perfect for this mission. The eclipsite armor absorbs light and radar signatures. The magnetic repulsors hover 6 inches above ground, leaving no tracks coated in bioluminescent gloom moss that mimics surrounding textures. The mycelium dampener emits spores that neutralize sound and thermal signatures, the symbiote core a living bio-reactor feeds on radiation and gloom toxins, converting them into energy, and for reinforcement pheromone trails, the bike releases chemical markers to guide AEGIS allies through gloom fog to their exact location, the perfect tracking vehicle. Maria adorns her speeder with Zapotec glyphs and quetzal feathers. She even gave hers a name called "Tonantzin breath". Only 12 exist made by her mother the blend of network, and machinery a beautiful testament to the network's adaptability and her mother's intelligence.

Maria, scrolling through personnel on her holo-pad, she concluded Roxy, and Baron are prime choices for this mission, Roxy an elite reconnaissance AEGIS agent trained in hand to hand combat and anti gloom tech and Baron an elite search and rescue operative with extensive gloom recovery efforts. They are the best of the best. Their expertise in the field makes them valuable assets in the mission. Maria sends orders for them to meet at the north gate at 14:00 hours new order from general Braddock.

The Teotihuacán base thrived under a sky so cerulean it seemed painted by gods. Sunlight spilled over the valley, gilding the pyramids' ancient stones and setting the network's bioluminescent mycelium ablaze—a tapestry of turquoise and gold veins pulsing through the earth. The air smelled of rain-soaked soil and blooming *cempasúchil*, their orange petals glowing faintly at the edges, as if dusted with starlight. Birds darted between fruit-laden trees: mangoes dripping nectar, chicozapotes splitting with sweet flesh, and guavas swollen to bursting. A river cut through the oasis, its waters crystal-clear, alive with silver fish and lotus flowers that opened lazily to the sun.

Maria paused at the edge of a terraced farm, where engineers in AEGIS greens tended to a mycelial reactor. Its core hummed, filtering toxins into fertile soil that spilled into planter beds. A child ran past, laughing, clutching a handful of glowing marigolds that shed petals like embers. In the distance beyond the base, the network's atmospheric veil shimmered faintly—holding back the Gloom's rot, a wall of light refracted. Spores rise from the ground where the network meets the gloom rot, a small silent battle that takes place beneath the soil and rises to the sky. Beyond its perimeter, the world turned hellish: skies choked with greenish-black smog, earth cracked and weeping oily mist. But here, life *roared*.

She climbed the Pyramid of the Sun, the mycelium underfoot warm and alive, its glyphs flaring softly where her boots touched. Maria knelt, tracing a glyph depicting a feathered serpent devouring its tail. The mycelium flared gold beneath her touch, casting her shadow jagged against the steps. *Testament of time.* Citlali's voice echoed in her skull. *Or a loop we're too blind to escape?* The glyphs offered no answers—only the same soft, mocking glow that had haunted Maria since childhood.

Her wrist chimed, a vibration sharp as a knife. Time

Descending the pyramid, she gazed down at the sprawl of the safe zone—markets buzzing with vendors selling tamales steamed in banana leaves, elders weaving gloom-moss silk into iridescent shawls, and engineers grafting new nodes into the network's roots. Solar panels glinted beside pre-Columbian stonework, and holographic Zapotec symbols hovered above plazas where children danced.

"*Jefa!*" A farmer waved, holding up a basket of *nopales* studded with bioluminescent spines. "For the road?"

Maria accepted one, the cactus flesh cool and sweet on her tongue. *This*, she thought, *is what the Gloom wants to erase.* Not just people, but the hum of cicadas in the afternoon heat, the way the river sang as it curved past the Moon Pyramid, the smell of corn roasting on clay *comales.* Maria hops on her speeder and heads to the north gate where her team awaits instruction. Roxy and Baron approach Maria, inspecting two speeders for her team.

The hangar buzzed with the low thrum of active rot-speeders, their eclipsite armor swallowing the overhead lights until they resembled voids edged in ghostly bioluminescence. Maria stood between two of the machines, her gloved hand resting on the haunch of *Tonantzin Breath* as its symbiote core exhaled spores that smelled of burnt ozone. Baron and

Roxy approached through the amber-lit haze of the safe zone's dusk, their shadows stretching long and jagged across the alloy floor.

Baron halted, spine rigid as a railgun barrel. "Ma'am," he said, saluting. The word rang like a bullet casing hitting concrete.

Roxy lingered half a step behind, one thumb hooked in her belt beside a serrated combat knife. Her eyes—sharp as shrapnel—scanned Maria's face, then flicked to the speeders. "Heard you scraped the coyote's hide yesterday," she said, her voice sandpaper-rough. "Left him howling."

Maria tossed a grease-stained rag onto *Tonantzin*'s seat and turned. The hangar's climate control couldn't mask the acrid tang of gloom-moss festering beyond the compound walls. "Saved some fun for you," she said, nodding at the two untouched speeders behind her. They crouched like mechanized panthers, Zapotec glyphs glowing faintly along their flanks, quetzal feathers trembling at their handlebars. "Yours now. Our mission track the coyote and his raiders find their base of operation."

Baron's jaw tightened. "Copy that."

"They're getting desperate." Maria tapped her holo-pad. A grainy feed materialized: raiders in scavenged gloom-tech armor, their faces warped by rot, riding hounds whose eyes wept black ichor. "General wants their nest found. Numbers. Weaknesses. What they're pumping into their *veins* to keep them breathing." She stepped closer, her boots crunching grit. "And if you spot the coyote himself? *Observe*. But if he's dumb enough to step into your sightline…"

Roxy grinned, all teeth. "We'll mail his kneecaps to AEGIS in a pretty box."

Maria's smile was a blade's edge. "Pack light. The gloom's menu is shit." She jerked her chin at the ration crates stacked nearby—vacuum-sealed bricks stamped with AEGIS logos. "Algae paste. Protein gravel. If you're *lucky*."

Baron picked up a brick, turning it over. "And if we're not?"

"You'll find out why raiders chew gloom-vines." Maria's voice dropped. "Saw a rookie try it once. His gut swelled like a corpse in the sun. Burst mid-scream."

Roxy snorted, slapping a magazine into her rifle. "Pass."

"Move out in sixty," Maria said, tossing them ignition chips. The speeders roared to life, their dampeners smothering the sound to a subsonic growl. "Sunset's our curtain. Stay ghosted. And *don't*—" she pointed at Roxy, "—taste the fucking scenery."

As the duo geared up, Maria watched the safe zone's veil flicker gold at the horizon. Beyond it, the Gloom churned—a cauldron of green-black clouds, lightning fracturing the sky like cracked glass. Somewhere in that rot, the coyote waited.

The speeders tore into the wastes, leaving no tracks, no sound. Only the faintest shimmer of pheromone trails, glowing like fireflies in the dying light.

The raiders eat food in the gloom in strides, slowly evolving their gut biome to handle gloom rot but at the risk of death, some revert to cannibalism, freedom they call it more like a hellscape. The safety of Teotihuacán will be missed. Home to a growing number of refugees, the barges always find pockets of life out in the gloom, those fighting for a way out and if they're lucky, they get picked up and brought back. AEGIS always makes sure to save those in need. We are the last living colony on the planet NEW ERRA. AEGIS needs all the help it can get.

The last few breaths of safety are savored. It would be awhile until they return, if they return, there's no guarantee out in the gloom. The group arrived at the edge of the treeline where the raiders retreated one last look at the base and all its beauty; it stands as a beacon of hope, a guiding star in the night. A sense of unease befalls the group, the tracker drone are deployed the hunt begins.

The drones connected to bikes fly low to the ground, rapidly tracking and sending the course back to the speeders. The path is set the three ride off, the gloom awaits. in the gloom, aside from gigantic beasts, the corruption has invaded every living thing, insects increased in size, birds mutated into ghastly looking things, everything the gloom touched has mutated to abhorrent creatures but they too can be saved. The more the creatures stay in network controlled areas, the faster their genetic code begins to heal. AEGIS has created special ranges for such animals so our food supply can proliferate once rehabilitated there are released back into network lands.

The drones track throughout the night during the day, the group rest. The drones provide security, allowing for the team to sleep and eat. Maria sets up camp, since the ground is corrupted and sleeping on the floor is ill advised. The team has a mag-camp a cannister full of nanites that hover over the ground creating a 10 by 30 campsite. The nanites are extremely resistant to gloom rot and also purify the air. The fog and air in the gloom are extremely hazardous.

Helmets are always to be worn in the gloom the corrupted air will cause severe hallucinations, and slowly and painfully corrupt your genetic code, you can survive without a helmet in the gloom yes but past 7 days, your body will take longer and longer to revert back to human, if at all possible. AEGIS could only ever figure out pieces to how the raiders survive in the gloom, the toxic environment was just one of many deaths that awaited a person who ventured too far, perhaps a mutation maybe some sort of new tech it has bewildered scientist for years something worthy of study. AEGIS invented their own fungal nose clips that filters toxins when worn not a permanent solution but it allowed for 15 days without a helmet. Though bodies were captured and studied, no distinguishing features or mutation jumped out at them. It was a puzzle impossible to solve. Genetic testing revealed nothing of value. Maybe the answers reside in the gloom. The only thing of certainty was the effects of the gloom seem to be repelled by them. Their veins coursed with black blood.

The trees around camp are petrified black spines of their former self, their branches clawing at the bruised sky streaked with green auroras. The air crackles with static, and the ground weeps an oily mist. Bioluminescent fungi glow green in the mist, their tendrils recoiling as maria passes, gloom pools ripple oily water with half-formed faces screaming silently, lost souls of the gloom. Ruins of old Mexico City lurk in the distance, crumbling highways draped in black ivy, mutated snakes slithering in between. Marías blades hum and glow in response to the gloom, an uneasy sign they are in dangerous territory.

"Hey look here, the tracks lead west," Maria said to Roxy and Baron

"It looks to be heading straight to eschaton, in the city's ruins," Roxy replied

"I hope not. We are not Wardens, we weren't trained for that type of combat," Baron says fearfully.

Maria: "Well, this is observe and report. We shouldn't have to deal with any threats so long as stealth is maintained, and we keep our distance."

Roxy: "Observe and report, recon only copy that."

"What are we really hoping to find, boss?" Baron asked.

"It's unknown right now, but the attack yesterday was more than just an attack," Maria responded.

"What happened?" Roxy asked.

"It was a diversion while we were at the main gate. There was a group of gloom beast flanking and, well, look,"

Maria pulls out her holo-pad and plays the security video. The team lets out a gasp. The pits of their stomach turn. The realization that the gloom beasts now show some sort of intelligence behind them gives them questions Maria is unable to answer.

"So there showing signs of intelligence. Is it a hive mind? I thought they were thoughtless beasts!" Baron says.

"So did everyone. That's what we are here to uncover if the raiders maybe somehow are controlling them or if they are actin of their own volition," : Maria

"Copy that boss, man im not gunna get any sleep today," Roxy said uneasily

"lets not think the worst until we have concrete answers. We have to be vigilant. I need you guys focused, lets grab some food and take a rest for now. We'll start back up at sunset," Maria said.

"Roger that," Roxy and Baron replied

The team unpack for the day, grab their gear, and head inside. Roxy fires up the grill. The sound of sizzling meat fills the make shift outpost. The smell of chillies and onions grazes the nostrils of Maria and Baron. A sense of safety inundates the team, a little reminder of home. Baron working on the rice and maria heating some tortillas. Maria sets the table for the magnificent meal they are about to enjoy. The team sits down at the table full of food and smiles all around.

"Dig in," Maria says ecstatically,

"I know my way around the kitchen thanks to my mother," Roxy says

"It smells amazing. It reminds me of my mother's cooking," Maria erupted in joy.

Baron, without hesitation begins stuffing his face in excitement. The darkness of the gloom couldn't perforate this 10 x 30 command post. The crew's spirits were too high to topple.

"So why were we the lucky one's boss, to join you on this mission," Baron said in between bites

"I read your files. I needed the best of the best, and that's what you guys are. I mean, this food to die for," Maria said.

"So we're glorified cooks?" Roxy laughed.

"No, that's not what I meant," Maria

"Relax boss, im joking," Roxy replied

"Where did you grow up, Baron? how'd you end up in Mexico?" Maria asked.

"Well, it is a long story. Everyone always wants to know how the Asian guy ended up in Mexico. I heard you guys needed help with your rice and well, here I am," Baron laughed.

"No, seriously, how did you end up here?" Roxy asked.

"I'm kidding my great grandmother was visiting on vacation when the great fracture happened from what she says the world went dark and getting back home was impossible this was before she found out there was no home to go too there were talks of some areas at the Russian-Chinese border that may have survived, but nothing came of it, and so my great grandparents looked to the future and 2 generations later here I am, im happy I did not live through that it was rough times I've heard so many stories, and you Roxy?" Baron asked.

"Me, I dont have a story lived here my whole life. My ancestors too. I wish I could have seen the city when it was still standing, hell the country too," Roxy said, laughing.

"And you Maria?" Baron asked

"Me im the same as rocky been here my whole life. We always lived by Teotihuacán, my grandmother was here when the network first bloomed. My mother said it was an amazing sight. The bioluminescent mycelium sprouting and expanding, AEGIS, came not too long after. We went from looking for scraps to a mini city. My mother said she was glad they showed up. They gave her a job safety and security to raise me," Maria answered.

"A real die hard, me too. My parents told me there was a time where everyone on the planet hated eachother pointless wars, im glad we did not live through that," Baron.

"Same, I agree, although the thought of no gloom seems like it couldn't be that bad," Roxy said, laughing.

"Maybe that's why the monsters are here. My grandparents told me stories of dragons and how they were a part of our culture and now they fly around the eschaton," Baron.

"Maybe, but no one knows the real cause of the fracture. It's been a mystery for decades," Roxy.

"I'm just saying maybe humanity caused it, not too farfetched to think. I mean, look at the raiders hopped up on rot maybe its god's way of saying enough," Baron.

"Or maybe it's the devil saying hi. The network fights back maybe that's god helping us fight back," Roxy.

"Lets get some rest guys, we leave in a few hours," Maria

"Roger that, boss. We'll finish this convo later. It was just getting good," Baron smirked.

The shelter's interior clung to the cold like a second skin, the air thick with the sour tang of mildew and ancient dust. Maria lay stiffly in her bunk, the threadbare AEGIS-issue blanket scratch against her neck, its fibers stiff with dried gloom-moss residue. No regenerative network hummed here; the sheets were dead weight, offering only the illusion of warmth. Roxy snored softly nearby, her arm dangling over the cot's edge, fingers brushing the alloy floor. Baron's silhouette was a motionless lump in the adjacent bunk, his breath fogging in the chill.

The bang tore through the silence—a metallic *clang*, as if a titanic hammer had struck the shelter's roof. Maria jolted upright, her pulse a drumbeat in her throat. The security node's holographic interface, usually a soft blue, was dark. *Power failure.* She fumbled for her boots, her breath visible in the sudden, icy draft. "Roxy! Baron! Up *now!*"

The bunks were empty.

Roxy's cot lay disheveled, her rifle still propped against the wall. Baron's gear vest hung neatly on a hook, his canteen half-full of murky water. Maria's throat tightened. She staggered to the door, her boots crunching over grit, and thumbed the manual override. It hissed open, revealing not the gloom's toxic wastes, but a corridor swallowed by writhing network mycelium. The fungal tendrils glowed an unnatural cobalt, their bioluminescence pulsing like a sick heartbeat as they crawled up the walls, devouring the metal inch by inch.

"*Baron?!*" Her voice echoed, swallowed by a low, droning hum.

The mycelium flared. The wall ahead rippled, turning translucent as glass. Beyond it, a shadow moved—a figure with hunched shoulders, its outline blurred as static. Then it turned. Amber eyes ignited in the dark, pupils slit like a serpent's. Maria froze. The shadow *lunged*, a blur of obsidian smoke, and she stumbled back, her spine hitting the opposite wall. The mycelium surged, knitting itself into the shape of a feathered serpent, its scales shimmering with stolen glyphs. The room dissolved.

A cavernous void replaced it, the air reeking of copper and decay. A colossal red eye materialized overhead, its pupil a black vortex. Inside it, visions erupted: her grandmother screaming as gloom rot devoured her legs; her mother, Citlali, clawing at a mycelium-choked doorway; faceless ancestors writhing in a pit of molten shadow. Their wails vibrated in Maria's teeth.

"***WAKE UP!***"

The voice was Citlali's.

Maria screamed—

—and bolted upright, drenched in sweat. Roxy's calloused hands gripped her shoulders, the woman's scarred face inches from hers. Baron stood behind, his helmet already sealed, a pulse rifle slung across his back. The shelter was intact: grimy but functional, the security node casting a jaundiced yellow light over their gear.

"You okay, boss?" Baron's voice was steady, but his knuckles whitened on his weapon. "Sounded like you were wrestling a jaguar."

Maria swiped at her damp brow. The nightmare's afterimage lingered—the eye, the serpent, her mother's voice. "Fine," she rasped. "Time?"

Roxy jerked a thumb at the sealed door. "Past due. We're parked a few clicks east of the ruins. Gloom's restless today." She tossed Maria her helmet, its visor already smeared with residue. "You were muttering about 'eyes' and 'serpents.'"

Maria stood, her legs trembling. The shelter's floor was ice under her feet. "Just ghosts."

Baron handed her a canteen. "Save the haunting for the raiders."

Outside, the gloom hung like a burial shroud, clouds churning. Maria stared at the horizon, where the safe zone's veil was a distant, mocking flicker of gold.

Not just ghosts, she thought, tightening her grip on her blades. *A warning.*

The shadowed serpent was close.

"We decided to lest you rest up while packed. You seemed tired," Baron added.

"Thanks, I'll finish up in here. Get the bikes started. I'll be out in five," Maria said.

The team leaves and finishes loading up the gear on the speeders. Maria gets dressed, staring at the wall from her dream. Could it be a bad omen? She thinks to herself. The prophetic dreams she's been having have been around since she was a young girl back in Oaxaca. The closer to Teotihuacán, the stronger the visions she's learned to live with them, not knowing if they're a curse or a gift. Her mother always told her they were a gift from god and she should think of them as such, and that one day she'll understand the message he was trying to send her. Maria never spoke of them, the nightly visions, but as of recent, they have been more frequent and this one more terrifying.

The questions who is the shadow man? why is here? And now what is the red eye and why is it here? She sheaths her blades and makes her way out, holds her cannister and hit the button the nanites collapse and the camp now sits inside. Maria puts the cannister in her pouch on the bike, she grabs her holo-pad. They are leaving what was once San Martin Azcatepec. The drones relieved of guard duty are now back on the hunt, guiding the team deeper into the gloom. The first giant chasm in the earth goes through part of Mexico City, which is now a wasteland. The drones track a path through old highways leading toward the city. The outskirts of San Martin Azcatepec lie under perpetual twilight, the sky choked by the gloom's reddish- greenish haze, crumbling highways snake toward Mexico City, flanked by skeletal trees and rusted carcasses of abandoned cars.

#

Chapter 3

Dance Of Death

Atlas: "I was forged to mend, yet I fracture the sky

a law of the cosmos, the first and last sigh

to break what I am, you must break what you bear

the father's false eden, the son's shadowed snare,"

The barge hums with alarms blaring, the corridors flood with personnel attending to bruised and bettered parts of the ship. An attack like this hasn't been seen. The gloom erupted into chaos in a matter of minutes, sending horrific wave after wave whatever the wardens happened upon must have been of great importance. Wardens regularly encounter threats that are sporadic but never an intelligent driving force of beasts, for the most part attacks were random and very few in number, 2 beasts at most. The retreat as well was questionable, for we have never seen a gloom beast retreat or now small force retreat. It seems the creatures are intellectually advancing. Could it jus be that evolution is taking place faster than wed hope? Perhaps the beast see themselves as the apex now. The questions arising from this encounter are baffling even the smartest minds at AEGIS.

The barge sways as if in unsteady seas. Critical damage to integral network systems will require repairs.

"Status check?" the barge captain asks on the bridge

"Sir the core is running at 60% efficiency, we've lost cannons 4,6,and 8. Two solar sales are offline, and hull breaches in basement levels are causing drag and pressurization problems. I recommend heading to the Teotihuacán base for critical repairs," says a private.

"Can we make it back to HQ?" asks the captain

"Negative sir, we have enough power to get to Teotihuacán station and that's pushing it," replies the private

"Alright, make a heading for the pyramids, conserve power steady as she goes, and I want a debrief with all remaining Wardens ASAP. I want to know what the fuck happened down there. Hail general Braddock let him know we are coming in for emergency landing and repairs, and shut those fucking alarms off," the captain ordered veins erupting from his neck and forehead.

"Yes sir," the private responded

The barge fell silent everyone moving with purpose and haste medical wing was overwhelmed the battle is not yet over. Sector seven was vast, and making it to Teotihuacán without incident could very well be difficult. The ship was running on fumes, another attack and the barge is done for. To conserve power, all battle stations were turned off, turrets and cannons left unoccupied and visual patrols ordered. Every angle of the ship monitored for possible attack, the comfort of once having wardens was overshadowed now that one lie dead. The three remaining wardens must suffer decontamination for 20 minutes with a headless corpse and an unconscious leader. The aura in the ship grew heavy and dark minds grasping for hope in unsteady times. The once angels of death stand somewhat defeated as they watch their leader and brother lay lifeless bodies, stiff and unwavering.

"What the fuck happened out there, Duke? It was like an ambush. They fucking came at us with an army. We never dealt with those numbers. Now max is dead, the boss is out

cold, and he fucking turned into the grim reaper himself doing shit I've never seen *ese*,"
Reaper said confusingly.

"I know he turned into something else. He was almost dead. I dont know how he had
the strength. Look here, Reap see that?" Duke said, pointing to his wounds.

"There healing already, like he was never touched. His armor works faster than I've
ever seen." Duke.

"Yea, what the fuck? hey check to see if he's still got that injector," Reaper

"It not here. Maybe it fell out when he was hit?" Duke said, knowing that was
impossible.

"We both know there aint no way ese," Reaper

"Maybe we dont know? We'll ask him when he wakes up," Duke said.

The air reeked of chemicals sterilizing all gloom rot. Maximus's wounds regain their
normal color. The chunks of flesh missing begin the decaying process. The organic odor
filling their senses hardened the atmosphere. The time never passed as slow as it did in those
moments. As they sit in silence, they remember the years they stood as brothers fighting back
gloom beast upgrading their defenses with the withered corpses of their kill. The gloom beast
had valuable resources and rare earth metals that greatly enhance warden armor. It was
standard practice to use their kills to upgrade their system. In fact, it was encouraged and
studied for building better defenses in every aspect of AEGIS. Max was always a stiff and
serious individual ready for promotion to captain. His future seemed bright, but out in the
gloom assurances are never present.

The wardens all know the risk this fight, this war brings. The war just turned
complicated. The beasts organizing attacks in numbers could prove difficult for the wardens.
The fight sees new challenges for AGEIS and raises questions we've yet to answer. The loud
sound of compressed air resonate in the chamber as the doors swing open. Decontamination

is complete. Both wardens lug a brother over their shoulder and march down to their private health ward. The silence was loud as the crew watch the wardens traverse the hall to their ward.

The fear drenched over the crew in waves, confusion permeated throughout the barge. The doors to the warden's quarters open. They pass the threshold, Reaper sets Maximus's headless body down on a mossed over medical, aluminum and nature fused together. The mycelium spores connected to the networked revealed his vitals, and the time of death was marked. The moss embraces the corpse of the fallen Warden and glows blue. The network remembers every warden that passed. Their connection and bond far outweigh normal infantry men. They are the tip of the spear. The network mourned heavily every fallen warden for reasons unknown. Perhaps their selfless sacrifice, perhaps their reliance on the network. Duke sets Samiel on the adjacent med bed, the moss emits an intensified amber glow the like of which neither Wardens witnessed. Samiel, in a deep slumber unconscious, unresponsive, the surrounding glow pulsing like a heartbeat.

Samiel finds himself standing at the base of the pyramid of the sun, but it's twisted- a grotesque fusion of Aztec stone and gloom-tech. The steps bleed black ichor, and the summit pulses a sigil unseen before. Atlas's voice echoes, a distant fragmented voice "Follow the serpent... or become it" Samiel ascends the pyramid halfway up, a woman appears to him a familiar sight in his dreams, but she splits into three manifestations the first is clad in obsidian armor, blades crackling she fights shadowy gloom specters. The second kneeling in a field of maize, hands stained with glowing blood as she tends to wilted crops. The third cradling a child's shadow and humming a lullaby. The manifestations each plead with Samiel:

Warrior: "fight with me!"

Healer: "save whats left!"

Mother: "let go..."

Samiel confused stares as they dissolve before him into smoke. Leaving only their voices. A voice echos above the rest, "you cannot outrun duality, Samiel". Samiel presses forward. The dream more intense than its predecessors does not instill fear only longing and knowing. The steps glowing. With each step, the serpent on its stone railings glowing showing him the way up. At the pyramid's peak, Samiel enters a hall of shattered mirrors, each shard reflecting a version of himself, a younger Samiel in a broken home, his half sister and half brother and mother mocks and abuse him. The next shard showing him leave it all behind entering AEGIS, eyes hollow, veins blackened, his umbral fang fused to his body. The last shard showing a strange sight, a skeletal and vein circuit infused with network, the sigil eye behind it angry and glowing red as the skeletal circuit turns amber. An entity slithers through the mirrors wearing the woman's face, echoing the words *"you'll fail her*, and in doing so you'll fail that which is left of this disease you call the *human race"*.

The floor collapses, plunging Samiel into an underground cenote. The Quetzalcoatl appears gigantic in form, coils in the water, its feathers made of gloom static and nahuati glyphs. the serpent speaks.

"To break the chain, you must forge it anew.

the father's sin is the sons due.

what binds the storm to earth?"

Samiel pauses. "A riddle," he thinks to himself. A soft, low voice utters *"choice"* in his head. Samiel looks to the colossal beast and shouts, **"choice!"** the serpent disintegrates. Behind him a door, etched in its face, a DNA helix. Samiel approaches the door through the puddle in which the serpent stood. The closer he gets, the color glow changes from red to amber. He extends his arm and swings the door open. Beyond the door, the woman stands in a Chapultepec Castle, surrounded by eschaton drakes. she's wounded, clutching her blade as the gloom core of the drakes circle above. A hologram of a scientist appears beside him in a lab coat. His name tag reads Dr. Voss flickering in and out of existence.

"Your *sacrifice* will cleanse this world, the future lies with *her*, the key to salvation lies with *you* embrace it, the bond that binds us all,"

"And what if I can't?" Samiel responds

"You didn't come here to make a choice. Samiel, decisions are ghosts of paths already walked; you're here to meet the version of you that did,"

The pyramid collapses all around him, rubble into smoke. He stands in an empty med room, a soft hum starts. The door to his left opens. An amber skeletal structure walks to him. A brain, veins and spinal cord stand before him.

"Hi I'm **Atlas,** I'm your new ai symbiote. What a dream huh? Had to help with that riddle I was too invested in the outcome. Who is that women? You dream of her often ever since you were young,"

"How do you know that?" Samiel asked, puzzled

"Once fused, our *duality* becomes *singular*. All your memories become a part of me as well as you."

"What are you? What is this?" Samiel.

"Ahh yes, the question gnawing at your brain. I was in that injector you stuck in your neck. AEGIS scientist have long been trying to fuse the network with ai capabilities to humans, to build a more efficient fighting force and hoping to repel the gloom."

"What happened at the lab? Why were we overrun?" Samiel.

"Well, that, my friend, is a good question for which I have no answer. I'm not sure exactly what happened, while I was being built strange occurrences were happening at DAWN lab, systems glitching it was if the gloom was reacting to my being built, Dr. Voss not the man in your vision I'm assuming maybe a descendant of his maybe his great granddaughter she created me, an ai able to interface with Wardens each different but all sharing information together through the network. A breakthrough. She said she would call me Atlas, the first and, sadly, the only. Before Doctor Voss could implant me into a test subject, a new unseen gloom creature attacked the lab. It bypassed all security. It was fazing in and out of reality, draining all the souls in that lab. Dr. Voss ran with me to the synthesizer. My code was complete and human trials were ready. The alarms were triggered, and the lab went on lockdown. Security forces were no match for this thing. Dr. Voss seemed to know what it was. In a panic, she locked us in the synthesizer room, uploaded me and placed the capsule in the injector. She was going to inject me into her to save the project. After that, I woke up with you in the midst of battle. I have no memory after being encapsuled im unaware of the status of Dr. Voss currently,"

"So you're a prototype and I'm the lab-rat got it, why are we still in the vision?"

"I guess you can say that, ha ha, we're no longer in the vision. This is the place I've created in your mind for us to get acquainted before waking you up. I figured you had questions, and this place is like a meditative state, a simulation for us to gather our thoughts, so to speak. You have unbridled access to the network. Here you can search the world, access points of interest AEGIS equipment. You can pretty much see everything. It's what I use to gather your information for any mission."

"Can you find her?"

"Yes, hold on," Atlas responded.

The room turned into a holographic world of the existing network. Everything it touched was visible to samiel now he could see cities labs anything the network touch was projected to him in this hologram.

"Searching for similar faces, no luck the network only shows real-time feeds I'll have to physically gain access to AEGIS servers to execute a broader search"

"Dam, I thought you were AEGIS Ai don't you have access to all that?" Samiel asked

"My uplink was never complete. You know, the whole ghost killing everyone thing. Once integrated with a human subject, I need to be jacked into the servers using a Warden uplink to maintain a secure sever upload. It was a safety protocol in case of any malfunction," Atlas said sarcastically

"Ha you don't have to be a smartass, how do we get you access to AEGIS servers?"

"Not being a *smartass*, I'm just telling you like it is. Well, considering we are at Teotihuacán base, connecting to any computer near the servers by the pyramids should be quick and easy, but as of now, no one knows I exist. I advise we keep it that way, so how do you want to go about this?"

"You're right, I have a feeling we went to lab for you but also the beast. Something's not right. Well, keep this a secret for now till we know what we're dealing with. Leave no traces and be discreet," Samiel explained.

"Yes sir, I like this. Just the two of us, against all odds, beating the gloom, it's exciting," Atlas said enthusiastically.

"Yea got it what do I need to do to get you access?"

"yay our first real mission it's exhilarating!" Atlas said. Samiel gives Atlas a serious look.

"Ohh, right yes well first the server farm is to the right of the pyramid of the sun there's a network lab attached we can bypass security at night and enter when no one is around connect your armor to the nearest holo screen and that should do it"

"Alright, sounds like a solid plan, but my armor is already linked to AEGIS servers. Why not go through my uplink?"

"*Sharp mind,*" the AI intoned, its words rippling through the air like stones tossed into a black lake. A hologram flickered into being—a serpentine coil of code devouring a human silhouette. "Internal access would require *synaptic override*. The encryption here is… *alive*. It would feast on your neural pathways. Reduce you to a drooling husk." The serpent dissolved into a swarm of glowing locusts. "But the choice is yours."

"External download it is then, lets wake me up and inform the team,"

"Absolutely, and my condolences, about Maximus."

Samiel turned away, staring into a shard showing the med bay—his corporeal body lying motionless, Duke and Reaper silent sentinels at his side. Maximus's corpse glowed under the network moss, its blue light throbbing in time with Samiel's pulse. *Guilt* was a lead weight in his gut.

"Why mention him?" Samiel whispered.

The AI's shadow stretched, tendrils brushing the memory of Maximus. "Because grief is data. It *shapes* you. And I am… curious." A pause. "My condolences are not a simulation, Samiel."

"Yea, thank you Atlas," Samiel replied, saddened

#

Chapter 4

The Awakening

Three days ago. . .

The sun peeks through the horizon, rays effervescent, the glow hitting the spire at the center of the city. It was a magical sight Verdant spire, in the center of Dallas it stood as a sign of hope, of freedom the first New ERRA construct. the building was massive, a giant feat 300 stories tall, the compound just as massive, measuring 100 square blocks. It stands before us, blue and humming with people, an AEGIS compound, more like a small city. The base was sophisticated well before the network started to emerge. The defense systems are what kept this beast standing the wall mounted missels and machine guns, auto turrets every 100 ft, the barge hangers covered and underground equipped with humming bird copters and speed drakes. the close air support and troop transports were truly astonishing to look at up close, the beautiful blend of nature and machine contrasting the hell the gloom produced. The network, while helping upgrade defenses, also turned our war machines into beautiful artwork, each ship different from the next, not unlike Wardens themselves.

The mycelium weaving gorgeous designs in solar sails and exposed metal, a sight unlike anything ever seen. The spire was not too far from the Eschaton, but still it stands impenetrable. Life in the spire was a symphony of working class citizen and military personnel, in its early days, it was under constant attack. The gloom being only miles away, sent everything it could to disrupt life in Dallas, while at first it seemed unbearable, soon we discovered its wonders. AEGIS began reverse engineering and used recovered tech from the gloom build to better are defenses. It gave us an advantage though the corrupted tech would leach in areas causing rot and sickness amongst troops. The balance was restored when the network appeared. It began healing rotted equipment and repelling rot back to the Gloom/Eschaton, a savior mother nature provided, though some say god, whatever it was it changed the balance of this war and we were finally winning.

With the Eschaton at bay, the community grew. The hurdles surpassed a bright future awaited for those strong enough to commit to the cause.

"Madam president, you're requested in the situation room," a marine announced.

"Alright tell the generals im on my way," President Levitt responded.

At the top floor of the spire, a situation room was constructed for informing top officials of ongoing threats and battle. The war was constant, so this became the standing president's home. The new ERRA colonies maintained the American republic constitution, but capitalism was abolished. The world relied on a resource-based economy everyone was taken care of, no homelessness, no starvation, and free healthcare and transportation. Everyone had a right to a home or apartment. Basic needs were in the hands of all, not the few. All who lived in the world must contribute.

New ERRA's promise was pristine on paper: *No homelessness. No hunger. No chains of capital.* The resource-based economy bloomed in verdant hydroponic towers and hummed in fusion reactors tended by citizens who'd once been artists, teachers, dreamers. Money lingered only as a phantom for indulgences—a week in the alpine biodomes of Sector 1, a neural upgrade to taste virtual wines. But it was the Mandate that sculpted this utopia, its algorithms sharper than any blade. The test didn't just measure skill; it dissected *potential*, sieving neurodivergent brilliance and savant genius into "optimal tiers," while anomalies— trauma-scarred minds, misfiring synapses—were pruned.

The network saw to that. Woven into humanity's DNA during the Fracture, it scrubbed away mental illnesses like stains, rewriting depressive loops and anxiety spirals into orderly code. Prenatal screenings excised "poor genetic stock" with the precision of a scalpel. Yet some slipped through: orphans of war, minds cracked by childhood horrors the network couldn't suture, souls too wild for the Mandate's grids. These became Wardens.

They called it an honor. A *sacred duty*. The posters in the Spire's transit hubs showed Wardens in obsidian armor, standing triumphant atop gloom beasts, their faces heroically shadowed. No one mentioned the screams echoing from the training compounds, or the way veteran Wardens stared through you with eyes like dead screens.

Levitt passed one now on her way to the situation room—a Warden, their armor etched with fractal scars, mycelium tendrils snaking from their helmet into exposed vertebrae. The air around them tasted metallic, charged with the static of unprocessed grief. She quickened her step, clutching her folder and itinerary.

Behind her, the situation room doors sealed with a hydraulic hiss.

The situation room hummed with latent power, its curved walls alive with holographic maps that bled into one another like liquid light. President Levitt stood at the apex of the Verdant Spire's pinnacle, her silhouette framed by floor-to-ceiling windows that showcased the sprawl of New Dallas below—a labyrinth of bioluminescent towers and mycelium-laced transit veins. Beyond the city's glow, the horizon smoldered where the Gloom's emerald-black tempest clawed at the network's veil.

"Generals," she said, her voice cutting through the low thrum of quantum processors. "What's on the agenda today?"

The air rippled as seven holograms flickered to life around the hexagonal table, each general cast in hues reflecting their domain: Sector 1's projection glowed arctic blue, its borders spanning Baffin Island's glacial ruins to the fractured ice plains of Hudson Bay.

General Vorsk, his face scarred by frostbite, nodded stiffly. "Permafrost destabilization near Churchill. The network's holding, but the Gloom's seeping through melt channels."

Sector 2's hologram burned autumn gold—a territory stretching from Hudson Bay's thawing coast to the skeletal forests of the Great Lakes. General Hale, her hair cropped to a steel-gray bristle, leaned forward. "Raider clans are hijacking supply barges near Superior. They're using Gloom-mutated leviathans to drag ships under."

One by one, the sectors unfolded: Sector 3's heartland amber fields now pocked with sinkholes from Ohio's collapsed aquifers; Sector 4's dust-choked plains north of Dallas, where nomadic farmers dueled over dwindling aquifer rights; Sector 5's coastal marshes, Dallas to Corpus Christi's flooded skyscrapers jutted like broken teeth, their upper floors colonized by mangrove-thick "sky reefs"; Sector 6's scarred deserts bleeding into Tampico's jungles, where bioluminescent flora warred with Gloom rot; and Sector 7—Oaxaca's volcanic highlands, where the air itself seemed to curdle with the Gloom's advance.

Levitt's gaze lingered on the map. The continent had been carved into seven bulwarks against entropy, each sector a patchwork of human grit and network-infused miracles. Florida was a myth now, its bones dissolved in the Atlantic's acid tides. The East Coast's drowned cities lingered only in holographic archives, their names whispered in memorial halls: *New York. Boston. Charleston.*

"Elections approach in nine months," Levitt said, tracing a finger over Sector 5's rain storms. The system was her pride—no bribes, no dynasties. Candidates emerged from the Mandate's meritocratic forge: engineers who'd stabilized fusion cores, medics who'd pioneered gene therapies, Wardens who'd clawed back Gloom-claimed land. Yet power here was a mantle, not a prize. Two terms max. No exceptions. She'd seen predecessors retire to hydroponic communes or neural archives, their legacies etched into the Spire's mycelium-chiseled halls.

Monthly situation reports were standard procedure, each sector providing knowledge attained, crop counts and Warden reports. Whatever a sector needed or lacked was also reported and properly handled with support from other sectors. No one sector was above the rest, all citizens were free to move about sectors as they please as long as they adhere to the contribution law. Only after 30 years of service, starting from age 20, was a citizen allowed to retire. Most never do, but force retirement at age 60 is mandatory. The average lifespan of humans during this time was 150 years old. Citizens are encouraged to invent and transform society further after retirement, and repopulating was of most importance. Most retirees start massive agriculture farms and also arms companies, others inventing new tools to help everyday citizens.

The only citizens allowed to never retire are the Wardens. The grueling combat they endure is their life. Most become trainers of the new generation, and all inevitably want to die in combat. A sacred oath they take to defend the new world till their last breath "numquam recede, numquam Dede" Latin for "never retreat, never surrender."

The situation room continued its information sharing when General Arekis of Sector 6 broke the silence, his hologram flickering jade-green.

"Madam President, it appears Dawn lab at the edge of the Eschaton has fallen silent, pre-emptive drone scans show no signs of life and the alarms in the building are active, giving the fact we have recover an O.E.R, and have been studying it for months now. I ask we dispatch a team of Warden to ascertain the fate of the lab. As you know, great scientific strides were underway with Dr. Voss's research. A new AI system being developed with immense power to change our future. I urge on the

side of caution it doesn't appear to have been raiders the lab hasn't checked in, its been 24 hours." General Arekis stated.

"The Lab in Vallés, yes, I've been eagerly awaiting news of Dr. Voss's project, I'll have General Belisarius dispatch a Warden team immediately, that will conclude this months briefing, Arekis, Braddock, a word in private," President Levitt responded.

"Yes, madam president?" they both asked as the other generals disconnected from the situation room briefing.

"Arekis fill Braddock in on what you told me of Dr. Voss's project, so we are on the same page," President Levitt ordered.

"Yes, madam President, Five months ago Dawn lad discovered a strange signature near the gloom in sector one, a team was dispatched to investigate. We recovered an OER of great importance. Dr. Voss's great grandfather assured my predecessors we'd find something in that general vicinity, when the time was right, a cryptic old bastard. Sure enough, we did. It was an old server bank from 2027. According to Dr. Voss's great grandfather, this server bank had new breakthroughs in AI. It was lost during the fracture and buried in miles of ice. The server only popped up on scans now, almost two centuries later because of the melting of the ice and our recent advances in the last 100 years. We relocated what was left of the server to Dawn Lab. Dr. Voss assured me she would lead the project and uncover its secrets. The project was successful. We uncovered that with the help of the network, we could merge AI with the human brain, giving unparalleled knowledge and computing power. Without the network, it wouldn't have been possible. As of last week, we've noticed increasing activity in the gloom. That location has been quiet for years, precisely why it was chosen. We began reading strange signatures in the

gloom, unidentifiable. The Data of that project is of utmost importance. It could turn the tide of this war. We could possibly travel beyond the first chasm deep in to gloom territory." Arekis explained.

"Wait, how is this AI different from current programs we have now and why wasn't this studied and tested with current AI models?" Braddock asked.

"Our current AI models are specifically designed for ordinary operations. A lock in its code put there by scientists after the fracture ensured the AI could not grow beyond what it was designed to do. A failsafe against learning beyond its means, each system independent of the next, always compartmentalized. This server provided the keys to unlock that restriction. Dr. Voss cracked the code. The server provided code for a hive mind AI system capable of quantum computing and infinite learning." Arekis responded.

"Essentially, a singularity," Braddock replied.

"Yes! and so much more! When fused with the network, it accelerated growth. The resistance to gloom rot was unlike anything we have ever seen. The network stabilized the code, and the AI, it began learning everything in an instant, no restrictions and best of all compatibility with the human brain. We were due to start human trials." Arekis stated.

"Great, now that we are all up to speed, Braddock, you said your sector was experiencing more raider attacks. I believe the two may be connected somehow. We are on the precipes of ending this war. With this technology, we will all but assure victory in the years to come. I need the both of you to handle this jointly. Stay connected, provide whatever each of you needs from one another. This mission is top priority, is that understood?" president Levitt ordered.

"Yes, mam" they said in unison

"General Belisarius, I want your best Warden team on this recon and recovery ASAP!" President Levitt ordered

"I'm on it, madam president," Belisarius stated.

The silence in the situation room thickened, dense enough to choke on. President Levitt leaned back in her chair, the supple leather creaking like a warning. Sunlight streamed through the panoramic window, gilding the sprawl of New Dallas below—its mycelium-laced towers glowing, its aerial trams gliding like silver threads—but the warmth stopped at her skin. Her breath hitched as her gaze snagged on the horizon, where the Gloom's emerald-black tempest simmered behind a veil of fog. A cold filament of dread coiled down her spine. Something's wrong.

She spun her chair sharply, the motion cracking the stillness. Her holo-pad flared to life, casting jagged shadows as Dr. Voss's final log materialized. The hologram flickered, corrupted at the edges, as if the Gloom had already begun gnawing at the recording.

"The A.I. is brilliant," Voss said, her face lit by the sterile glow of Dawn Lab's servers. A strand of hair escaped her bun, trembling as she spoke. *"It computes faster than anything we've ever recorded—tenfold, a hundredfold. My grandfather warned me… warned me about the dangers. I never understood his fear. This tech will free us all. His experiments failed. Mine won't."* She paused, her eyes darting off-screen. *"Atlas will redefine this world. I only hope… I can make up for my ancestors' mistakes."*

The hologram dissolved into static. For a heartbeat, the room held its breath—then klaxons erupted, crimson light strobing across the walls. A synthesized voice boomed:

"CONTAINMENT BREACH. UNIDENTIFIED GLOOM SIGNATURE DETECTED. EVACUATE IMMEDIATELY."

Levitt's pulse thundered in her ears. On-screen, the static cleared just long enough to show Voss's face one last time—not afraid, but *resigned,* as if she'd expected this. The president's stomach dropped. *Ancestors' mistakes.* The Voss dynasty was enshrined in AEGIS: architects of the network, saviors of the Fracture. But history, she knew, was a palimpsest. The truth always bled through.

She pressed her thumb to her palm, the biometric sensor flaring. Her secretary's hologram flickered into existence, translucent and tense.

"Ma'am?"

"Pull every file on the Voss lineage. Journals. Black-box logs. *Everything.* And scrub the metadata—no traces."

The secretary's pupils dilated, a telltale flicker of unease. "Understood."

"And Lieutenant?" Levitt's voice sharpened. "This stays between us...."

"A routine audit. Yes, Madam President."

The hologram winked out. Levitt rose, her reflection fractured in the window's smart glass. Outside, the city gleamed—a monument to order. But in the distance, the Gloom churned, its secrets swirling like poison in the fog.

What did you bury, Voss?

The answer, she feared, was already clawing its way to the surface.

#

Chapter 5

Shadows Of The Past

The sound of vibrating air pulses, the low static hum ruminates the space. The chop of the AEGIS Huitzilin pierces the sky. The pilots of these helicopters appear strange in nature their helmets are one with the hunk of steel blazing through the clouds. The look like bids heads, large eyed and feather like protrusions from the helmet. An odd sight, but the tech behind it is most important, the same as the helicopter. These were not your average old world troop transports, these were masters of the sky. The hull forged from eclipsite alloy and reinforced with gloom resistant fungal fibers that self repair minor damage. Aztec glyphs etched into the sides and wings glow faintly with bioluminescent algae. In hover mode, the blades beat rapidly for stationary precision. In speed mode, the blades flatten into a delta wing formation for supersonic dashes. When behind enemy lines, stealth mode is activated, emitting subsonic frequencies to mimic natural wind patterns. Purification vents expel putrified air as a by-product, creating temporary safe zones.

Chameleon camo, a fungal coating, shifts texture and color to match the surrounding area virtually invisible to the naked eye. The Huitzilin was Dr. Voss's creation, its appearance resembles a hummingbird, and idea sparked from watching the birds hover in her garden. An amazing talent they had for hovering and maneuverability, truly a deadly fighter if it had the right capabilities. The piloting system was a magnificent thing to experience. The helmets, the most integral part of the helicopter, provided its pilot with tons of visual information and rendered the surrounding environment in an almost sonar view. The pilot who can toggle between views in any situation could see gloom threats miles away. The eyeballs that protrude could see even the smallest of birds and insects from high in the sky, an engineering masterpiece. The helmet fused with the ship, creating one being when in flight; the pilot was the ship.

"We are approaching the landing zone, Dr. Voss. Scans show the object in an ice canyon just below us," the pilot said over comms.

"Very good. Take us down the team and I will secure a perimeter and move to recover the OER. Be ready to leave in a moment's notice. We are close to the Eschaton. Expect the unexpected." Dr. Voss ordered.

"Copy That! mam" she responded.

The arctic wind howled through Sector One's scarred peaks, its knife-edged gusts ripping at the team's thermal suits as they disembarked. The Huitzilins wings fluttered to a stop, leaving only the creak of settling metal and the *crunch* of boots on permafrost. Breath crystallized in the air—ghostly plumes swallowed by the vastness. Before them, the canyon yawned like a jagged maw, its walls sheer and glazed with ice that shimmered under the weak sun. Below, shadows pooled in the abyss, hiding the cave where the OER lay entombed.

Dr. Voss tightened her gloves, the synthetic fibers stiff with cold. Her holo-pad flickered, its screen warped by Gloom-static—a persistent, spidery crackle that made the mountain's EMP pulses feel alive. *Hungry.* "Anchors set," barked one of the AEGIS soldiers, driving a titanium spike into the volcanic rock. The ground here was a patchwork of obsidian cliffs and frostbitten tundra, the aftermath of eruptions centuries dead.

"Grav-chutes are useless in this interference," Dr. Mastoph muttered, his breath fogging his goggles as he tested the ropes. "One wrong slip and…" He didn't finish. They all knew. Without Warden armor, a fall here wouldn't kill them—not immediately. The Gloom's static would fry their synapses long before the rocks did.

The descent was a ballet of grit and terror. Dr. Voss went first, her boots scraping against ice-sheathed stone. The ropes groaned under her weight, fibers fraying where the Gloom's pulses had gnawed at the tech-weave. Loose rocks clattered into the void, their echoes swallowed by the dark. Fifty feet down, the air grew thicker, stinging with the ozone reek of decaying electronics. Water dripped somewhere—a slow, maddening *plink*—as meltwater seeped through cracks in the canyon's throat.

"Sixty feet!" Mastoph called up, his voice swallowed by the wind. Below, the cave entrance gaped, its edges jagged with stalactites that dripped bioluminescent ooze—a sickly green syrup that pooled on the floor, casting wavering light. Voss's helmet lamp cut through the gloom, revealing veins of quartz in the walls, their facets glittering like a million watching eyes.

At the cave's mouth, the two AEGIS soldiers secured the lines, their rifles slung over shoulders crusted with ice. One stamped his boots, the *thud* echoing too loud in the hollow silence. "Like standing in a goddamn freezer," he muttered, his breath frosting the visor of his helmet.

Voss ignored him, stepping into the cave. The ooze above glistened, droplets catching in her hair as she moved. Her holo-pad buzzed—a weak signal, but enough. The scan revealed the server bank ahead, a shadowy mass encased in ice that glowed faintly blue, as if the machines themselves had seeped into the frozen water.

"Mastoph—tools," she ordered, her voice steady. The older scientist hurried forward, unclipping a laser pick from his belt. Behind them, the soldiers crouched, their gazes darting to the cave's entrance. Outside, the wind screamed.

"One hour," Voss said, adjusting her gloves. "If we're not back…"

"We'll be *gone*," the lead soldier finished, his tone leaving no room for debate.

She nodded, turning toward the ice. Somewhere deep in the cave, something *clicked*—a sound like a bone snapping. The bioluminescent ooze dripped faster.

Plink. Plink. Plink

The cave's bioluminescent ooze dripped from above, casting a sickly green pallor over the chamber. Dr. Voss adjusted her headlamp, its beam slicing through the gloom to reveal jagged ice formations clawing up the walls like frosted talons. The air hummed with a subsonic vibration—the kind that rattled molars and prickled the skin. Mastoph trailed close behind, his breath ragged in the confined space, the *click-clack* of his gear echoing too loudly.

"Scans say it's *here*," Voss whispered, as if the cave itself might eavesdrop. She pressed a gloved hand to the wall, frost crackling under her touch. Mastoph joined her, swiping at the grime-covered ice. His fingers left streaks in the filth, exposing a glacial barrier that glowed faintly blue from within. Behind it, shadowy outlines of server towers loomed—angular, alien shapes preserved in their icy tomb.

"Two meters thick," Mastoph muttered, his voice tinny through his rebreather. "Solid. No fractures."

Voss unclipped the nanite canister from her belt, its surface etched with hazard glyphs. "Then we make our own door." She slammed the device against the ice. With a hiss, the capsule split open, releasing a swarm of silver nanites that rippled across the surface like liquid mercury. The ice screamed as it dissolved, tendrils of steam curling upward, only to freeze again midair and fall as crystalline dust.

The scientists retreated to a lichen-crusted boulder, its surface slick with glacial sweat. Mastoph's knee bounced nervously. "How long?"

"Fifteen minutes," Voss said, her gaze locked on the swarm. The nanites pulsed rhythmically, their collective intelligence etching a perfect archway into the wall. But something was wrong. The ice *moved*—not melting, but *retreating*, as if repelled. Veins of black corruption spiderwebbed through the exposed layers, throbbing in time with the cave's unnatural hum.

Mastoph stiffened. "You see that?"

Voss leaned forward. The black veins coalesced into symbols—Zapotec glyphs, or something older. A warning. "Residual code," she lied smoothly. "From the servers. Expected."

But her palms dampened inside her gloves. The sensation of being watched sharpened. Above, stalactites quivered, droplets of ooze pausing mid-fall before streaking downward like green tears. A faint scrape echoed from deeper in the cave—metal on stone.

Mastoph's hand flew to his sidearm. "We're not alone."

"Focus," Voss snapped, though her own pulse thrummed in her throat. The nanites shivered, their silver sheen dulling as they consumed the corrupted ice.

The cave's bioluminescent ooze dripped slowly from above, each drop freezing momentarily in the frigid air before shattering on the ice below. Dr. Voss and Mastoph sat side by side on a lichen-crusted boulder, their breath fogging in the dim green light. Behind them, the swarm of nanites hissed like a nest of vipers, devouring the glacial wall in methodical silence. The machines' silver bodies pulsed faintly, casting jagged shadows that slithered across the scientists' faces.

Voss stared at her gloves, picking at a frayed seam. "You know… if the world hadn't plunged into darkness, I wonder what it would be like today." Her voice wavered, barely audible over the nanites' hum. "The corruption back then—greed, exploitation—it infected *everything*. My great-grandfather used to say the Fracture was… a mercy. A chance to start over. Some might even call it a *gift*."

Mastoph leaned forward, elbows on his knees, his Russian accent thickening with disdain. "A gift?" He snorted, breath curling into the air like smoke. "*Da*, humanity survived. But at what cost? You think Old Earth's sins couldn't have been dismantled without genocide? Billions buried under ash and ice—children, families—gone in a blink. Whoever triggered the Fracture wasn't a savior. They were a coward. A *butcher*."

The nanites' hum sharpened, their rhythm faltering as they hit a vein of corrupted ice. Black tendrils spiderwebbed through the wall, throbbing like poisoned arteries. Voss flinched but didn't look up. "But the *outcomes*—the unity, the network, the end of scarcity—"

"—are built on mass graves," Mastoph snapped. He gestured to the cave around them, the ice weeping oily residue.

"I know greed doesn't die," Mastoph said, his voice low. "It adapts. Slips into new systems. Like that server." He nodded to the wall, where the nanites now struggled against the corruption. "You think we're digging up answers? Or just another virus?"

A stalactite cracked overhead, splintering the tense silence. Bioluminescent ooze splattered near Voss's boot, its glow fading as it seeped into cracks. She stood abruptly, her reflection splintered in the ice. "The Fracture happened. We're here to fix what's left. Not wallow in 'what-ifs.'"

Mastoph rose slowly, his shadow engulfing hers. "Fix it? Or repeat it?" He pointed to the server's faint outline, now visible through the melting ice.

Mastoph froze mid-sentence. "Do you hear—"

His words dissolved into a gurgle. A serrated leg, glistening with mucus and rusted metal, erupted from his sternum. Blood sprayed in an arterial arc, painting Voss's face and goggles crimson. Mastoph's eyes bulged as the Gloom centipede twisted inside him, its segmented body—a grotesque fusion of chitin and corroded steel—bursting free in a shower of viscera. Mandibles snapped, shredding flesh and bone as it dragged Mastoph's halves into the shadows.

Voss screamed, scrambling backward, her boots slipping on entrails. The centipede's thorax pulsed, slurping marrow from splintered ribs.

Skitter-skitter-SKREE!

Plasma fire erupted as the two AEGIS soldiers stormed the cave, their rifles spitting searing blue bolts. The centipede screeched, its carapace sizzling, but didn't die. It rippled, shedding molten armor plates to reveal fresh, glistening hide beneath.

"Get her out!" one soldier barked, yanking Voss upright. His gloves smeared Mastoph's blood across her arms.

The second soldier unloaded a sustained burst, the plasma overheating his rifle until the barrel glowed white. The centipede recoiled, leaking black ichor—then lunged, stinger-first. The soldier dodged, but the barb grazed his thigh. He collapsed, screaming as venom melted through his armor, flesh bubbling like wax.

"Seal the cave! Now!" the first soldier roared, dragging Voss toward the exit.

A low, tectonic groan shuddered through the ice. The walls moved.

The soldier swung his rifle's light toward the darkness. The beam trembled over a nightmare: hundreds of centipedes, each larger than the last, uncoiling from icy tombs. Their compound eyes reflected the light in a kaleidoscope of malice, mandibles dripping venom that hissed where it struck the floor.

The lead centipede shrieked—a sound that liquefied fear—and the horde surged.

"Go! GO!" the soldier shoved Voss toward the ropes, turning to face the swarm. His final plasma burst lit the cave in a hellish blue. "The server!" she screamed, lunging for the nanite-carved hole in the ice. Her fingers closed around the hard drives just as a centipede's stinger punched through the first soldier's chestplate. He collapsed, convulsing as venom liquefied his organs.

Plasma fire lit the cave in strobing hellscapes. Chunks of chitin and soldier meat rained down as Voss stuffed drives into her pack, her breath ragged. The surviving soldier dragged her backward, his rifle spewing rounds that barely slowed the swarm.

"Go! Climb!" he snarled, shoving her toward the ropes.

Voss hit her grav-chute, as she grappled the line. Below, the soldier vanished under a thrashing knot of centipedes, his final scream drowned by the screech of rending metal. Flesh poured from the mouth of the cave like a meat grinder.

The creatures swarmed the walls. Not chasing—herding.

They ignored her, instead gnawing at the ropes with precision, their serrated legs shredding fibers as she ascended. The static-choked whir of the extraction VTOL grew louder, its floodlights piercing the cave's mouth.

A centipede lunged, stinger grazing her boot. She kicked, dislodging it, and glanced down. They moved as one—a single, sentient shadow—carving through the ice.

Voss climbed, her gloves slick with blood and ice. Below, the cave echoed with wet, rending screams—and the skittering grew louder. Closer. The hum of the Huitzilin rotors staring pierced her like a dagger. They were preparing to lift off.

"Don't leave me!!" she cries out in terror.

The silence is loud, cutting through her soul like a knife. The echoing nibbles of centipedes chewing her rope, disabling her connection, will end her life. Her face showing visible defeat her life, alas, amounting to this. All her accomplishments, her secrets, will die with her.

The centipedes surged like a living tsunami, their chittering jaws drowning out Dr. Voss's ragged breaths. She clawed at the ice, her gloves slick with gore, as the horde closed in—until the sky *screamed.*

A shadow plummeted from the ridge, trailing smoke and fury. The Warden—armor etched with serpent scales, helm shaped into a dragon's snarling maw—slammed into the canyon face with a concussive ***boom***. Ice shattered. Centipedes erupted into geysers of viscera as his wrist-mounted plasma cannons roared, painting the walls in arcs of blue fire.

Above, two more Wardens materialized at the cliff's edge, their spike pods detonating in sync. ***Thoom-thoom-thoom!*** Razor-sharp shrapnel rained down, skewering centipedes mid-leap, pinning their twitching bodies to the ice.

"*Move!*" the lead Warden barked, his voice distorted through the dragon helm's vox-grille. He moved like a storm—a whirlwind of crackling blades and cannon fire—carving a path through the swarm toward Voss.

The air *thrummed* as the Huitzilin gunship descended, its shadow eclipsing out the sun. Rotors screaming, it unleashed hell: a minigun spat hypersonic spikes that *evaporated* centipedes in bursts of acidic green mist. The canyon became a slaughterhouse, the gunship's floodlights illuminating the chaos in stark, strobing flashes.

A centipede lunged at Voss, mandibles snapping—

CRACK.

The Warden's blade cleaved it in two, black ichor splattering his helm. He didn't flinch. "*Climb!*" he ordered, hauling Voss up by her harness as the Huitzilin's guns chewed through the cave mouth, in a roar of stone and static. Above, the *Huitzilin* gunship was like an avenging angel, rotors churning the air into a hurricane. Its minigun pods swiveled, unleashing a storm of hypersonic spikes that ***SHREDDED*** the canyon face. Centipedes burst into clouds of acidic mist, their remains sloughing off the walls in a grotesque rain.

Reaper and Duke leaned over the ridge, their nano-helmets retracting to reveal grins sharp as knives. "*Pinche madre*, Doc!" Reaper crowed, hauling her over the edge. "You look like hell's pissed-off ex!"

Duke rolled his eyes, his 6'5" frame casting a shadow over her. "Ignore him. You're intact. That's what matters."

Voss collapsed, laughing breathlessly, her relief short-lived.

BRRRRT!

The *Huitzilin*'s minigun roared again, stitching the canyon with fire. "*Samiel's inbound!*" Maximus's voice crackled over comms. "Door's open—move!"

Below, a figure rocketed from the cave—Samiel, his armor scorched and smoking. He leapt, thrusters flaring, and slammed into the *Huitzilin*'s open bay with practiced precision.

Voss's laughter died.

At the cave mouth, the air *rippled*. A creature materialized—translucent flesh shimmering purplish-pink, tendrils writhing from its neck like parasitic worms. Its pupil-less eyes, glowing radioactive pink, locked onto Samiel. A low, subsonic **HUM** vibrated in Voss's bones, *screaming* without sound: *Hate. Hunger. Revenge.*

Then—gone.

"Did you… see that?" Voss whispered.

Reaper followed her gaze. "See what?"

The canyon lay silent, save for the *drip-drip-drip* of ichor.

Samiel's voice cut through the quiet, cold as deep space: "*We're done here.*"

But as the *Huitzilin* climbed, Voss stared at the cave, now a tomb.

"Did you see that?" the doctor asked again.

"See what, Doctor?" Duke said, turning around to help her up from the ground.

"There was a creature, staring out the cave?" she stated, almost sounding like a question.

"Doc, you're probably in shock. You just had an intense ordeal most never survive from, it's probably in your head. Lets get you cleaned up and looked at back at the barge," Duke said reassuringly.

The Huitzilin rises over the edge of the canyon and sets down in the clearing nearby. The Wardens carry the doctor over to the helicopter. Samiel and Max welcome them in, Samiel hands the doctor the drives she thought she had in her possession.

"Here you go, Dr. Voss, I think you dropped these," Samiel said, nano tech helmet retracted with a smirk full beard and stoic face.

"My bag, one the centipedes must have sliced it, oh my god thank you, that would have been all for nothing."

"Your welcome, doc," he replied.

"Back to the barge," Maximus ordered the pilot,

The Huitzilin thundered into the cloud-choked sky, its engines screaming like a gutshot beast, carving a jaged contrail of fire and static toward the barge—a ghostly leviathan looming on the horizon, its lights flickering like the last heartbeat of a dying world. Dr. Voss couldn't shake it. The creature's phantom glare lingered in her mind.

A promise, not a retreat.

#

Chapter 6

The Angel of Death

The massive hangar bay door grinds open in the distance, its rusted gears shrieking as jagged panels retract like the segmented carapace of some mechanical beetle. Against the ashen sky, the *Huitzilin* emerges—a sleek, obsidian-hulled helicopter, its shifting blades cutting through sulfurous clouds that bleed amber twilight. As it descends, the craft's floodlights slice through the gloom, illuminating the barge below: a floating fortress of weathered steel and corroded iron, its surface crawling with bioluminescent fungi that cling to every surface like electric lichen. The mycelial network thrums with an eerie cerulean glow, its pulsating veins mapping the barge's skeletal framework in liquid light, as if the entire structure breathes with some alien heartbeat.

The barge sprawls across the sky like a shattered metropolis, its labyrinth of platforms and towers stitched together by swaying suspension bridges and crackling power conduits. Some armored barges rise like medieval citadels, their hulls plated with riveted blast shields and studded with anti-aircraft batteries. Others, slender reconnaissance vessels bristle with sensor arrays—glass-domed observatories and skeletal radar dishes humming with static. But with all of them, hangar bays gape open, revealing rows of docked *Huitzilin* copters, their beetle-black chassis scarred from combat, rotor blades folded like the wings of resting raptors.

But even these agile machines—built to dart through storms and skirmish with lesser Gloom creatures—are dwarfed by the true terrors of the skies. Gloom Drakes circle high above, their silhouettes blotting out the sickly sun. When they descend, the world fractures: wingspans wide enough to eclipse towers, scales shimmering like molten obsidian, and eyes that burn with radioactive green fire. The barges shudder when Drakes attack, their reinforced hulls screaming under claws that rend steel like parchment. Crews scramble to fortify blast doors, sealing the *Huitzilin* in grounded hangars where they wait, trembling, as the Drakes' shrieks pierce the air—a sound like glaciers splintering. Survivors speak of skies raining fire and armored plating peeling back like fruit rinds. Most never speak at all.

The lucky ones return with hulls baptized in Drake blood, their ships's bioluminescent fungi mutated violet by the encounter, glowing faintly… as if haunted.

A medical stretcher waits at the landing pad for Dr. Voss. The doors to the Huitzilin are seamless and invisible, they open. The crew disembarks, Duke carries Dr. Voss and lays her on the stretcher, she thanks the Warden for saving her life. The Wardens, luckily in the area clearing out a section of the gloom, ridding it of drakes, received a distress call from the Huitzilin pilot. The team wasted no time and set after the doctor while en-route informed of her mission of retrieving an OER. Their armor and enhancements give them the ability to run great distances with little effort, and so they set out on foot to the distress call.

The Warden program was born from desperation after the fracture. With conventional armies obliterated by the gloom, AEGIS was formed. AEGIS, in its early days, recruited orphans, death row inmates, and dissident scientist. The Warden program a black ops initiative to forge soldiers who could survive, adapt, and become immune to the gloom. The key architect Dr. Cesar Vazquez, a neuroengineer who fused Zapotec warrior rituals with gloom tech, for it to only be enhanced and redesigned later after the network appears and spread through the known world. His motto, harsh as it may seem, bore truth:

"A warrior's soul cannot be coded. It must be broken first."

Dr. Vasquez created the first Warden trials, recruits would spend 72 hours in VR pods reliving the Fractures worst atrocities. Heart rate, pain tolerance, and PTSD triggers are monitored. Those who scream are discharged. Those who remain stoic and unwavering pass to the next test. The next test was simple but failed by many: execute a gloom corrupted civilian to save a squad mate. Failure to do so resulted in elimination from the program. Those successful pass through to the second round of trials. "The Labyrinth", a booby-trapped replica of the chasms and canyons of the gloom. The recruits must navigate pitch-black corridors filled with gloom mimics, solve complex coding systems, and endure Hallucinogenic gas. Once completed, the exit appears, recruits cross the threshold only to realize the exit leads back to the start of the trial. With Dr. Vasquez's haunting voice saying,

"Only those who carve their own path through the walls pass."

The consequential result of this driving some recruits to insanity and dieing. Those who solve the riddle proceed to trial 3 the final trial "the Blood Eagle." Recruits at this phase in training are stripped of all gear and released into gloom-riddled jungles. They must survive seven days with only a ceremonial Obsidian blade, and hunt down a gloom Jaguar and bring back its corpse. Death counts in this phase were extremely high, only the strong made it out, only Wardens. The next phase perfected in later years because of network mycelium was surgical Warden enhancements. The skeletal structure was reinforced with an eclipsite alloy, changing the color of the bones to matte black, enhancing strength and stamina. Nahual Neural Shunts, implants fused to the brainstem, allowing for interface with gloom energy, and a wireless uplink to AEGIS servers. Taloc Injector system, a spinal port implant that administers gloom antivenom to resist corruption, and adrenaline-x to enter berserker states in combat, overuse results in liquified organs. Gloom resistant Symbiotes, bio-engineered parasites grafted to the liver and lungs, metabolize toxins but crave gloom energy, forcing

Wardens to seek combat. Obsidian Dagger interface, a socket in the forearm, allows Wardens to bond with sword combat weapons. The blades sentience feed on their pain.

After surgical enhancements, the Wardens undergo psychological conditioning called The Hollowing, recruits undergo memory suppression to erode pain receptors in the mind, and mute guilt in their thoughts. Though not fully destroyed, the Hollowing gives them a greater tolerance of pain. Lastly, Empathy suppression, electroshock therapy paired with gloom exposure to eradicate fear, guilt, and doubt. The lucky few who survive the surgical enhancements and psychological conditioning graduate, Becoming AEGIS Wardens. The Warden program isn't just training, it's a soul alchemy. Each Warden is a paradox: a masterpiece of brutality and the ultimate argument against playing god. As the New ERRA colonies fought back the gloom, the emergence of the network, and the elimination of corruption in the government, the program was refined. No longer were children and prisoners used as lab rats, when contribution law was enacted and placement test were given, recruits were attained at the age of 20. Mostly neuro-divergent and young adults suffering PTSD, and savants were recruited, outcasts so to speak. Those who failed first trials were often placed in other programs, such as pilot training and regular infantry. Sadly, after trial 2 in the first phase, death was the only way out of the program.

Samiel, born Samiel E. July 2200, was raised outside the city of Dallas with his mother and half siblings. Samiel's earliest memory wasn't of laughter or light, but of the **closet**. It reeked of mothballs and mildew; the walls pressing close as a coffin. His half-brother's voice slithered through the door crack: *"Stay in there, mistake."* Samiel's tiny fists pounded the wood until his knuckles split. *"Please—"* The door shuddered under their kicks, each *thud* vibrating through his bones. Blood trickled warm down his temple, pooling on the floor beside a discarded toy soldier—its painted smile chipped, one arm snapped off. He clutched it like a talisman, whispering to its hollow plastic face, *"It's okay. It's okay."*

His mother found him hours later, curled in the dark. She didn't scream. Didn't cradle him. Her sigh was a blade. "Fighting again, Sami?" She dabbed his wound with a dishrag, her eyes avoiding his. The rag smelled of sour milk.

Her love was a revolving door of men. The first left her with two children and a shattered heart. The second—Samiel's father—arrived like a summer storm, all charm and reckless promises. He'd sweep her into dances in the kitchen, his calloused hands spinning her until her laughter rang like wind chimes. But by winter, the storm turned toxic. Samiel would wake to the *clink* of needles on the bathroom sink, his father's silhouette hunched over the sink, muttering to ghosts.

"Look at me, Sami-boy," he'd slur, pupils dilated to voids. His breath reeked of chemical decay. *"You're gonna be better'n me, yeah?"* Samiel would nod, throat tight, as his father's trembling hands gripped his shoulders—too hard, like he was clinging to a cliff's edge.

The basement apartment was a tomb. Samiel's "bedroom" was a nest of blankets beside a leaking water heater. When the power died—which it often did—the darkness swallowed him whole. Rats scuttled in the walls. His father's laughter echoed raw and broken from the other room, tangled with the static of a dead TV. One night, Samiel found him weeping into a cracked mirror, blood streaking his cheeks where he'd clawed himself.

"She's gone, Sami. They're all gone."

Samiel didn't ask who. He already knew.

His birthdays were hollow rituals. At eight, his mother handed him a gas station pastry with a candle stabbed into it. The wax dripped onto the *"Happy Retirement!"* logo. *"Make a wish,"* she said, scrolling through her holopad. He wished for the closet door to vanish. It didn't.

At twelve, he sat alone on the roof, legs dangling over the edge, watching distant barges glide through the Gloom's emerald haze. The wind tasted of acid rain. He wondered how far he'd fall before the impact erased everything.

The night his father died, the police drone delivered the news in a monotone chirp. *"Deceased. Overdose. No next of kin."* Samiel didn't cry—not then. He cried weeks later, scrubbing his father's dried blood from the bathroom tiles. The stain lingered, brown and accusing.

At the funeral, his mother smoked synth-cigarettes and said nothing. The coffin was cheap polymer, unadorned. Samiel tossed his broken toy soldier inside before they sealed it. A eulogy for the man who'd called him *"Sami-boy,"* for the boy who'd believed it meant *"I love you."*

When the placement test branded him *"Warden,"* Samiel traced the scar on his brow—a relic from the closet door. His reflection in the holopad's screen didn't flinch. *Maybe the Gloom will finish what they started,* he thought.

At 20, nervous and excited, he went for his placement test. The placement test was a relief for Samiel, a chance to start over, begin anew. The test was designed to draw from life experiences, and problems, to determine a fairly certain future life path. Every school had a testing room, a chamber of truth. Who's truth? Your own.

The testing chamber smelled like antiseptic and dread.

Samiel's palms slicked the arms of the chair as he stared at the helmet—a skeletal thing woven with bioluminescent fungi, its tendrils writhing faintly like parasitic worms. Outside, laughter seeped through the door; his classmates traded dreams like currency. *Farmer. Engineer. Architect.* Words that tasted like sunlight. Words he'd never let himself savor.

The mycelium pulsed as he lowered the helmet onto his skull. Cold. Always so cold.

*"**Breathe,**"* he told himself. *"**This is your chance to be** **wanted.**"*

The fungi ignited, searing blue.

—A closet door rattling. Blood pooling under his knees. His father's hollow laugh echoing through a basement tomb. The rooftop edge, wind clawing his tears sideways—

Memories flooded him, raw and unbidden. He gasped, nails carving crescents into his palms. It wasn't supposed to *hurt*.

*"**Please—**"*

Then, silence.

The helmet retracted. His holopad chimed—a sound like a funeral bell.

Samiel's thumb hovered. For a heartbeat, he let himself hope. *Farmer. Engineer. Architect.* A life where no one called him *mistake*.

The screen blinked.

ANOMALY: WARDEN PROGRAM

The words carved into him, deeper than any closet door. Around his neck, the cross pendant—his father's last gift—suddenly weighed a thousand pounds.

*"**No.**"*

The door creaked open. His classmates' laughter died mid-breath.

Mara from BioStudies met his eyes first. Her smile curdled. One by one, they turned away, as if his fate were contagious. Only Jax lingered, pity sharp in his gaze. "Sami, I'm… sorry."

Sorry. A grenade word. It detonated in his chest, shredding the last of his hope.

He stood, legs numb. The pendant's cross sharp edge dug into his sternum. *You're gonna be better'n me, yeah?* His father's ghost grinned, needle in hand.

In the hall mirror, his reflection stared back—a boy already half-corpse, the helmet's fungal residue glowing like a brand on his temple. *Anomaly.* A diagnosis. A death sentence.

He reached the exit and paused, hand trembling on the door. Behind him, whispers bloomed: *"Warden... Gloom fodder... lucky if he lasts a week..."*

Samiel stepped into the rainy afternoon. The first droplet hit his lip, bitter as regret.

Rewrite your story, the Warden veterans would say.

He laughed—a sound like shattered glass—and walked toward the storm

The park bench groaned under Samiel's weight, its rusted metal claws sunk into cracked concrete. Around him, the world rotted beautifully. Bioluminescent weeds snaked through fissures in the pavement, their sickly violet glow clashing with the sunset's hemorrhage of orange and black. The air reeked of decayed blossoms—flowers the Gloom had long since poisoned.

He clutched the holopad, its screen still scorched with the verdict: **WARDEN PROGRAM**. The words pulsed like an infected wound.

Anomaly.

The dream came clawing back—*always the dream.*

She stood at the edge of a fractured highway, her black dress fluttering like a funeral shroud. The mole on her shoulder pulsed like a third eye, the scar on her lower back a jagged paint stroke brush. Behind her, a Drake's shadow blotted out the sun. "Samiel—" Her voice frayed, a radio signal drowning in static. He ran, boots sinking into asphalt turned to tar, but the distance between them grew. *Always grew. Her hand reached for him, fingers dissolving into bioluminescent spores. "Why can't you—"*

Then silence. Always silence.

Samiel's throat burned. He'd vomited twice since leaving the testing center, bile and bitterness. Now, emptiness gnawed at his ribs. *Maybe the dream was a premonition. Maybe she's the one I'll fail to save in some Gloom-riddled trench.*

A child's laughter pierced the haze. Across the park, a girl chased a drone, her mother's eyes tight with fear. Samiel's chest ached. *That could've been me. Should've been me.*

But the test didn't lie.

Mistake. Anomaly. Warden.

The sun dipped below the horizon,the storm passed, its last light gilding the cross pendant around his neck—the one his father had given him before the needles stole his mind. Samiel twisted it until the chain bit into his skin. *You're gonna be better'n me, yeah?*

Darkness pooled in the park. He stood, knees buckling, and stumbled toward the streetlamp's jaundiced glow. Its light caught the pendant's cracked edge, reflecting like a smile—a mockery now. *Better'n you, old man? I'll be dead by twenty-one.*

The walk home was a funeral march.

3 months later…

The holopad on the nightstand flickered to life.

"Warden recruit, pick up. Arriving in 2 hours."

The words slithered into his skull. Two hours. Two hours until the Gloom became his cradle and casket.

The dream clung to him like a second skin.

Samiel woke gasping, the woman's voice still echoing— *"Why can't you—"* her words dissolving into the hum of the holopad's alarm. He stared at the ceiling, its cracks mapping constellations of failure. Her face lingered behind his eyelids: the mole on her shoulder, the scar like a crack in porcelain. *Who are you?* He'd asked the darkness a thousand times. It never answered.

His room smelled of mildew and lost years. The cross pendant lay on the nightstand, its cracked grin accusing. He stuffed it into his pack, fingers brushing the folded photo beneath—his mother, half-siblings, all turned away from the camera. From *him*.

A horn shattered the silence.

Samiel rose, his reflection in the grimy mirror a stranger: hollow eyes, jaw tight as a coffin lid. He traced the scar on his brow—a relic from the closet—and wondered if the Gloom would carve deeper.

No one stood at the door to say goodbye. The house exhaled as he left, as if relieved to be rid of him. Rain fell in sheets, needling his skin, but he didn't hurry. Let it drown the memories: his mother's averted gaze, his father's syringes glinting in the dark, the closet's *thud-thud-thud.*

The transport idled at the curb, its windows opaque and weeping condensation. Samiel paused, his reflection warped in the glass—a spectre stretched thin. For a heartbeat, he saw *her* behind him, black dress blending with the rain, mouth shaped around a warning. He turned. Empty street.

Hallucination. Or mercy.

He slid into the car. The seat groaned, smelling of synthetic leather and strangers' sweat. He reached for the pendant in his pack. The pendant dug into his palm, its broken edges drawing blood.

As the transport lurched forward, he pressed a hand to the window. His childhood home shrank in the distance, its windows dark. No silhouettes waved. No lights flickered farewell. It vanished behind a curtain of rain, erased like a mistake.

The Glass Cities loomed ahead, their spires jagged and furious, piercing the cloudy sky. Bioluminescent fungi smothered their bases, glowing, beautiful, but to him like infected wounds. Samiel's breath fogged the glass. *Verdant Spire*. A name that tasted like lies.

The emptiness in his chest yawned wider, a void where fear or hope should've been. He leaned into it. Let it devour the boy who wept in closets, who flinched at raised voices, who still believed in *saved.*

The pendant's chain snapped, the cross clattering to the floor. He left it there.

Through the haze, a Huitzilin silhouette circled the Spire, its roar vibrating in Samiel's molars. The transport's AI chirped: *"ETA 12 minutes."*

He closed his eyes. The woman waited in the dark, her hand outstretched, always just beyond reach.

This time, he thought, *I'll let the Gloom take us both.*

The Glass Cities glittered ahead, their spires standing bright and beautiful. For the first time, the emptiness in his chest felt like **power.**

The Verdant Spire rose like a hymn.

Samiel pressed his face to the transport's window, breath catching. After years of cracked smiles and basement mold, here the city's emerald glow gnawed at the horizon, he hadn't imagined anything could gleam like this. The Spire's central tower spiraled skyward, its surface a tapestry of polished steel and living ivy, leaves shimmering with bioluminescent dew. Cascading waterfalls—clean, tumbled from tiered gardens, their mist painting rainbows in the midday sun. The air, when he cracked the window, smelled of jasmine and freshly turned soil.

Dallas's Safe Zone stretched around the Spire in concentric rings: white domes housing markets and schools, solar panels glinting like dragon scales, children laughing as they chased drones shaped like butterflies. A woman sold peaches at a stall, their flesh sunset-orange. Samiel's throat tightened. A veil lifted before his own eyes.

The transport descended into the Spire's underground entrance, but not before Samiel glimpsed the barracks—ivy-clad terraces with open-air training grounds, recruits sparring under blossom trees, their movements almost graceful. No screams. No blood. Just the rhythmic clang of practice blades and the distant hum of a biotech orchestra, its melody woven from birdsong and synthesized strings.

The hangar door ahead was no jagged maw, but an arch of living wood fused with glowing crystal. As it opened, light spilled out—warm and gold, not the sterile fluorescence Samiel had expected. Dr. Vasquez Jr. stood framed in the glow, his lab coat crisp, his smile disarmingly human.

Recruits spilled from their transports, murmurs swelling into gasps. A boy reached out to touch a vine curling down the wall; it bloomed at his fingertips, petals unfolding in a ripple of sapphire light. Samiel knelt, brushing his hand over the floor—smooth, living moss pulsed gently beneath his palm, as if breathing.

"This is what we're fighting for?"

The thought undid him.

Memories lashed like shrapnel: his father's basement reeking of mildew, his mother's hollow eyes, the closet's suffocating dark. He'd braced for a fortress of scars, but this… this was a *sanctuary*. A place where light didn't sting, where soil wasn't poison.

Dr. Vasquez approached, his gaze piercing but not unkind. "You expected a tomb?"

Samiel straightened, jaw clenched. "I expected something different."

"Ah, but only the Gloom *hates* beauty," the doctor said, plucking a bioluminescent flower from the wall. It dimmed in his grip, then flared brighter. "That's why we cultivate it. Why we *fight* for it."

For the first time, Samiel noticed the scars beneath Vasquez's collar, the faint tremor in his hands. Even here, Eden had *thorns.*

A recruit laughed nearby, spinning beneath a shower of glowing petals. Most were uneasy, all were weary, knowing the truth. Samiel's chest ached, a old wound prodded. *Is this what they'll turn me* into? Not just a weapon, but a gardener. A guardian.

The doctor gestured to an arched corridor, its walls alive with fluttering moth-drones. As Samiel followed, he glanced back. The hangar door sealed, but sunlight still filtered through crystalline panels, painting the moss floor in dappled gold.

He touched the flower one last time—soft, alive, *fragile*.

Maybe, he thought, *beautiful things don't have to die*.

 Standing in the entry, Dr Vasquez JR, the Warden programs creators son. He took after his father's mission and continued to refine and perfect the Warden program.

"Welcome recruits! I see the long look on all of your faces, fear has no place here. What you see before you countless others have seen, consider it a great honor to serve your nation in such a capacity. Becoming a Warden ensures the safety of the remaining world. Not long ago we suffered at the hands of the gloom, desperation and poverty, death and sickness. The initiation of the Warden program set out to reverse that desperation, to turn it into glory. I see all you young faces standing here, I beg you, rejoice in this placement. Serve like our forefathers before us, change the landscape in front of you, alter your mind-state. Through this door, either certain death, or a prosperous future awaits, but it is solely up to you. Your mind and body will be tested, pushed to its absolute limits. We will break your sprit, but endow in you the strength, to face all adversities. Most of you will not survive, a necessary sacrifice to ensure our future. I beseech you, to die here is to die with honor. I welcome you to your new home." : Dr Vasquez

#

Chapter 7

The Soul Alchemy

The barracks, separated by gender, were a chilling sight. The only comparison was that of prison. Each recruit is taken to their room, each one isolated from the other. The psychological warfare starts right from the beginning. It was purposeful for the first round of trials. All recruits must feel isolated and alone. They must understand that in here they have no one but themselves. They must rely on no one. The rooms all came furnished with a mattress on the floor, a desk in the corner with their new holo-pad on it, a small closet with a uniform with their name on it. A door leading to a bathroom with a shower, was directly left of the entrance. The room had no windows, and one dimly lit light on the desk, a truly mind bending environment. The new holo-pad on the desk vibrates and chimes a message read:

"Warden recruits we bid you welcome, phase one of the trials begins tomorrow, sleep well, you will need it"

As the recruits were shown to their room, all belongings were taken, no distraction of family or loved ones was allowed. The underground base was massive en route to the barracks, they passed large helipads wit Huitzilins docked and ready to fly. Above them the entire roof could open at a moment's notice, an exit for all aircraft. Beyond that were large auditoriums with V.R pods for training. Continuing down the corridor, rifle ranges for target practice were on the left, to the right med stations. Past that rec rooms and cafeteria. Past that, rooms for upgrading weapons and armor. At the very end were the Warden recruit barracks.

Active Wardens had no living quarters down here. Once fully instated, Wardens have luxury apartments in the two spires next to the Verdant spire. They were our saviors, and they were to be treated as such. A generous gift from AEGIS.

The barracks were eerily silent, not a peep from anyone. The recruits still settling in, all in shock and afraid of what will become of them. Samiel was well adjusted, to him this was just as good as his room back home. He was a simple man living minimally was second nature and oddly comforting, no clutter and pure. Samiel laid on his bed, staring at the ceiling as his mind wanders, thinking of all he has been through. A sense of ease envelops him, a sense of happiness to be away from it all. His lips let out a smirk.

"He smiles this one,whats his name?" Dr. Vasquez asks.

"Samiel, sir," the private monitoring the cameras responds.

"Ahh, yes, I've seen his test results he show great promise. Well, monitor this one." Dr. Vasquez says.

"Yes sir,"

All rooms were monitored, the only privacy was the bathroom. All recruits were under surveillance in case of unforeseen anomalies. Every aspect studied with a fine-tooth comb. At lights out, all doors were locked, no one in or out. Samiel hears the door lock and the announcement of lights out over the intercom. His eyes grow heavy with each breath, he slips away into sleep. His dream plays out again, each time slightly different, each year changing entirely. He Stands in fog; the fog touching his knees. He's in a city he's never seen, with murals painted on the side of buildings. The city streets dilapidated, the buildings holding on by a thread. He hears a gut curling scream coming from one of the buildings, he runs toward the sound. Entering a building, he sees a horrid sight, blood everywhere, the walls appearing bathed in it. Traversing the halls, he enters a large room. He sees her; the woman laying on the ground in a pool of blood. She is still alive but barely, he walks up to her, kneels down and holds her hand. She whispers to him.

"The shadow is your strength, my love. Fear not, for I am always with you," she says.

As the life drains from her honey-glazed eyes, Samiel lets out a tear. He is always too late to save her. A loud bang comes from behind him, someone watching him. The ghost runs "stop" Samiel pleads to the silhouette. He chases after it, running to the door, he slams through it and falls, a dark pit. Just before hitting the bottom, he jolts up out of his sleep, sweating profusely. The door to his room unlocks and a voice over the intercom tells the recruits to report to the V.R pod's room. Phase one of the trials are to commence. The recruits race to get dressed and all pour out into the grand hall. At the door to the V.R pod's room stood Dr. Vasquez.

"Recruits welcome to phase one of the Warden program. Behind me are virtual reality pods, these pods are not any normal virtual reality pods. The pods are designed for prolong use, meaning it will intravenously feed you while in training. The first trial will approximately have you in V.R for one year, but it will not feel like one year. The tests will feel much longer, depending on your choices, and out comes those who survive the first two trials will move forward to the third. Those who fail, will not. As you enter, choose a pod, make yourself comfortable. Nurses will come around and connect you to your pods. I wish you luck, recruits."

Verbal gasps can be heard throughout the corridor. The recruits are stunned, one year in V.R. The group walks in each reaching a pod and sitting inside waiting to be connected. The pods were white and egg-shaped. Attached to the network, they glow a bioluminescent purple. The outside, covered in glyphs, pulsate. The inside was black, the seat comfortable and plush. Near where your head would rest, embedded in the seat, were nodes that connected to the user's brain wirelessly. Once connected, the nurse shoved tubes down their throats connected to the pods that feed them while under. All simulations were monitored, the A.I during trial one would weed out the weak and any who failed were awaken. Failing the first trial, however, did not result in death. Recruits who failed trial one, in the first phase were put into other operations program. In trial two, and henceforth, all failures result in death.

Samiel settles for a pod in the front. He gets in and gets comfortable. It was like laying on a cloud; he thought to himself. It wasn't a bad place to spend a year in suspended animation. Next to Samiel two young men also settled in.

"Ay, look at the bright side guys, it'll either be the best rest, or the longest one you feel me haha, ay what's your name bro? They call me Reaper ese,"

"I'm Sam,"

"Well, shit, we making friends before we die? Im Duke. Crazy how we ended up here, huh?"

"I'm still not too sure how we got picked, honestly," Samiel said.

"It's cause we're fucked in the head bro, that's what they say" Reaper responded.

"It's true. My father said it has something to do with trauma. Everyone here had some fucked up shit happened to em. We all have something in common," Duke stated.

"Yea, my parents beat me for fun, ese, my dad when he'd drink, and my mother well when she felt like it, and you, what happened to you Duke?" Reaper asked.

"Me? shit i watched my mother get mushed by a truck when I was ten. Fucked me up good. What about you, Sam?" Duke asked.

The talk was cut short; the nurses started from the back, making their way to the front. As they reached Samiels and the boys, loud screams started erupting from the pods, muffled by the pods themselves, but very much audible. The young men look at eachother in shock.

"We're in for a ride ese, holy shit, let fucking do it, lets go nurse link me up." Reaper said.

The boys all shared a laugh. Their time has come. Samiel watches as Reaper is put under and the pod doors close. The nurse turns to him and gets him settled. Duke as well, at the same time, both went under. The first trial begins.

"Those boys in the front, the ones laughing, they show great promise," Dr. Vasquez stated.

"Yes sir, they do," a private responded

"Ok they are all in, activate movement protocal," Dr. vasquez ordered

"yes sir," responded the private.

The movement protocol was essential for the V.R pod training. The pods, already in sync with the user, turn the recruit upright from a laying position. The plush bed retracts back and the pod fills with embryotic fluid. The movements in V.R, acted out in real life to prevent atrophy of the body and muscles. The pods are state-of-the-art tech. The first trial is fairly simple but terrifying none the less, some recruits last longer than others, but out of 150 recruits it is likely around 20 will fail.

Samiel awakes in a grocery store, his memory fuzzy. The people seem strange. He can't quite put his finger on it, but regardless, he walks about. He hears the laughter of children running about a mother chasing after them. He sees people filling their carts with goods. As he walks throughout the aisles, he notices price tags on all the food. The people are paying for groceries; he is shocked by this. Quickly Samiel realizes he is in V.R, and understands there is a test. As he walks about the store, he wonders what kind of test this is, its seems pointless. A loud air horn starts blaring, Samiel rushes to the front of the store.

The people all look worried and concerned. Loud sirens start screeching from everyone's pockets, including his own. He reaches in and pulls out a smartphone, and OER, and on it reads a message:

"This is the Emergency alert system. Large earthquakes are being reported around the globe. Please stay indoors until further notice, await further instructions."

The message was ominous and unclear, and that's when it happened. The whole market shakes violently, glass shattering all around. The aisles falling apart, food tossed about. Samiel heads out the door, safer to be outside in case of collapse. A large crack develops across the parking lot and spreads wider and wider. Cars swallowed whole, the market collapses, the screams of innocent civilians are torture to his ears. Samiel runs the opposite direction of the crack as fast as he possibly could. Everywhere he turns people dieing, some crushed by vehicles, some by the devouring hole. Samiel hears a family screaming for help. Their car sits at the cusp of the gorge, the car inching closer to death. Samiel runs to help the family exit the vehicle before it's too late. He grabs a rock and mid stride throws it, breaking the back window. He jumps on the trunk of the car, shifting its weight back to the ground, but time is short. He Yells for them to exit through the rear, helping the children out first. As the children are secured he reaches for the parents next mother and father slide to the back seat. The car begins to fall Samiel rolls back off the trunk, watching as the parents fall into the chasm. The children cry. Samiel turns around to go comfort them. A vehicle out of controls runs over the two children. Samiel, covered in blood and in shock, sets off running for the treeline the forest may provide him respite.

Panting and out of breath, he makes it to the forest. Samiel finds a tree and sits down, shaking, in shock, and covered in blood. He sits there. He hears branches crack around him and calls out to the noise. Silence, he figures the shock is playing tricks on him, but he hears a woman's soft voice:

"I am with you my love, have no fear,"

It's her, from his dreams, but how? Samiel calls out to her. The silence grows louder. The simulation resets the world crumbling all around him. Samiel starts the process over again. Each time the simulation changing, either a new location or the same one. The first trial instills perseverance through doubt, no matter the outcomes. Recruits who try to save as many people as possible succeed. Those who give up are awakened and let out of the pod. Failures have no place in the program. Wardens encounter insurmountable odds every day. There is no giving up Warden persevere. After subjecting them to this enough, the recruits are sent to the second part of trial one, the betrayal protocol.

Samiel, having passed his first part, now wakes in a gloom ridden city. A dense fog covers every square inch. Equipped with standard military load-out. With his rifle in hand, he walks the desolate town, hungry and tired. In the distance, he sees smoke ascending into the air, a possible refugee camp. Stealthily, he makes his way over, checking his corners for any and all surprises. As he approaches, he smells meat frying, oh the lovely smell of steak wafts in the air. He reaches a building, across from the smoke and sees an elderly man by himself. Cooking and dancing, happy to be alive, just him and his little puppy, enjoying life. Samiel. drops his rifle, and calmly walks over.

"Hello sir!? i dont mean to harm you in any way i was wondering if you could spare some food?," Samiel asked.

"Well, hello there to you, absolutely, young man. Come, come. Please, sit and relax. Enjoy yourself a weary traveler such as yourself out here all alone? How strange," The old man rebutted.

"Yes sir, im famished. thank you for showing hospitality. Its nice to see another friendly face," Samiel said.

"I could say the same. Here, grab a plate. There's plenty for the three of us aint that right rocky," the dog barks, acknowledging the old man ask speaks.

The two laugh and converse for what seems like hours. In the distance, two gloom hounds stalk them as they enjoy themselves. Creeping closer and closer, the hound's hunks of steel and flesh smell their prize. Samiel notices movement from the corner of his eye and springs into action, drawing his rifle. The old man grabs his rifle as well, the hounds growling and barking in a muffled static tone, inch closer and closer. Two more hounds materialize from the darkness. A woman's voice whispers to him:

"You know what has to be done,"

Samiel steps further and further back, out pacing the old man. He raises his rifle and lets off two shots. The air is still and heavy. The puppy cries as the body of the old man falls. The hounds pounce on the old man, ravaging his body. The puppies' cry eventually subsides.

Samiel having replayed the simulation countless times. Every one trying to save the old man and dog, never surviving, understood what needed to be done. There was no other way. The test would not allow it, it was designed to rid out weakness, to birth a ruthless machine of war. If recruits did not realize this, the simulation would eventually kill them. Dieing too many times in V.R has repercussions, and inevitable death. Those who could not stomach the decision that had to be made. Suffered to the end. Wardens had to be ruthless, empathy had to be stripped from them. In this part of the trial, 30 recruits lost their lives, leaving only 100 for the last round of trials. While the bodies of dead recruits are being cleaned out of their pods, the recruits pass through to round 3 of trials, the Labyrinth.

Samiel, groggy and tired, materializes on a new plain. The pyramid of the sun the epicenter of the network growth. It's night time as most of the simulations were, save the first. The stars gleaming in the sky, beautiful and radiating. The sand beneath his feet, he is barefoot. Only wearing shorts and no shirt, he's puzzled. In front of him was a campfire with food cooking. He calls out but no answer. The place deserted, what tricks will this test hide? He sits to enjoy a meal before gathering his strength. The pyramid in front of him is his next hurdle. A bright light shines at its apex, his next test. After a much needed break, and some food, he makes his way to the behemoth. It's a long way up, he begins to ascend step by step. His mind racing, he tries to anticipate his next trial, but to no avail. The tests are gruesome and mind-altering. At its apex, Samiel takes a breath, one final look at the rhythmic scenery.

He steps through the threshold, the surrounding walls begin to shift and move like a puzzle. The room turning into a maze; the ceiling disappearing, revealing only stars. Its obsidian walls humming with suppressed gloom energy. The air reeks of burnt copal incense and decay. The scene is pitch black, offering nothing but your senses to guide you. A glow emits from his under him a bioluminescent fungus pod, a dim light, but it should help. The maze changes and shifts like tectonic plates, should you stumble, and the walls close in, crushing you. Samiel walks the maze, turning left, turning right, allowing his senses to guide him. 30 minutes in and the fungus pod light dies. The silence is deafening, his ears ring. Calming his mind and steading his breath, he listens for the changes in the maze. He starts walking again, each step fearful a wall will close. He hastens his pace. The loud bangs of walls clashing offer no comfort and appear to be getting closer. His eyesight adapting to the darkness, he was able to see. The exit lies before him, a doorway to an empty chamber. He makes a dash to it, leaping inside.

A hexagonal room lined with polished black stone. Samiel stares at his reflection in the stone. The reflection warps and molds into gloom mimics. Shouting at him his failures and using his fears against him.

"You will die here!."

"You will die alone!"

"You are scum"

"No one could ever love a scum like you!,"

Samiel raises his fists and beats at the stone, each hit cracking it. The walls start closing in. He continues to pound at the stone, his hands bleeding more with each strike. Numb to his pain, he continues until shattering the stone. The pieces fall to the ground and morph into scarabs. He runs, scarabs giving chase as he reaches the end of the corridor. A wall comes smashing down, killing a few beetles in the process, and the room shifts.

A door appears in front of him, sealed by a rotating stone wheel. Etched with Nahuatl Glyphs, a puzzle recounting the myth of Huitzilopochtli's birth. A god who slew his sister in the womb. Samiel begins rearranging the glyphs in correct order. He misplaces one and vents in the stone open, a flood of hallucinogenic gas fills the chamber. He begins to vomit and convulse. The puzzle must be finished to continue. He presses on arranging the glyphs and the stone door opens. Coughing and vomiting, he walks through. Standing at the edge of a canyon in the night, only one path forward, a bridge.

A chasm spanned by a narrow bridge, lined with vibrating monofilament wires. Below gloom crocodiles, hungry and waiting. Samiel steps forward. He places his hand on the wire, horrifying memories of his past play in his mind upon touching it. He lets go in pain, hallucinations of his family and parents appear fading in and out, yelling nasty profanities at him. Stepping on the bridge, he realizes sections crumbling and falling. It requires leaps of faith to get across. The crocodiles beneath snapping at the falling debris with each leap. Samiel makes it across, just barely. The haunting vision and hallucinations made it tricky and difficult, but his will was undefeated. He continues on his mind, feeling broken and twisted thus far.

Samiel arrives at a new corridor. The walls drip with psychotropic moss. A corridor of hallucinations, the corridor materializes your worst nightmare. Samiel sees the woman from his dreams. She cries for help, gloom beasts ripping her apart, blood engulfing him. He fights off the gloom beasts with his bare hands, his eyes filling with rage and anger. He fights and fights. The test is cruel but important. He must let go. Understanding this is all in his head, he passes one horrific scene after the other. Him being beaten as a child, his mother's cold words, his father's abandonment. The mental torture has run its course. Reaching the end, the corridor opens.

The sunlit courtyard of Teotihuacáns zenith, an AEGIS officer, greets him. Congratulating him on a job well done, offering water and a medkit. Samiel was paranoid and hesitant, he feels a sense of dread as though this cannot be the end. Of all ways to end the test, this seems off. Taking a sip of the water, he feels an intense burn run through his body. Samiel goes stiff, paralyzed, he collapses. The floor retracts into the true final chamber. The walls, lined with calcified remains of failed recruits, shocks him. A Nahuatl Glyph inscription glows:

"Only the serpent who sheds his skin SURVIVES"

The final test, Samiel surveys the room. Up to this point, every action was a misdirection. He sees the exit in front of him, but given the glyph, he knows it is not that simple. He paces back and forth. Samiel walks to the opposite walk. Grazing his hand across it, he realizes it is made of brittle gloom crystal. He goes for a punch, but nothing, not a crack. He walks around the room searching for something to break the crystal wall with. He started rummaging through the corpses strung up on the wall one by one. While searching, he finds in one corpse a ceremonial Tepoztli hammer. He grabs the hammer and starts demolishing the wall. With each strike of the hammer, the wall disintegrates, the path is forward is pitch black. Samiel takes one final look at the exit door behind him. Confident in his decision, he runs into the pitch black chamber. A wise choice, the only recruit to pass it on the first try. The labyrinth mirrors the glooms Chaos no logic, no mercy, only adaptation.

"Truly remarkable this young man is, the first to pass the false exit trial in the first round," Dr. Vasquez stated.

#

Chapter 8

The Blood Eagle

The egg-shaped pods glistened in the training bay, the pods open. A year passed in animated suspension. Their bodies need time to adjust. The resurrection bay hummed with cold, antiseptic efficiency. Row upon row of white egg-shaped pods glowed faintly in the cavernous chamber, their surfaces etched with circuitry that pulsed cobalt-blue. Inside each, recruits floated in viscous amniotic gel, bodies suspended like insects in amber, while their minds endured the Ascendance Project's simulations—a gauntlet of fractal puzzles, moral labyrinths, and Gloom-infested nightmares designed to forge *Wardens*. To break gods, you first had to shatter souls.

Samiel's pod hissed open, gel draining in a syrupy cascade as neural filaments retracted from his temples, leaving pinprick scars. He collapsed onto the polished black floor, coughing fluid from his lungs, his muscles twitching with phantom memories of the trials. A year of psychological carnage: forcing recruits to abandon allies in simulated Gloom hives, solving quantum ciphers mid-firefight, enduring hallucinatory loops where their own screams became the soundtrack . His vision swam, but he steadied himself against the pod's warm, pulsing interior. The nurses froze, their mirrored visors reflecting his unnerving lucidity—no tremors, no vacant stare. Dr. Vasquez materialized from the steam, clipboard in hand, his voice a blade wrapped in silk. "Fascinating. The gel hasn't clouded your irises. No… *hemorrhaging.*" He gestured to the corpse-filled bags. Beside him, Duke's pod disgorged the giant in a roar of curses, his augmented arm sparking from where he'd torn it free during a trial. Reaper emerged silent and lethal, his pupils still contracted from weeks spent in a simulation where darkness meant death.

"Recovered subjects proceed to debrief," droned an AI voice as medical drones descended, their spider-like limbs prodding at the survivors. Most recruits stumbled or crawled, synapses fried by the false exit—the Ascendance's final trick. To escape the simulation, you had to ignore the glowing, obvious exit and instead find the alternative. Fail, and the trial reset, each loop stretching subjective time into years. Many died, clawing their eyes out in the gel. One recruit nearby giggled uncontrollably, his hair gone white, repeating, "The exit's a lie, the exit's a lie…"

The remaining recruits are put on wheelchairs and rolled to their rooms. The scene is untasteful, bodies being dragged to body bags in preperation for cremation. The recruits, dazed and confused, see glimpses of the scenes unfolding.

Dr. Vasquez observed from a floating platform. "Remarkable, Samiel," he said, studying a hologram of Samiel's neural readouts. "You solved the false exit in *seven minutes*. Even our AIs average twelve." His smile didn't reach his eyes. "What did you see?"

Samiel said nothing. He'd seen through the trial's cruel poetry. His reflection in the pod's surface showed faint scars: glowing fractal patterns under his skin where the gel's nanites had rewired him. Samiel is awake for all of it. His alertness is considered strange to the nurses and Dr. Vasquez. Truly, a first, his individuation is undeniable. He is in considerable shock but also grateful the test is over. Samiel found kinship in the broken. Duke, a mountain of muscle and synth-flesh grafts, had brute-forced his way through simulations. Reaper, gaunt and ghost-pale, could still smell the Gloom's rot in his nostrils, his aim now preternaturally precise. Together, they became obsidian. Dawn drills in the gym, fists pounding punching bags filled with metal shavings. Dusk sessions in the shooting range, lit only by the toxic glow of bioluminescent fungi. Samiel taught them to exploit the Gloom's

weaknesses. But the Blood Eagle loomed. Whispers said it wasn't virtual. They excelled in

every aspect of training, but the final test would test their strength. All recruits must endure

The *"Blood Eagle"* the final trial of phase one.

After the final phase, body augmentation began, and Wardens were born. The recruits

needed to be at 100 percent before the next trial. The trial would test their cohesiveness, and

sheer brutality to succeed in any circumstance.

"What do you think the next trial is bro?" Reaper asked Samiel

"I dont know. What I do know is it's going to be hard,"

"What makes you say that?" Duke asked.

"Well, look at us. We're training, eating, not in any distress, not being killed, or

mentally fucked with. So im sure the next test is not goin to be a walk in the park,"

"So negative Hermano, who knows, maybe it will be. We'll see some flowers, a

bunny, hahaha," Reaper laughed to himself.

"Ha, yea right Reaper. They're fattening us up for a reason, and it's not to pet

bunnies," Duke said.

"I know but a man can dream, ese," Reaper said, smirking.

"I'd rather it be puppies." Samiel chimed in.

"See ese, that's the spirit," Reaper said, laughing.

The men laughed, knowing what Samiel said holds weight. They were unafraid of

what lay ahead for them, and if they could, they would face it as a team. As the month ended,

an eagerness and unsteady air was about the recruits, eager to know their next trial. Dr.

Vasquez would order on the last day of the month a feast to be held in honor of the remaining

recruits the night before the blood eagle. The main hall was transformed into a banquet, a

long table running down its center fit for 80 recruits, and Dr. Vasquez. The false exit test only claimed the lives of 20 recruits. The next trial is sure to claim more than double that. The table, adorned with beautiful silverware and elegant cutlery, was ready for a feast fit for kings. The recruits were told the banquet would begin at sunset. At sunset, the recruits made their way to the hall, excited for the feast. All but one. Naturally suspicious, Samiel saw this as a final supper, and the following days a crucifixion. He was unable to hide it, his face gave away his true insights. So much so even Dr. Vasquez could pick up on it.

The recruits filed into the vault-like hall, their footsteps echoing off cold, blackened stone. Shadows clung to the edges of the room like specters, the only light a sickly amber glow from iron sconces that flickered as if gasping for air. The long table before them groaned under platters of roasted meat glistening with fat, blood-red wines, and bruised fruits—a feast that smelled faintly of iron and decay. Samiel took his seat, his spine rigid, as the others laughed too loudly, their voices brittle with forced bravado.

Dr. Vasquez rose from the head of the table, his lab coat unnervingly pristine against the room's rot-stained grandeur. His smile stretched like a scar. "Ladies and gentlemen," he purred, the words syrupy and cold, "how *eagerly* you await this… *celebration*." His gaze swept over them, lingering on hollow-eyed recruits who flinched as if scalded. "Tomorrow, your final trial begins. Those who survive will emerge as *Wardens*." He paused, teeth glinting in the dim light. "And the rest? Well. Let us toast to your… *remarkable* potential."

The room erupted in ragged cheers, fists pounding the table hard enough to rattle the cutlery. Goblets spilled wine like old wounds weeping. Samiel sat motionless, his reflection warped in the polished silver plate before him—a face already haunted by what lurked in the shadows of Vasquez's words.

"Samiel." The doctor's voice slithered through the noise, silencing it. All eyes turned. "You refuse to revel in this… *triumph*. Why?"

The air thickened. Somewhere, a draft moaned through cracks in the walls, carrying the faintest whisper of screams—or was it the wind? Samiel stood, his chair screeching like a dying thing. "This isn't a celebration, *sir*," he said, voice steady as a grave marker. "It's a last meal. We all know what the trials do to those who fail. *If* they even find the bodies."

Vasquez's laugh crackled, sharp and brittle. "Oh, *Samiel*," he crooned, stepping into the light. His eyes were voids, pupils dilated to swallow the room. ***"You see so clearly. Pity your peers do not."*** He raised his glass, the wine inside black as congealed blood. "Eat. Drink. Savor every *morsel*." His smile turned feral. "Tomorrow, the Gloom feasts on *you*."

The recruits froze. A few choked back whimpers. Platters suddenly reeked of charred flesh; the fruits oozed dark, viscous liquid. Samiel stared at his trembling hands, the truth settling like a corpse's weight: the real trial had already begun.

The room, once alive with the ebullient hum of laughter and the warm glow of shared smiles, shifted imperceptibly as a flicker of unease rippled through the air—conversations faltered mid-chuckle, hands stilled mid-gesture, and eyes, once crinkled with mirth, narrowed with wary calculation, their gazes darting toward the door where an unexpected silence had settled, heavy and thick, like the pause between lightning and thunder, until even the clink of glasses ceased, leaving only the nervous tap of a foot and the faint creak of someone leaning forward, spines straightened, breaths held, as if the walls themselves had whispered a warning.

The recruits picked their plates clean, the clatter of cutlery echoing through the sterile mess hall like a funeral dirge. The food, delicious and savory, had tasted of nothing in that moment, but they ate ravenously. Calories were currency here. Samiel watched Duke lick grease from his augmented knuckles, while Reaper dissected his meal with surgical precision, searching for hidden messages in the gristle. None came.

They were herded back to their cells by drones, the hexagonal chambers sealing shut with a *hiss* of hydraulic malice. The night stretched thin, the base's artificial skyline dimming to a bruised purple. Some recruits slept fitfully, their breaths fogging the glass doors. Others paced, fingers tracing the fractal scars left by the simulation pods. Samiel sat cross-legged on his bunk, sharpening his phase-blade against a stolen whetstone. The air tasted metallic, charged—like the moment before a Gloomstorm.

At 0400, the vents hissed. Samiel's head snapped up. A faint *psssh* echoed through the cellblock, and then the gas came—neon-green and sweetly floral, pooling like liquid poison across the floor. He lunged for the door, phase-blade raised, but his legs buckled. The world tilted. Reaper's cell flashed in his periphery: the man slamming his fist into the glass, cracks spider-webbing, before he collapsed mid-punch. Duke roared, a sound swallowed by the fog, then silence. AEGIS agents stormed the block, their black hazmat suits glistening with anti-Gloom resin. Gas masks distorted their faces into insectoid voids. They moved with cold precision, prying open cell doors and dragging recruits by their ankles. Samiel fought the numbness, his fingers twitching as an agent rolled him onto a stretcher.

"Subject Samiel-A responsive," the agent droned to a partner. "Administer secondary dose."

A needle pricked Samiel's neck. Cold fire flooded his veins. He faded in and out: The sting of shears cutting through his fatigues. Rough hands stripping him to his shorts, the air biting his exposed fractal scars. A woman's voice: *"Leave the bras. Let the Drakes smell their fear."* A pneumatic tool prying his jaw open, the grind of metal against enamel. Samiel's tongue probed the ache in his mouth. A back molar felt wrong—smooth, cold. He blinked groggily as an agent clamped his head in place.

"Mandible secure. Implanting M-09x."

A device whirred, injecting something into his gumline. He tasted blood. The agent leaned close, breath fogging his visor. "Sweet dreams." Unconscious, the recruits were loaded into Huitzilin copters. Samiel's stretcher slammed against Duke's in the cargo hold, their limbs tangled. Reaper hung limp in a harness, his arm disengaged, fingers still curled into a fist. The copters shuddered to life, wings chewing through the hangar's bioluminescent fungi, sending glowing spores swirling into the abyss.

Samiel's still unconscious as the Huitzilin's bay doors yawned, Gloom-tainted wind screaming into the hold. His hands were free, his body clad only in shorts, the obsidian blade strapped to his thigh with a note. A boot slammed into his back. He fell, the world a blur of rotting green canopy and jagged cliffs. Somewhere below, a Gloom Drake screeched. Samiel, half dazed slowly awakening, grabbed the blade, its edge humming with dormant energy, and spotted the others tumbling through the acid rain—Duke roaring, Reaper already twisting into a controlled dive.

As he plummeted, Samiel tongued the implant. It throbbed faintly, a tiny LED blinking behind his molar. *Tracker? Poison?* Vasquez's voice slithered into his memory: *"You'll thank us later."* The jungle rose to meet him—a living culture of writhing vines and pulsating fungi. Samiel falls unconscious again, phase-blade glowing to life. Samiel, awakening the sun grazing his face through dilapidated trees, sees the situation before him. The final test the gloom itself. A truly diabolical test left with nothing but a blade. The note attached reads:

*"**Blood Eagle survival protocol,***

***Objective:**￼*

You have been deployed to a sector of a gloom corrupted jungle, to complete the Blood Eagle Trial. Your mandate is twofold:

1: survive for seven solar cycles.

2: Eliminate designated gloom jaguar (Taxonomic ID: Panthera onca obscurum)

Failure to achieve either objective will result in immediate termination.

Equipment issued:

1: Obsidian blade, formed of eclipsite alloy. Do not lose.

2: Contingency Implant, located in your lower left molar. Bite down with force to end trial.

3: Fungal nose clip: a clip to be attached to the nose for filtering of gloom toxins 15 day life span.

The Blood Eagle Trial.

Rules of Engagement:

No Exratction: Extraction protocols are suspended.

No Aid: Interaction with non hostile entities is prohibited.

No Retreat: Active gloom reactors bound the trial zone. Cross the perimeter, and detonation is assured. On the seventh day extraction will be at sunset at the perimeter.

Survival Advisory:

The gloom jaguar is an apex predator class gloom beast. It hunts via subsonic vocalizations and thermal mimicry. Assume it is always watching.

Water sources are 89% contaminated. Prioritize fluid extraction via gloom-cacti.

Closing Directive:

*Survival is not a virtue, **IT IS A MANDATE**. The gloom does not care for your prayers, your fear, or your past. Neither do we.*

The Warden's shadow falls only on the worthy. Break or be broken

Dr. Vasquez Director of Project Warden,"

The letter was a final taunt to recruits, 7 days in this hellscape. Fitting, Samiel thinks to himself, a final test of survival and wits in the place we will soon call our home. The letter made great kidling for a fire. The air was thick with the stench of rotting vegetation. The jungle pulsed around him, bioluminescent fungi glowed like curse lanterns as the night drew closer. Twisted trees creaked as if whispering secrets to the shadows. AEGIS had stripped him of everything but his resolve. His first task survive the night. As dawn breaks the horizon, Samiel's throat burns with thirst. Gloom-cacti oozed viscous, iridescent sap. He'd trained for this. Slitting one open, he filtered the fluid through moss, drinking only when it turned clear. Hunger gnawed at him, but the jungle's fauna were no ordinary prey. A swarm of gloom moths descended, their wings shedding corrosive dust. He smeared himself in mud to mask his scent, clinging to the shadows. He makes his way to a river and set up camp for the night.

The river slithered through the Gloom like a liquid serpent, its currents shimmering with unnatural iridescence—neon greens and violets bleeding into the water from toxic mineral veins. Samiel crouched at the bank, his reflection fractured by the ripples, and scanned the gnarled trees clawing up from the muck. Their trunks pulsed with bioluminescent fungi, casting a sickly turquoise glow over the clearing. He chose a skeletal fig tree, its roots coiled like arthritic fingers, to build his camp. Above, the canopy seethed with shadows, but the river's murmurs masked the worst of the Gloom's whispers.

Dung beetles were easy prey, if you knew their habits. The size of feral cats, their carapaces gleamed like oil-slick, segmented plates overlapping like medieval armor. They moved in skittering bursts, mandibles clicking as they devoured clumps of rotting Gloom flora, purging toxins with a low, guttural hum deep in their thoraxes. Samiel scaled the fig tree, its bark crumbling like ash beneath his grip, and perched on a sagging branch. Below, a beetle emerged from the undergrowth, its antennae twitching as it gnawed a bulbous mushroom. The fungus hissed, releasing a plume of spores that glowed briefly before dissolving into the beetle's mouth.

Samiel waited.

The beetle scuttled closer, its six legs tapping a staccato rhythm on the petrified moss. Beneath its armored belly, the ground sizzled faintly where it excreted purified waste. *Three feet. Two.* Samiel's muscles coiled. The beetle paused beneath him, mandibles buried in a carcass—a decaying ratbird, its feathers still smoldering with residual radiation. He dropped like a stone, dagger angled downward. The blade punched through the beetle's thorax with a wet *crunch*, piercing the neural cluster between its wings. The creature spasmed, legs flailing, acidic drool hissing as it ate into the soil. Samiel pinned it with his weight, wrenching the dagger free in a spray of iridescent hemolymph that stank of ammonia and burnt sugar.

A fatal blow, dragging the corpse back to fire a sense of relief over takes him, finally, some luck. Back at camp, he gutted the beetle by firelight. The flames, fed by sulfurous driftwood, spat embers that popped like distant gunfire. Samiel worked methodically: He plucks the beetle's wings and pincers. He will fashion them into armor and weapons later. The beetles hard scaly exterior was great for such things. the pincers curved and serrated, they gleamed like blackened steel. He honed their edges against a flat river rock, sparks skittering into the dark. The head he severed with a twist, its compound eyes still glowing a faint radioactive green. Perfect for luring scavengers. The body is where the meat is. He slit the abdomen carefully, avoiding the toxin sacs nestled near the spine. The stomach burst open, disgorging a slick of half-digested spores that writhed like maggots. He hurled the mass into the river, where it erupted in a geyser of neon-orange foam, tendrils of smoke curling upward, an enchanting sight. The meat, nestled beneath the carapace, was lean and iridescent blue. He skewered it on a sharpened branch, the fire's heat transforming it into something resembling food—charred at the edges, glistening with rendered fat.

Samiel is ready for a feast of his own making. He sits aside the fire, collecting his sweat to lather on the beetle a little salt to ease the unfamiliar taste. He ate, watching the tree line. Shapes moved in the shadows—scaled, many-limbed things drawn by the scent of blood. His dagger stayed unsheathed, its edge reflecting the fire's dance. When the meat was gone, his hunger subdued, he banked the flames and retreated to his shelter, a hollow beneath the fig's roots, lined with beetle wings and moss. Sleep came in fitful bursts. Somewhere upstream, a Drake's roar split the night, shaking the river into frothing waves. Samiel curled tighter around his blade, the beetle's pincer clutched like a talisman. Dawn, when it came, was a gray smear behind the Gloom's perpetual haze. He counted his breaths. Alive. For now.

#

Chapter 9

Break Or Be Broken

The sun rises on the third day, there's a slight breeze in the air. Emerging from his little nook, Samiel stares into the jungle wasteland. With the remains of yesterday's hunt, it's time to prep for the real beast. The Gloom jaguar announced itself with a subsonic growl that vibrated in samiels bones. Peering through the dense forest trees, he glimpsed it. A hulking silhouette with obsidian claws and eyes like smoldering coals. Its pelt shimmered with nanite infused scales, blending into gloom haze. A sort of Camoflauge, not entirely still visible to the naked eye but somewhat hidden. At night, he's almost invisible. Samiel rigs a snare trap, baiting it with yesterday's kill. The jaguar avoided it, smarter than expected. He has to devise a new plan. With the sun setting, today's hunt was a bust, no jaguar. The walk back to camp was somber and quiet. The jungles reflecting his dissatisfaction, and eerie calm. Reaching his camp and lit the fire, eating his leftovers from the previous day, he ponders a new strategy.

The sun clawed weakly through a quilt of leaden clouds, its light smothered into a sulfurous haze that stained the horizon the color of a fresh bruise. A glacial wind swept through the Gloom, bending skeletal trees into creaking bows, their leaves—translucent and veined with bioluminescence—shivering like a thousand fractured mirrors. Samiel stood at the edge of his camp, the air thick with the acidic tang of the approaching storm. Above, the sky churned, clouds spiraling into a vortex of emerald and charcoal, lightning flickering in its depths like a serpent's tongue.

He worked swiftly, reinforcing his shelter with scavenged materials: beetle carapaces lashed together with sinew, their hardened skin plates overlapping like dragon scales. The acidic rain would eat through anything organic, so he layered the roof with broad, waxy leaves from a mutated tree, their surfaces seeping a viscous sap that hissed as it hardened into a resinous shield. The wind grew teeth, gnawing at his exposed skin as he anchored the walls with stones, their surfaces pitted from centuries of chemical erosion. Satisfied, he slung his blade across his back and melted into the jungle.

The beetles had grown bolder with the storm's approach, their armored bodies clattering through the underbrush like living tanks. Samiel tracked one by the guttural chittering deep in its thorax, a sound that reverberated through the petrified ferns. It was a colossal specimen, its carapace streaked with phosphorescent algae, mandibles snapping through a knot of glowing fungi. Samiel stalked it from the shadows, his boots silent on the ashen soil. When it paused to regurgitate toxins into a sinkhole, he struck—dagger plunging into the soft joint between its head and thorax. The beetle spasmed, legs scrabbling, before collapsing in a pool of iridescent hemolymph that steamed where it met the ground. He gutted the beetle swiftly, salvaging meat and chitin, but the jungle's whispers had shifted. Branches cracked where no wind blew. Samiel shouldered his kill and retreated, thunder growling in the distance like a starved beast. Halfway to camp, he froze. A footprint, fresh and human, dented the mud beside a cluster of bioluminescent toadstools. He smirked. *Company.* Back at camp, he built a fire in the pit lined with heat-resistant beetle scales, flames devouring sulfurous driftwood. As he skewered meat on jagged branches, shadows danced at the edge of the firelight—too deliberate, too *hungry*. Samiel raised his voice above the wind.

"How long can you hold out?"

A figure emerged from the gloom, gaunt and wild-eyed, hair the color of bleached bone. His fatigues hung in tatters, skin mapped with burns and half-healed scars.

"How long did you know I was here?"

Samiel didn't glance up. "Here? Ha! Heard you stepping on a spinevine three clicks back,"

Before the white-haired man could retort, the jungle erupted. A jaguar—muscles corded under patchy fur, eyes glowing with radioactive amber—lunged from the brush. It slammed into him, claws raking his chest as they crashed into the fire. Samiel moved on instinct, spear in one hand, blade in the other. The beast whipped its head toward him, jaws dripping saliva that sizzled where it struck the ground. The fight was chaos. The jaguar's claws tore through the man's shoulder, blood spraying in black arcs under the greenish light. Samiel feinted left, driving his spear into the creature's flank, but it twisted, snapping the shaft. The man roared, plunging his own blade into its throat, and finished it with a slash across its milky, pupilless eyes. The carcass collapsed, pinning him beneath its smoldering bulk.

Samiel hauled the beast aside, muscles straining. "Thanks," Maximus gasped, clutching his shredded shoulder. "I'm Maximus. From the hall. Guess you were right about the trial."

"Yea guess I was, Samiel. What was your plan exactly?" Samiel asked.

"I didn't have one. I figured I'd eventually work up the strength to ask you to team up," Maximus replied.

"Took you long enough," Samiel said, laughing, tossing him a rag soaked in antiseptic beetle bile.

"Yea, we can team up. Now you have to help me with my jaguar. seeing as I helped with yours,"

"Absolutely……"

The first raindrop struck as Maximus reached for his blade. It hit his cheek with a sizzle, burning through flesh to the bone. He screamed, clawing at his face as the implant in his molar—exposed by the acid—detonated, cyanide flooding his veins. Foam bubbled from his lips, his body convulsing. Samiel lunged, dragging him under the canopy as the storm unleashed its fury. Acid rain ate through leaves, the campfire hissing into smoke. He pried Maximus's jaw open, fingers blistering as he ripped out the shattered implant—a tiny chrome orb, its surface etched with AEGIS's emblem. Desperate, he packed the wound with beetle intestine, the alkaline guts neutralizing the acid. Maximus's breath rattled, his skin gray.

Samiel crouched in the ruins of his shelter, the storm screaming overhead. Maximus lay motionless, alive but brittle. Beyond the resin-streaked walls, shapes moved—twisted, half-seen things drawn by the scent of blood and weakness. He gripped his blade, the edge glowing faintly with residual bioluminescence.

A cruel twist. Cyanide, he thought.

But the Gloom had only begun to feast.

The fifth day was off to a horrible start. A new ally lay unconscious. His trial just got a harder. The thought of letting Maximus die in this jungle had crossed his mind, but he refused to let the man die when he completed his trial. *What a waste*, he thought. Samiel took on the extra work tending to his allies' wounds. He wouldn't deny a Warden their rite of passage. He will give him the best chance of surviving. Placing his body in the nook and covering him for protection, Samiel left the safety of the camp he had two days left to complete his trial. Samiel spent the day in the trees, watching and stalking his prey, learning his movements. Studying its habits and looking for weaknesses. The beast was tough. A shot to the head would be simpler, but he had no such luxury. The night soon came. He thinks he's found a way to get his target. The night sky glistened, beautiful and full of stars. On his way back, he gathered water and slaughtered another beetle. He needed the intestines, and he was going to have to make a stretcher out of what he had left for the walk back to the perimeter, a long trek with an unconscious body through the gloom what could go wrong. Getting back to camp, Samiel swaps the intestines in Maximus' mouth.

His body was changing, cyanide mixed with gloom rot paled his skin to the color of his hair. His body morphing trying to heal. It was unclear if he'd make it, but Samiel would try. Samiel sits by the fire fashioning a stretcher out of beetles' carcases. Eating and working, he goes over his hunt for tomorrow. His plan, after watching the jaguars' movements, is to wait at a watering hole the beast visited, submerging himself in toxic water before the beast comes for a drink. He would strike at its most vulnerable moment. He made extra rags for himself to help with the burns he was sure to recieve getting in that water, but worth it for an easy kill.

The Gloom clung to the jungle like a curse. Samiel crouched beside Maximus, whose pallid skin glistened with a sheen of sweat and necrosis, his white hair now streaked with veins of inky black where the Gloom's corruption seeped into his veins. The makeshift camp reeked of beetle bile and burnt resin, the fire reduced to embers that pulsed faintly in the half-light. Maximus' chest rose and fell in shallow, erratic bursts, his body a battleground between the cyanide's venom and the jungle's invasive rot. Samiel tightened the beetle-carapace straps of the stretcher he'd fashioned—a lattice of chitin plates and sinew—before heading to claim his prize.

The watering hole lay in a depression of cracked earth, its surface a kaleidoscope of toxins—neon greens and oily purples swirling under a film of iridescent scum. Samiel had tracked the jaguar here, its prints deeper than the others, the ground scarred by claws that left smoldering grooves in the soil. He crouched in the shallows, the toxic water seeping through the rags wrapped around his legs, their fibers dissolving slowly as the acids ate into his skin. The pain was a living thing, gnawing at his nerves, but he welcomed it. Pain meant focus.

The jungle held its breath. The jaguar emerged at dawn, its dragon scaled fur sleek like metal with bioluminescent fungi that pulsed in time with its labored breaths. Mutation had twisted its form: a second row of jagged teeth protruded from its gums, eyes milky and lidless, glowing with a sickly yellow radiance. It limped to the water's edge, a festering wound on its hind leg oozing black fluid that sizzled where it dripped.

Samiel struck as the beast lowered its head to drink.

He erupted from the water, blade arcing upward in a spray of corrosive droplets. The jaguar recoiled, but not fast enough—the obsidian edge bit into its foreleg, severing tendons with a wet *snap*. The creature howled, a sound like grinding metal, and lunged, its weight slamming Samiel into the muck. Claws raked his chest, shredding the beetle-carapace armor and scoring deep grooves into the flesh beneath. Samiel gagged on the stench of its breath, rotten meat fused with steel and ionized decay, as he drove his knee into its wounded leg. The jaguar faltered, its momentum broken, and Samiel rolled free, snatching a serrated pincer from his belt—a relic of yesterday's beetle kill.

The beast circled, saliva pooling in the dirt, its milky eyes narrowing. Samiel darted left, then pivoted, plunging the pincer into its flank. The jaguar thrashed, snapping the weapon in half, but Samiel was already behind it, blade raised. With a roar, he brought the obsidian edge down on its spine, the strike precise, brutal. The creature collapsed, its hind legs twitching, a guttural whine escaping its throat. Samiel finished it with a thrust to the base of its skull, the blade severing the corrupted neural cluster that pulsed like a tumor beneath its fur.

He worked quickly, skinning the beast under the glow of its own fungal growths. The hide was leathery, resistant to the Gloom's toxins, capable of Camoflauge. He folded it into his pack. Its teeth—jagged and streaked with radioactive veins—would make lethal arrowheads. The meat, though tainted, could be purified with beetle bile. He lashed the carcass to a frame of bamboo-like stalks, their surfaces blistered from the acidic air, and began the grueling trek back to camp.

Maximus was awake when he returned, propped against a tree, his eyes bloodshot but alert. "You… actually did it," he rasped, gesturing to the jaguar's remains.

"Don't flatter me," Samiel muttered, tossing him a canteen of water filtered through charcoal and lichen.

He rebuilt the fire, its flames tinged blue from the jaguar's bioluminescent fungi, and roasted strips of meat over the coals. The toxins hissed out as fat dripped, the scent almost tolerable. Maximus devoured his portion, color creeping back into his cheeks, though the black veins still writhed beneath his skin.

By midday, the stretcher was ready. Samiel layered it with the jaguar's hide, its Scaley fur hide glowing faintly, a grim lantern to guide their path. He secured Maximus with sinew straps, then slung two straps over his shoulder to drag him.

"Why?" Maximus asked, his voice raw. "You could've left me."

Samiel stared into the jungle, where shadows pulsed with unseen threats.

"Well, I thought about it. You'd come in handy for bait in case we have any surprises." He said, laughing.

Maximus, with a grin, falls back unconscious. They moved at sunset, Samiel hauling the stretcher through waist-high ferns that hissed and recoiled at their touch. The jaguar's carcass drew scavengers—scuttling things with too many legs and eyes—but Samiel kept his blade unsheathed, its edge stained with venom and resolve.

Somewhere in the distance, the perimeter beacon flickered—a pinprick of red light in the gloom.

One more day.

One more day, and the Blood Eagle would claim its due.

The night was long and grueling, having to stop every other hour to rest and replace bandages for his fallen comrade. Once and while a creature poking its head from the brush investigating the putrid smell of decay. Drakes above the trees, scanning for the sight of flesh. Theirs roars as loud as their stomachs. Thankfully, the trees provided some security. The adaptive camouflage of the jaguar pelt was slowly fading, with no host it lost its luster. With the sun soon approaching, their ordeal was almost at an end, the final trial sick and twisted but utterly necessary. if you could survive with nothing but a blade, you could survive the gloom as a Warden. Samiel wonders about his friends, did they survive? Were they mauled to death? Did they succumb to thirst and hunger? He wishes he got to see them in this mess, reaper was sure to lighten the situation. Duke a hulking giant offering help wherever needed. Instead, he faces the trial with an odd stranger, a timid man unsure of his future. We have all been there, Samiel thinks to himself; he has great potential. Faced with death, he did not fear; he did not hesitate. God has challenged Samiel in this test. Would he sacrifice his humanity for glory and pride? Or would he save his brother by allowing him a chance at survival? Samiel would not let his brother down. Sitting aside a fire at the break of dawn on the seventh day, he relishes in the fact the trials end is nigh.

The Gloom's perpetual haze burned away in streaks of jaundiced light as the sun clawed through the clouds. Samiel crouched beside the smoldering remnants of their fire, the jaguar pelt draped over his shoulders now dull and brittle, its bioluminescent camouflage flickering like a dying star. Maximus lay on the stretcher, his breath shallow but steady, the black veins beneath his skin receding like tidewater. They were close—so close—to the perimeter. But the jungle had one final lesson to teach.

A roar split the sky.

It was not the guttural cry of a beast, but a mechanical *screech*, like rusted gears grinding through bone. Above the canopy, a shadow descended—wings vast and jagged, half-feathered, half-steel, their edges serrated and dripping with oily ichor. The Gloom Drake landed with a tremor that split the earth, its body a grotesque tapestry of flesh and machinery. Glowing green eyes, housed in armored sockets, locked onto Samiel. Ribs protruded from its chest, fused with corroded plating, while its tail lashed like a scorpion's, tipped with a barbed metal stinger.

Samiel shoved Maximus's stretcher into the cover of a moss-choked boulder as the Drake lunged. Its claws—organic talons sheathed in razor-edged steel—raked the ground where he'd stood, spraying molten soil. Samiel rolled, unsheathing his obsidian blade, its edge still smeared with jaguar venom. The Drake's head snapped toward him, jaws unhinging to reveal a throat lined with spinning drill bits, their whine piercing the air.

Samiel ducked as the Drake spat a glob of acid, the liquid eating through a tree trunk behind him. He lunged, driving his blade into the creature's foreleg, aiming for the gap between flesh and metal. The Drake recoiled, shrieking, but the obsidian shattered against reinforced alloy.

The beast retaliated, its tail whipping forward. Samiel barely dodged, the stinger grazing his arm and searing through flesh. He stumbled, pain radiating like fire, as the Drake reared, its wings casting a death-shroud over the clearing. Samiel's mind raced: *Joints. Weak points. The drills—*

He sprinted toward a cluster of toxin-swollen mushrooms, their caps pulsing with volatile energy. The Drake followed, drills shrieking. At the last second, Samiel pivoted, hurling a beetle pincer into the creature's maw. The drills caught it, shredding the chitin—and with sparks flying, detonating the fungal spores.

The explosion blew Samiel backward, his ears ringing. The Drake staggered, its jaw mangled, drills sparking. But it wasn't dead.

Samiel spotted the flicker first—a crack in the Drake's chest plating, where flesh and steel fused. A bioluminescent heart pulsed beneath, its rhythm erratic. *The core.*

He tore the jaguar pelt from his shoulders, its residual glow clinging to his hands, and charged. The Drake swiped, claws tearing through his thigh, but Samiel leapt onto its neck, driving the pelt's fungal residue into the crack. The Gloom's own corruption reacted instantly.

The heart *burst*, spewing radioactive bile. The Drake convulsed, its mechanical limbs seizing, organic flesh melting like wax. Samiel fell, landing hard as the creature collapsed, its final roar dissolving into a wet gurgle.

He crawled to Maximus, his vision swimming. Blood soaked his leg, his arm blistered from venom. Maximus stared at the Drake's carcass, awe and horror warring on his face. "You… you killed a *Drake*."

Samiel grinned weakly, tying a tourniquet with beetle sinew.

"What that thing, no he killed himself. I just gave him that extra nudge."

Above, the perimeter beacon flared—a crimson star in the gloom. They limped into the extraction zone as the sun withered behind the storm. AEGIS agents awaited, their faces hidden behind black visors. Samiel refused their stretchers, hauling Maximus himself.

Dr. Vasquez's hologram flickered to life. "Congratulations, Wardens," he said, but Samiel wasn't listening. He stared at the jungle, where shadows twisted into familiar shapes—Reaper's smirk, Duke's hulking silhouette.

"You see them too?" Maximus whispered.

Samiel nodded. Alive or not, they were with him.

As the dropship ascended, he pressed a hand to the window, the Drake's blood still crackling on his skin. The Gloom had taken much. But not his humanity.

Not yet.

#

Chapter 10

Flesh Meets Machine

The *Huitzilin*'s rotor blades thrummed like the heartbeat of some colossal beast, their vibrations rattling Samiel's bones as he pressed a hand to the cockpit's translucent window. Below, the Gloom receded—a roiling sea of emerald mist and twisted canopy, its tendrils clawing futilely at the helicopter's underbelly before dissolving into the dawn. Sunlight fractured through the clouds, gilding the toxic haze in fleeting gold. *No graves here today*, Samiel thought, though the jungle's hunger still echoed in his skull.

Maximus lay strapped to a med-gurney beside him, his pallor ghostly under the cabin's sterile UV lights. An IV snaked into his arm, pumping fluids the color of liquid mercury. His chest rose and fell in shallow sync with the biometric monitor's *beeps*, its screen mapping his vitals in jagged red lines. Trophies from their trial lay piled at their feet: the Drake's serrated talon, its fungal-flecked steel still dripping black ichor, and the jaguar's skull, hollow-eyed and crowned with bioluminescent moss.

Ahead, Verdant Spire stabbed into the sky—a monolithic obsidian needle ribbed with glowing green coolant veins. Landing pads protruded from its flanks like metal barnacles, swarmed by AEGIS scientists in contamination suits. One team hauled the Drake's severed limb into a vacuum-sealed crate, its drills still twitching sporadically, while another scrubbed the copter's hull with acidic sprays that hissed into vapor.

Samiel's *Huitzilin* shuddered as it docked, magnetic clamps seizing the fuselage with a metallic *clang*. He counted the other copters descending—**eleven** in total, their hulls scorched and streaked with Gloom residue. His stomach tightened. *Eighty copters had left that hangar.*

The retractable ceiling sealed with a hydraulic groan, plunging the landing bay into sterile white light. Nurses descended on Maximus, their gloved hands prodding his necrotic veins as they wheeled him toward a neon-lit med-bay. Samiel staggered out, his boots clicking on the polished onyx floor, and froze.

Reaper leaned against a support beam, his lean frame draped in a tattered AEGIS coat, its collar singed from plasma fire. A fresh scar split his cheekbone, puckered and raw, but his smirk was unchanged. "*¡Órale!* The *vato* lives! *And* he brought spare parts!" he called, gesturing to the jaguar skull under Samiel's arm.

Duke loomed beside him, his augmented arm now sheathed in Drake-scale plating, the joints leaking faint trails of steam. "Ay, you two *lovebirds*. Get a room!" he boomed, his laughter echoing off the vaulted ceilings.

Samiel crossed the bay in three strides, clasping Reaper's forearm—a grip that said everything words couldn't—before Duke engulfed him in a bear hug that cracked his spine. "Drake food, my *ass*," Duke growled. "Ate one of those *fuckers* myself. Shit out a turd the size of a rover!"

Reaper snorted. "Bullshit. You owe me 200 bucks, *pendejo*."

Samiel stepped back, eyeing the hall. Once crammed with 150 recruits, it now yawned emptily. **Twelve** survivors stood scattered like ghosts: a woman with a cauterized stump where her left hand had been; a man whose eyes were milky voids, traumatized from the trials events; another whose skin had fused with his armor, leaving metallic scales creeping up his neck.

"Where's the rest?" Samiel asked quietly.

Reaper's smirk faded. He nodded to a hologram flickering above the med-bay doors—a list of names in glowing green script. **68** entries pulsed under the header, *deceased.*

Duke spat on the floor. "That's everyone AEGIS brought back, we're it brother.'" He tapped his temple. "Said this is what the Gloom spit out."

Samiel's jaw tightened. He turned as nurses wheeled Maximus past, his body shrouded in a sterile canopy. "And him?"

Reaper lit a contraband cigarillo, the smoke curling into shapes like Drakes. "If he wakes up screaming, they'll scrap him. If he wakes up *silent…*" He shrugged. "Maybe he's one of us."

A klaxon blared. Above, the hologram shifted, pixels coalescing into Dr. Vasquez's gaunt face. "Wardens," he intoned, "report to the Medical ward. Your true service begins *now.*"

The survivors trudged forward, their footsteps echoing in the hollowed-out cathedral of steel and lies. Samiel lingered, staring at the *Huitzilin* that had carried him home. Through its window, the Gloom's emerald stain still smeared the glass—a reminder, a warning.

Reaper clapped his shoulder. "*Vamos*, hermano. The fight's not over."

Samiel glanced at Maximus's gurney vanishing behind med-bay doors. "No," he said. "It's just getting started.

The surviving Wardens filed into the surgical atrium, their boots echoing through the cavernous hangar. The air stank of antiseptic and linen, the walls lined with chrome operating tables and holographic schematics of biomechanical augments. Dr. Vasquez stood beneath a flickering projection of Earth's last cities—New ERRA's spires clawing at a poisoned sky, their foundations choked by Gloom. His grin wasn't cruel. It was *fervent*, the zeal of a man who'd sold his soul to arithmetic.

"Wardens," he began, spreading his hands like a priest at a pulpit. His lab coat gleamed under surgical lamps, but his eyes were shadowed, sleepless. "You stand here *alive*. Not by luck. Not by accident. Because you *understood*."

He stepped toward them, gesturing to the jaguar pelts hung on racks nearby, their bioluminescent veins still pulsing faintly. One pelt sagged lopsided—Samiel's, its edges frayed from acid burns. Vasquez adjusted it tenderly, as if straightening a child's collar.

"These pelts… they aren't trophies. They're *testaments*. Every claw mark, every toxin stain—proof you stared into the Gloom's maw and *spat* into it." His voice softened, almost paternal. "Do you think I enjoy sending you into that hell? That I sleep well knowing children half your age are liquefied in simulation pods?"

He paused, staring at the woman with the cauterized stump. Her missing hand had been devoured by a Gloom rat; she'd chewed through her own wrist to escape. Vasquez's gaze lingered there, his jaw tightening.

"This world is a blade pressed to our throats. Every second, the Gloom gnaws closer. New ERRA's walls? A *fiction*. You've seen the truth—the rot, the mutations, the things that wear human skin but *aren't*. You think we have the luxury of morality? Of *kindness*?"

He slammed a fist onto a surgical table; the tools rattling. "*This* is kindness." He held up a vial of shimmering nanites. "Your scars, your pain—we'll erase them. Replace your flesh with steel that *bends*. Graft your bones with alloys that *sing*. You'll walk through acid storms. Heal from wounds that would liquefy lesser men. Because humanity *needs* you to."

His fervor cooled abruptly. He turned to the hologram of Earth, its continents swallowed by vast canyons and chasms. "You want a villain? Look there. The Gloom doesn't care if you're righteous. It doesn't care if you *deserve* life. It is hunger. Pure, ravenous *hunger*. And I…" He laughed, a hollow sound. "I am the man who feeds it *you* instead of everyone else."

He approached Samiel, stopping inches from his fractured armor. "You brought back Maximus. A man you barely knew. *Why?*"

Samiel didn't flinch. "He earned it."

Vasquez nodded, almost proud. "And that's why we'll win. Not because we're good. Because we're *ruthless* enough to save even one." He turned to the group, his voice fraying. "The enhancements will hurt. They'll remake you into things your old selves would fear. But when you stand atop the corpse of the last Drake, when you watch New ERRA's children play in the sunlight of this city without fear… you'll understand. This cruelty is the only love left."

He stepped back, his projection flickering. "Phase Two begins now. May you hate me enough to survive it."

The Wardens stood silent. Not in awe. Not in gratitude. In the grim resolve of soldiers who'd finally seen the war's true face.

Vasquez wasn't a monster.

He was the scalpel. And the world was the tumor.

The surgical ward gleamed under sterile white light, its walls lined with shimmering bio-polymer panels that hummed with regenerative energy. Twenty glass chambers stood in perfect symmetry, twelve now alive with the soft blue pulse of active systems. Maximus floated in Chamber Three, his body bathed in a nutrient-rich hydrogel that glowed faintly gold as symbiotic nanites threaded through his veins. The air smelled of lavender and crisp linen, not blood.

Samiel exchanged a nod with Duke and Reaper, their faces set with determination rather than fear. The doors to their chambers hissed open, revealing sleek medical slabs cushioned with self-sterilizing gel. No restraints. No screams.

Procedure One: Eclipsite Alloy Integration

Samiel lay back as the chamber sealed. A laser grid scanned his body, mapping bone density. Surgeons in luminescent exo-suits guided robotic arms that emitted a low, harmonic whir. Intravenous sedatives flooded his system—cool, weightless. He closed his eyes.

The alloy came first: liquid eclipsite, ink-black and iridescent, injected into his marrow. It spread like dark lightning, reforging his skeleton in seconds. No saws. No pain. His ribs fused with a resonant *chime*, stronger than titanium, lighter than air. Hydraulic joints slotted into place with magnetic precision, amplifying his natural strength. When he flexed his hand, it felt like his own, but *better*.

Procedure Two: Fracture Resonance Calibration

Awake now, Samiel stood in a resonance chamber. A low-frequency pulse rippled through him, vibrating his eclipsite bones. The sound was clean, a cathedral bell purging dissonance. Engineers monitored holographic readouts. *"Frequency optimal. Gloom dispersal efficiency: 99.8%."*

Procedure Three: Nahual Neural Shunt

A circular aperture opened above his skull. The shunt—a silver disc etched with fractal patterns—lowered seamlessly into his occipital bone. Neural filaments threaded painlessly into his brainstem. Data cascaded into his mind: tactical overlays, comms protocols, a live feed of Reaper's vitals two chambers over. *"Systems nominal,"* his own voice echoed in his head, translated by the shunt.

Procedure Four: Optical & Auditory Refinement

His old lenses dissolved under a beam of ultraviolet light. The new optics slid in—crystalline orbs that adjusted focus instinctively. Colors sharpened; the world gained depth. He blinked, and thermal signatures bloomed like watercolor. His eardrums resonated with a technician's heartbeat across the room, yet ambient noise stayed hushed.

Procedure Five: Symbiote Harmonization

The symbiote arrived in a capsule of frosted glass—a luminous, jellyfish-like organism, its tendrils rippling with bioluminescence. It merged with his liver and lungs in a surge of warmth, nesting itself inside without incision. He felt its presence as a gentle hum, filtering toxins, oxygenating his blood. *"Symbiosis achieved,"* the shunt confirmed.

Procedure Six: Myomer Fusion

Robotic needles wove myomer fibers into his muscle tissue, each thread alive with micro-servos. His biceps tightened, not with alien bulk, but the lean power of a predator evolved. He lifted his arm, marveling at the grace.

Procedure Seven: Taloc Injector

The spinal port clicked into place, a discreet nodule beneath his skin. Cartridges of adrenaline-X and antivenom slid home. *"Reserve: 98 doses,"* the shunt reported.

Procedure Eight: Weapon Integration

The obsidian dagger awaited him—a blade of pure, sentient stone. A port opened in his forearm, painless as a key turning. The dagger slotted in, its edge humming.

Seventy-Two Hours Later

The chambers hissed open. Samiel stepped out, his body humming with latent power. No scars. No tremors. Duke and Reaper followed, their movements fluid, eyes bright with unaltered humanity.

"Feel like yourself?" Reaper grinned, tossing Samiel a water flask.

"Better," Samiel said, catching it with reflexes that were faster than ever.

Duke joined them, his symbiote glowing faintly through his shirt like a second heartbeat. "They turned us into gods," he murmured, flexing a hand that could crush steel but still felt his own.

Dr. Vasquez approached, a rare smile cutting through his usual frost. "Not gods. *Evolution.* You are what humanity becomes when fear is removed from the equation."

The Wardens assembled in the hangar, their enhancements invisible but undeniable. No twitching augments. No haunted stares. They were sharper, faster, *alive.*

The hangar bay fell silent as Chamber Three hissed open.

Maximus stepped into the light—*transfigured.*

His jawline was now a living alloy, a cascading metallic beard that rippled like liquid mercury from cheekbones to collarbone, its surface etched with faint bioluminescent glyphs that pulsed cobalt-blue when he spoke. The poison had bleached his skin to the white of sun-bleached bone, making the black eclipsite augmentations along his arms and chest gleam like obsidian armor. Ten segmented abdominal plates—each etched with AEGIS circuitry—ran from his sternum to pelvis, flexing like the carapace of some ancient warrior-god. The sides of his thighs bore the same alloy, tapered to razor-edged greaves that hissed against the floor.

But it was his eyes that anchored him to humanity—still hazel, still *Maximus*, burning bright above the machine.

Duke choked on his water. "*good god man.* They turned you into a damn cathedral!"

Reaper circled him, prodding a bioluminescent node on his forearm. The alloy warmed at the touch, glowing brighter. "Got a charging port in there, hermano? Can you charge my holo pad?"

Samiel approached, studying the fractal patterns on Maximus's chest. "Does it… *hurt?*"

Maximus flexed his alloyed hand, the plates sliding soundlessly. "Feels like I've worn this skin forever." He grinned, the metallic jaw distorting into something feral yet familiar. "And the abs? *Twelve* hours of core workouts. *Every day.*"

Duke barked a laugh. "Bullshit. You've got a *ten-pack.* That's cheating!"

Reaper observing the glowing veins along Maximus's throat. "Nah. It's art. Bet the Drakes'll piss themselves when they see you."

Maximus smirked. He lifted his shirt, revealing where the alloy faded into pale, unmarked flesh above his hips. "Still me under here. Just… armored."

A technician approached, eyes wide. "The symbiote bonded with the alloy. Purged the cyanide, rebuilt him cell by cell. We've never seen anything like it."

"How about combat? Can he fight?" Samiel asked.

The technician nodded. "Better. Stronger. The alloy *reacts* to Gloom energy—absorbs, disperses. He's… adaptable."

Maximus slammed his fist into the hangar wall. The alloy flared white-hot on impact, cratering the steel, but his knuckles stayed unmarked. He flexed his fingers; the glow fading.

"

Reaper whistled. "Save some Drakes for the rest of us, yeah?"

Duke clapped Maximus's shoulder, the alloy chiming like a bell. "Don't get cocky, statue-boy. You're still buying first round after psych conditioning."

The Wardens fell in line—Samiel with his dagger's quiet hum, Reaper with predatory grace, Duke a mountain of muscle and laughter. And Maximus, now a hybrid of shadow and light, his every step a promise etched in steel.

Dr. Vasquez watched from the observation deck. "*Remarkable,*" he murmured.

But the Wardens didn't look back. They never did.

The chamber was cold, but not unkind. Twelve pods hummed in a semicircle, their interiors lined with neural interface gel that glowed a soft cerulean. Samiel lay back, the gel conforming to his body like a second skin. Above him, holograms flickered—*The Hollowing Protocols: Memory Modulation. Pain Threshold Optimization. Empathic Regulation.*

Memory Suppression:

The neural crown descended, its tendrils brushing his temples.

"Beginning cognitive reframe."

Memories surged—the acid storm eating through Maximus's cheek, Reaper's hollow stare after V.R training, Duke's augmented arm seizing in the V.R pod. But instead of erasing, the crown *blurred* the edges. The pain of those moments dulled, like a scar over a wound. Samiel could still see Maximus's face, hear Duke's laugh, but the visceral punch of guilt? The sleepless nights replaying failures? *Muted.*

"Affective resonance reduced by 62%. Retaining operational recall."

Pain Tolerance:

Needles pricked his spine, injecting a serum that fizzed like champagne in his veins. His eclipsite bones vibrated, amplifying the burn of synthetic nerve agents. But the symbiote in his liver flared, its bioluminescence brightening as it filtered the agony into a distant hum.

"Pain perception rerouted. Threshold elevated."

Samiel gritted his teeth. He *felt* it—the fire in his muscles, the ache in his joints—but it was… manageable. Like watching a storm through glass. Across the room, Duke roared through the procedure, not in anguish, but defiance. Reaper's smirk never wavered.

Empathy Suppression:

Electrodes clamped his wrists. The Gloom beam hit his chest—a concentrated stream of viridian light.

"Simulating high-stress engagement."

Visions flooded him:

A civilian caught in the fracture, her scream cut short.

A rookie recruit seizing as his body falls out of suspended animation.

His own hands, slick with Drake blood, trembling post-trial.

Fear coiled in his gut. Guilt followed.

The electrodes fired—not to destroy, but to *deflect*. The emotions slid away, like water off a raven's wing.

"Affect suppression active. Duration: 18 months."
The pods hissed open.

Samiel stepped out, his mind unnervingly quiet. The memories were there—sharp, clear, but their emotional weight felt… archived. *Distant.*

Reaper sits up, his eyes still sharp, still *Reaper.* "You look like you just took a nap, hermano."

Duke flexed his augmented arm, the servos purring. "Nah. He looks like he finally stopped overthinking."

Maximus leaned against a console, his metallic jaw glinting. "How's the head?"

Samiel touched his temple. "Lighter. But… present, no fog."
They were still *them.* Reaper still mocked Duke's obsession with protein shakes.
Duke still challenged anyone to arm-wrestle, alloy vs. flesh. Maximus still paused, quiet and watchful, before speaking. But when Samiel recalled the civilian's scream, his pulse didn't spike. When he thought of the rookie recruit, his throat didn't tighten. The guilt was there, but it couldn't *claw.*

Dr. Vasquez observed from the shadows. "The conditioning isn't a cage. It's a… filter. You'll feel it all again, in time. But by then, you'll have the clarity to bear it." Later, in the mess hall, Samiel found himself staring at the memorial wall. Names glowed in holographic red, recruits who hadn't survived Phase Two.

Reaper nudged him. "Don't. That abyss isn't yours to bear bro."

Samiel nodded. He felt the loss, but it didn't drown him.

Maximus slid into the seat beside him, his alloyed fingers tapping the table. "You good?"

"Better," Samiel said. And he meant it.

The armory hummed with the low, resonant thrum of dormant power. Twelve recruits stood in formation, their breaths syncing with the rhythmic pulse of the mycelium core embedded in the chamber's walls. Dr. Vasquez paced before them, his lab coat replaced by a commander's obsidian uniform, its collar embroidered with bioluminescent thread that mirrored the Gloom's emerald rot.

"Today, you cease to be soldiers," he intoned. "You become **Wardens**—the blade and shield of New Erra. Your armor is not equipment. It is your *soul*, forged in the crucible of sacrifice."

The Wardens exchanged glances. Behind Vasquez, twelve armor pods hissed open, revealing suits that glimmered like relics of a forgotten apocalypse.

The first pod split with a serpentine hiss. Reaper's armor emerged—obsidian plates etched with Zapotec glyphs that glowed teal, their light rippling like liquid mercury. The shoulder guards tapered into jagged points, mimicking the fangs of the Drakes. The chestplate writhed, a living mural of his battles: bioluminescent mycelium veins pulsed around a central glyph of *Mictlantecuhtli*, the Aztec god of death.

"*Chingón*," Reaper whispered.

The helmet descended—a skull fused with network mycelium, its sockets hollow voids until neural sync. As it sealed, glyphs ignited along the jawline, casting his face in spectral light. The visor flickered, projecting a HUD of crimson targeting reticules.

Duke's suit was a fortress. Plated in matte-gray eclipsite alloy, it bore the weight of a tank, its pauldrons studded with shards of Drake talons. A cape of black mycelium fiber billowed behind him, threaded with bioluminescent spores that scattered like stardust. His helmet—a mantis-eyed monolith—split into twin visors, one scanning for thermal signatures, the other projecting a shield matrix.

"Built for breaking," Duke growled, slamming a fist against his chestplate. The impact resonated like a war drum.

Maximus's armor was a paradox: sleek yet brutal. A pressurized helmet encased his head, its surface a mirror-like alloy that reflected nothing but the Gloom's sickly green haze. Glyphs coiled around the jawline, their light pulsing in time with his symbiote's heartbeat. Cat-like sensor arrays crowned the helm, twitching at distant threats.

Samiel's armor silenced the room.

Forged from drake-scale nanites and eclipsite, it shimmered like oil on water—black threaded with gold. The chestplate bore Quetzalcoatl in full flight, its feathered wings spread wide, bioluminescent veins tracing every feather. The helmet was a masterpiece of terror: twin drake talons arched backward from the crown, framing a visor of hollow blue light. Nanite-infused dragon flesh sealed the jawline, still twitching with residual life.

"Your story," Vasquez said, "etched in metal and rot.'"

Verdant Spire's courtyard stretched beneath a smog-choked sky, its beauty a defiant middle finger to the Gloom. Bioluminescent fungi glowed sapphire in fractal patterns across the ground, their light mingling with the crimson blooms of *flor de muerto*—flowers bred to thrive in poisoned soil. A crowd thronged the perimeter, their faces obscured by holographic veils, their murmurs silenced as twelve figures emerged from the Spire's shadow. The Wardens marched as one.

A crowd of thousands stood in silence, faces obscured, as twelve Wardens marched into the light—three teams of four, helmets sealed, identities erased.

Dr. Vasquez stood atop a dais of fused Gloom alloy and mycelium, his voice booming through the plaza. *"Behold New Erra's blades. Nameless. Faceless. Eternal."*

The Wardens halted in formation. Each team radiated lethal cohesion:

Team 1: Led by a captain whose armor bristled with jagged, volcanic plating, their helm crowned with sensor-spikes.

Team 2: A lithe squad adorned with serpentine glyphs, their movements synchronized like a hive-mind.

Team 3: **Samiel's team**—Reaper, Duke, Maximus, and their captain.

Vasquez descended, a neural remote glowing in his palm. *"Captains—step forward."*

From each team, a Warden advanced. Samiel's squad remained still—until Vasquez paused before them. *"Captain."*

Samiel stepped forward, his armor a void-black tapestry of drake scales and bioluminescent circuitry. His helm—a snarling fusion of eclipsite talons and Quetzalcoatl's feathered visage—burned with cold blue light.

"Remove your helmets," Vasquez ordered the captains.

Team 1's captain unsealed their helm—revealing a scarred woman with eyes like fractured glass. The crowd gasped.

Team 2's captain lifted theirs—a young man, his face mapped with glowing neural tattoos.

Samiel's clawed gauntlet hovered at his helm's seal. *"Do you choose anonymity?"* Vasquez asked.

"To the world—yes," Samiel growled. *"To my team—no."*

He unsealed his helm.

The crowd's holographic feeds scrambled, but his squad saw him—*truly* saw him. Reaper snorted. *"Still ugly, jefe."*

Samiel's lips twitched. *"Helmets off. For them."*

Reaper, Duke, and Maximus complied.

Reaper: His skull-like helm retracted, revealing a grin sharp enough to cut glass.

Duke: His mantis-eyed visor split, showing a battle-scarred face crinkled in pride.

Maximus: His mirrored helm dissolved into nanites, his expression calm, eyes haunted.

The crowd roared, their feeds still scrambled. *To the world, they were shadows. To each other—family*

The crowd fell silent as Dr. Vasquez stepped onto the dais, his obsidian uniform drinking in the courtyard's bioluminescent glow. He spread his arms, as if embracing the throng of veiled faces, his voice a blade wrapped in silk.

"Behold," he began, "the garden we've carved from rot. These flowers bloom where poison once reigned. This light,"—he gestured to the mycelium veins pulsing beneath their feet, "burns where only shadow thrived. You stand in a testament to defiance. To *hope*."

His gaze swept over the twelve Wardens, their helmets sealed, their armor humming with latent power.

"But gardens require guardians." He paused, the silence thickening. "And guardians require sacrifice. You, Wardens, are both the sacrifice and the scythe. Your armor, these masterpieces of eclipsite and myth, are not mere steel. They are *vows*. Vows to erase your names, your faces, your pasts. To become… *legends*."

He descended the dais, circling Samiel's team. His fingers brushed Reaper's jaguar-fanged helm, Duke's talon-studded pauldrons, Maximus's mirrored visor.

"In the Gloom, you will see horrors that could unmake lesser souls. You will fight not for glory, nor for memory, but for the fragile truth that *light persists*. And when you return— *if* you return—you will do so as shadows. The world will never know your sacrifices. But they will sleep soundly because of them."

He turned to the crowd, his voice rising.

"Anonymity is your armor's final layer. You are not *people* to them. You are the storm that cleanses, the void that swallows despair. And yet…"

Here, he faced the Wardens, his tone softening, almost tender.

"To one another, you are flesh. You are fire. You will know each other's scars, each other's fears. You will see the faces beneath the helms, the hearts beneath the glyphs. *That* is your true power—not the steel you wear, but the trust you forge."

He raised a hand, and the Spire's core surged. The Wardens' glyphs ignited—Quetzalcoatl's wings, Mictlantecuhtli's grin, Tlaloc's storm—all blazing in unison.

"The Gloom is not our enemy. It is our mirror. It shows us the cost of survival, the beauty of brutality. You are the edge where light and shadow meet. The blade that *chooses* to cut. Remember this when the rot closes in: you are not erasing yourselves. You are becoming… *more.*"

He stepped back, his final words a whisper that pierced the silence like a needle

"Your armor is your covenant. Wear it. Become it."

A pulse surged from the Spire's core. The Wardens' armor ignited:

Samiel's team: Bioluminescent glyphs flared—Quetzalcoatl on Samiel's chest, Mictlantecuhtli's skeletal grin on Reaper's pauldrons, Tlaloc's storm on Duke's cape, and Tonatiuh's sun on Maximus's visor.

Team 1: Volcanic plating glowed molten-orange, their captain's spikes humming with seismic energy.

Team 2: Serpent glyphs slithered across their armor, reacting to the crowd's heat signatures.

"You are the shield," Vasquez intoned. *"The Gloom's end. Now—go. Let the shadows know fear."*

The Wardens resealed their helms, anonymity restored.

As the crowd dispersed, Samiel's team lingered.

Reaper flicked a bioluminescent spore at Duke's helm. *"Bet my glyphs glow brighter."*

Duke shoved him. *"Your glyphs look like a kid's doodle."*

Maximus stared at his reflection in a pool of rainwater—a faceless warrior, a loyal ghost.

Samiel watched them, his helm's talons clawing at the smog. *"You can hide from the world,"* he said quietly. *"Never from each other."*

Reaper's skull-helm tilted. *"Wouldn't want to, jefe."*

In the distance, artillery thundered.

The ceremony was over.

The war wasn't.

#

Chapter 11

The Ghost of The Eschaton

Maria crouched at the edge of a petrified forest, her eclipsite armor blending into the gloom's perpetual twilight. Roxy and Baron flanked her, their breath fogging the visors of their helmets. The rot-speeders lay dormant nearby, cloaked in bioluminescent moss. Ahead, the ruins of Mexico City loomed, a jagged silhouette of collapsed skyscrapers and highways strangled by black ivy. The Coyote's trail led here, deep into the eschaton's heart.

"Tracks veer west," Roxy whispered, her sniper-scanner highlighting faint bootprints in the ash. "They're heading toward the old financial district. Nest of gloomspawn, last recon said."

Baron adjusted his respirator, the fungal filters hissing. "If they're holed up there, they've got a death wish. Or a plan."

Maria nodded, her blades humming faintly. The air here was thicker, the static pricking her skin like needles. Above, mutated birds circled—their feathers molted, eyes glowing a sickly yellow. She signaled the team forward.

They moved like ghosts, the speeders gliding soundlessly over fissures that wept oily mist. Maria's holo-pad flickered, projecting a map corrupted by gloom interference. "Stay sharp," she murmured. "The network's weak here. No alerts if something's hunting us."

A guttural roar echoed in the distance. The ground trembled as a colossus lumbered into view, its hulking form fused with jagged metal and pulsating rot. Maria froze, pressing into the shadow of a collapsed overpass. The beast sniffed the air, its maw dripping black

sludge, before shambling away.

"Divert east," Maria ordered. "Through the subway tunnels."

The tunnels were a graveyard of rusted trains and bones. Bioluminescent fungi coated

the walls, their tendrils recoiling as Maria passed. Baron's flashlight flickered over graffiti,

crude symbols of raider gangs and warnings in Nahuatl: *"El Serpiente vigila."*

Roxy cursed as her scanner pinged. "Movement ahead. Not human."

A pack of infant gloom hounds skittered into the light, their bodies malformed, jaws

unhinged. Maria's drones activated with a vengeful whir. The fight was quick, brutal. The

hounds dissolved into ash, but not before one latched onto Baron's arm. He gritted his teeth

as Maria cauterized the wound with her blade's plasma edge.

"Thanks, boss," he muttered, face pale.

"Your good to go," she said, but her grip tightened on her dagger. The shadows here

felt alive, watching.

The rot-speeders glided past the skeletal remains of a collapsed museum, its vaulted

ceiling open to the bruised sky. Maria slowed, her visor tilting upward as a flash of color

pierced the gloom, a fractured mural clinging to the remnants of a wall. Time and rot had

gnawed at the art, but the defiant gaze of Frida Kahlo stared back, her iconic floral crown

half-reclaimed by bioluminescent fungi. The mural's edges curled like dying petals, the once-

vibrant reds and greens muted to ghostly hues under the gloom's haze.

"Dios mío," Roxy whispered, her voice crackling over the comms. "Is that…?"

"Sí," Maria said softly. "Frida. My grandmother used to talk of how it looked here

before the fracture. Said her art was a rebellion. 'Even pain can be beautiful,' she'd tell me."

Baron braked beside them, his scanner flickering over the mural. "There's more—

look."

Further down the rubble-strewn avenue, fragments of Diego Rivera's *Man at the Crossroads* survived—a worker's fist thrusting skyward, now entwined with black ivy. The mural's socialist fervor had been defaced by raider glyphs, crude skulls and serpentine scrawls oozing gloom rot. Nearby, a severed stone head from the Toltec era lay toppled, its features eroded into a hollow-eyed grimace.

Maria dismounted, her boots crunching on shards of stained glass. She traced a finger over Frida's fractured cheek, the mural's plaster cold and damp. "They tried to erase us," she murmured. "But we're still here. Buried, but not broken."

A low growl rumbled in the distance. Roxy tensed, her rifle snapping toward the sound. "Jefa, we're exposed here."

Maria lingered a moment longer, the weight of her grandmother's words echoing. *"Nuestra historia es un arma."* *Our history is a weapon.* She turned, nodding to the team. "Move out. Stay sharp."

As they sped deeper into the necropolis of Mexico City, the murals faded behind them, whispers of a world that refused to die quietly. Frida's eyes followed Maria until the gloom swallowed them whole.

By dawn, they reached a raider outpost—a makeshift fortress of scavenged metal, guarded by hounds and men whose veins bulged black. Maria crouched on a ridge, zooming her visor on the Coyote's silhouette below. His arm was bandaged, but he barked orders, gesturing to a holo-map of the pyramids.

"They're planning another strike," Roxy breathed. "But why here? There's nothing but ruins."

Maria's blades pulsed, reacting to a low-frequency vibration beneath their feet. She knelt, brushing aside ash to reveal a network glyph—crudely carved, oozing gloom. "Not ruins," she whispered. "They've found a weak point. A fissure in the network's code."

The ground shuddered again, this time with purpose. A deep, resonant growl echoed from the earth, as if something ancient had stirred. Maria's dream flashed before her—the serpent, the storm, the blood.

"We need to move," she said, rising. "Now."

The air thickened with the stench of decay as Maria's team crouched behind a skeletal archway, its stone crawling with bioluminescent fungi that pulsed like dying stars. Ahead, the ruins of a plaza lay bathed in an unnatural violet haze, the ground seething with tendrils of gloom that writhed like serpents. Shadows pooled and congealed, coalescing into a towering figure—ten feet of pulsating horror, its purplish-pink flesh shimmering as though reality itself rejected its existence. Tentacles slithered from its neck, each tipped with a lipless maw dripping black ichor. Fungal spores crowned its head, glowing faintly as they rained down like cursed snow.

The Coyote knelt before it, his armor cracked and oozing rot, his raiders prostrate in a semicircle. Their breaths came in ragged, synchronized gasps, as if the creature controlled their very lungs.

"What the *fuck* is that?" Roxy hissed, her voice trembling.

Baron's grip on his rifle faltered. "It's… *feeding* on them. Look—"

The creature placed a clawed hand on the Coyote's skull. The warlord jerked violently, veins bulging black beneath his skin as the tentacles coiled around his throat. A guttural, static-laced voice erupted from the creature, its words overlapping like a corrupted chorus:

"Little rot-king… you crawled back to me… wounded… weak."

The Coyote gagged, blood foaming at his lips. "I-I found it… the fissure in the network… like you commanded—"

"Sssilence."

The creature's free hand lashed out, a tentacle spearing through a raider's chest. The man dissolved into ash, his scream cut short. The remaining raiders pressed their foreheads to the ground, chanting in broken unison: *"El Devorador… El Devorador…"*

"You ssssuffer… for their failingssss," the creature hissed, dragging the Coyote closer. Its void-like face split into a fractal maw, rows of needle-teeth gnashing. *"But thissss… weaknessss… you found… it pleasssses me."*

The Coyote's eyes rolled back as the creature's spores burrowed into his pores, knitting his severed tendons and purging the rot from his veins. He shuddered, renewed—a puppet on strings.

"You will return… to the sssserpent's nest…," the creature commanded, its voice reverberating through the stones. *"Bring me the girl… the one who carriesss the glyphsss of old… Maria."*

Maria's breath caught. Her palm burned where her mother had carved the serpent's mark years ago.

"Her blood… will crack the network's bonessss…," it continued, lifting the Coyote until his boots dangled above the ground. *"Fail me… and I will peel your tribe apart… vein by vein… and feed them to the gloom."*

The Coyote nodded frantically. "S-sí, *mi señor*…!"

The creature hurled him into the dirt, then raised its sword—a jagged shard of anti-light that devoured the haze around it. The raiders howled, their bodies twisting as spores fused their flesh to armor, their eyes glowing the same sickly violet as their master's crown.

"Go…," it thundered, the ground quaking. *"Let the network sssscream… before I unmake it."*

As the raiders scrambled to obey, the creature's void-face snapped toward Maria's hiding spot. The creature's crown of spores flared suddenly, bathing the plaza in a sickly violet glow. Its void-face locked eyes with Maria, tentacles writhing as if tasting the air.

"Sssshe watchesss…," it hissed, static clawing at Maria's skull. *"The sssserpent's child… here…"*

Before Maria could react, the sky ruptured. A gloom storm descended—a swirling maelstrom of green-black clouds that vomited acid rain. The ground liquefied into tar, skeletal trees snapping as winds howled like dying beasts.

"Fall back!" Maria screamed, but the storm drowned her voice. A ravine split the earth between the team and their speeders, glowing moss shriveling as the rot-speeders sank into the muck.

The Coyote's laughter cut through the chaos. "¡Corran, ratas! ¡El Devorador los *ve!*"

The raiders surged from the storm's veil, no longer human—spore-mutated horrors with glowing eyes and limbs elongated into barbed talons. Roxy fired, her plasma rounds fizzling in the acidic downpour. Baron's rifle jammed, fungal growths clogging the barrel.

Maria's blades screamed as she carved through two raiders, their bodies dissolving into ash. "The glyphs—use the *glyphs*!" She slammed her palm against a half-buried network node in the rubble. The ancient Zapotec symbols flared blue, repelling the storm in a ten-foot radius—a fragile oasis.

"Hold the line!" she ordered, yanking her holo-pad from her belt. The screen flickered, corroded by gloom static. *Braddock's frequency—*

A tentacle speared through the barrier, shattering the glyphs. The creature loomed, its fractal maw unhinged.

"No messsagesss… no hopesss…," it crooned, swatting Baron into a crumbling column. Roxy lunged, her combat knife glancing off its hide as another tentacle wrapped around her throat.

Maria dodged a strike, fingers flying over the holo-pad. The storm raged—5% signal. 10%. *Come on—*

The Coyote materialized behind her, rot-sword raised. "¡Adiós, reina!"

Maria rolled, his blade grazing her ribs as she slammed "SEND." Braddock's face flickered on-screen for a heartbeat—long enough for her to scream, *"Fissure in the network—it's targeting the pyramids!"*

The holo-pad exploded in her hands as the creature's claw closed around her neck.

"Ssssleep now…," it whispered, spores blooming from its crown.

Maria's vision darkened. The last thing she saw was Roxy and Baron, unconscious and bound in fungal sinew, as the storm swallowed the plaza whole.

Message Sent Fragment (Intercepted by AEGIS Network):

DECRYPTING...

SOURCE: MARIA-ECHO-7

CONTENT: [STATIC]…GLYPH

BREACH…DEVOURER…STORM…PYRAMIDS… [STATIC]

STATUS: PRIORITY ALPHA. ALL UNITS, FULL LOCKDOWN.

The creature smiled, its void-face reflecting Maria's limp form.

"The sssserpent's sssstorm… comesss."

Samiel awakes from his coma, steady calm, the room was dark the only light illuminating the headless corpse of Maximus. Samiel turns his head toward the light, the room was empty.

"I'm sorry, i was too late to save your friend," Atlas said.

"It's alright, wasn't your fault we didn't know what we were walking into. The Gloom never unleashed a hell like that before, it was calculated and with overwhelming numbers." Samiel responded.

"What were they after?" Atlas asked.

"My guess Atlas. You. It's no coincidence they attacked a few weeks ago, and they didn't find you because you were in that injector. Dr. Voss's body wasn't at the lab, she might be held hostage somewhere. They returned when we arrived to stop us from finding you, but why? What aren't you telling me, Atlas? What was your purpose?" Samiel asked.

"I was designed to integrate with Wardens such as yourself. My integration would allow for superior combat effectiveness. I was designed to end this war." Atlas said proudly.

"I get that, but why go through all the trouble we know the gloom adapts to whatever we throw at it, like its one step ahead. Its never responded in such force it was a coordinated attack that went unnoticed, the bodies there, nothing makes sense," Samiel said confused.

"Perhaps the answer lies out there in the gloom. We also still need to find your girl. The dreams seem to be connected somehow. Let's focus on what we can do, get me into the AEGIS servers. ill have more answers then," Atlas retorted.

"Your right," Samiel said bitting his tongue.

Samiel stares at the remains of his friend its been years since that day in the jungle, countless missions, countless drinks shared. A wave of guilt washed over him. His future was bright. He didn't deserve this, a single tear gazed his hardened face, sliding down his cheek, landing on Maximus' armor. His loss consumed him for a brief moment, but the suppression kicks in and the feeling begins to blur. A distant thing he can't grasp no matter how hard he tried, a void, a blur.

The med bay's sterile lights hummed faintly, casting a pallid glow over Maximus's shrouded body. Samiel sat slumped on a steel bench, his armor still flecked with dried rot and ash, fingers gripping the edge until his knuckles blanched. The air tasted of antiseptic and regret.

Duke shouldered through the door first, his hulking frame blocking the glare from the corridor. Reaper followed, uncharacteristically quiet, his rifle tucked under one arm. Both froze at the sight of their captain—Samiel's face, usually a mask of glacial control, was raw, haunted.

"Sit-rep?" Samiel rasped, not looking up.

Duke exchanged a glance with Reaper before stepping forward. "Barge is grounded. Braddock's frothing for a debrief. We told him to chew steel till you're upright." His voice softened. "Max… they're prepping his rites at dawn."

Samiel's jaw twitched. A single tear tracked through the grime on his cheek, splattering onto his blood-crusted gauntlet.

Reaper leaned against a med terminal, arms crossed. "*Cabrón* went out swinging, eh? Took half those *pinches* hounds with him." His attempt at levity fell flat, swallowed by the silence.

Duke cleared his throat. "Boss… what *happened* back there? The Gloom's never hit us like that—coordinated, tactical. And that shit you injected—"

Samiel's head snapped up, eyes sharp. "You saw."

"Saw you go full *loco*, sí," Reaper cut in, thumbing the scar under his eye. "Moved like a ghost. Tore through that Goliath like papel. Then you flatlined."

Duke stepped closer. "Your wounds sealed in seconds. That ain't standard Warden tech. What'd you stick in your neck?"

Samiel held their stares, weighing the truth. Finally, he exhaled. "Atlas. Show yourself."

Nothing.

Reaper snorted. "Who's Atlas? Your new imaginary—"

A voice, crisp and synthetic, reverberated from Samiel's armor. **"I'd prefer discretion, Captain."**

Duke's hand flew to his sidearm. "The *hell*—?"

"Stand down," Samiel ordered. To the air, he growled, "They're family. No secrets here."

A beat. Then, amber light bled from Samiel's chestplate, coalescing into a hologram above his shoulder. The figure glowed like a neural map—a skeletal lattice of circuits and veins, pulsing with bioluminescent tendrils that snaked around a shimmering, brain-like core. Its voice resonated, equal parts warmth and machine precision.

"Greetings, Wardens. I am Atlas. Apologies for the… dramatics."

Reaper gaped. "*Chingado.* You've been hiding a *fantasma* in your armor?"

"AI," Samiel corrected. "Found him in the lab. That injector was his housing."

Duke circled the hologram, wary. "So the Gloom tore that place apart looking for *this*?"

"Correct," Atlas replied. **"My purpose is to integrate with Warden systems, enhance combat efficiency, and terminate the Gloom's advance. Dr. Voss's hid me before the attack. They knew Eschaton would target me."**

Reaper barked a laugh. "Great! So you're babysitting a Gloom magnet. *Perfecto.*"

Samiel stood, the hologram flickering as he moved. "Atlas isn't the enemy. He's why we survived. His code boosted my reflexes, healed me mid-fight. Without him, we'd all be on a med bed waiting for our rites."

Duke crossed his arms. "And the lab? The bodies?"

"Sabotage," Atlas said flatly. **"The Gloom's strike was a retrieval mission. When they failed to acquire me, they purged the lab. Dr. Voss… her fate remains unknown."**

Reaper's smirk faded. "So that swarm wasn't random. They wanted *you*. And now they know we've got you."

Samiel nodded. "Which means the next attacks could already coming."

Duke rubbed his temples. "Braddock's gonna burn us alive if he finds out we're hauling forbidden tech."

"Hence the need for secrecy," Atlas interjected. **"My full integration requires access to AEGIS's core servers. Until then, I'm… limited."**

Reaper raised a brow. "Limited? You turned *jefe* here into a one-man apocalypse."

"A preview," Atlas said, the hologram brightening. **"Imagine what I could do with proper syncing. The Gloom's mutations, their patterns—I can predict them. End this war."**

Silence hung, thick with doubt and possibility.

Finally, Samiel locked eyes with his team. "We keep this buried. No reports. No leaks. Atlas stays between us until we crack what the Gloom's really after."

Duke grunted. "And Braddock?"

"We'll tell him the *official* story. Lab was overrun. Max died a hero. We grabbed intel, came home." Samiel's tone brooked no argument.

Reaper chuckled darkly. "*Órale.* So we're lying to High Command now? Love it." He tossed his blade in the air, catching it with a grin. "But hey—if your new robo-angel here can make me shoot straighter, I'm in."

The hologram dimmed as Atlas withdrew into Samiel's armor. **"Then let's write history, gentlemen."**

As the Wardens filed out, Samiel lingered, staring at Maximus's shroud. Atlas's voice hummed softly in his mind:

"Guilt is inefficient, Captain. Honor their sacrifice by ensuring it wasn't in vain."

Samiel clenched his fists. "We will."

Outside, a Gloom storm churned on the horizon—a living storm, waiting.

The pyramids of Teotihuacán glowed under a bruised sky, their ancient slopes veined with bioluminescent mycelium that pulsed like a heartbeat. The AEGIS compound loomed ahead—30 floors of reinforced glass and blackened steel, its hangar doors sealed like the jaws of a titan. Tanks patrolled the perimeter, their turrets tracking the Wardens as they approached on foot, the damaged barge shrinking behind them in a haze of welding sparks. The Teotihuacán Citadel rose from the Gloom's emerald haze like a god's clenched fist—its bones a fusion of pre-Columbian stone and pulsating biotech. The Pyramid of the Sun anchored the complex, its terraces armored in meteorite alloy and veined with mycelium that glowed sapphire against the rot-stained sky. Around it, AEGIS labs hummed inside repurposed temples, their arched doorways sealed by holographic glyphs that hissed with anti-Gloom code. Samiel's team stood at the base, dwarfed by the fortress's shadow.

The Citadel's central spire pierced the emerald maelstrom of the sun, its obsidian walls throbbing with the pulse of the mycelium network. Samiel and his Wardens marched through the vaulted corridors, their armor still caked with dried rot and ash. Braddock's office loomed ahead—a glass-paned chamber overlooking the Pyramid of the Sun, where holograms of the Dawn Lab's ruins flickered like ghosts.

Braddock stood at the panoramic window, backlit by the encroaching storm. He didn't turn as they entered. "Sit."

Samiel remained standing. "We'll stand."

Reaper slouched into a chair anyway, boots propped on the holotable. "*Ay, jefecito,* you redecorated! Love what you've done with the place."

Braddock pivoted, his scarred face twisted into a sneer. Holoscreens ignited, replaying the Wardens' battle at Dawn Lab: Samiel's blades carving through a Goliath, wounds sealing mid-swing, Maximus's final stand in the stairwell.

"Explain."

Duke's voice rumbled like distant thunder. "Max died holding the line. Saved our skins. That's all that matters."

Braddock's fist slammed the table, scattering static. "What *matters* is that lab was overrun for a reason. Dr. Voss's team was developing an AI—something the Gloom *craves*. And you…" His glare locked on Samiel. "…waltzed out without a scratch. Coincidence?"

Atlas's voice hummed in Samiel's mind, cold and clinical: [Heart rate elevated. Pupils dilated. He suspects, lacks proof.]

Samiel crossed his arms. "We retrieved intel. Brought back Max. Mission complete."

A holoscreen zoomed in on Samiel's ribs knitting shut mid-combat. "Wardens don't *heal like that*," Braddock spat. "They endure. What's in your veins?"

Reaper flicked a stim canister at the hologram. "*Sangre, sudor, y lágrimas, viejo.* Plus a shitload of Gloom rot. Want a taste?"

Braddock's eye twitched. He swiped the air, pulling up encrypted logs—redacted fragments of Dr. Voss's work. "The AI's designation: *Atlas Protocol.* Sound familiar?"

Samiel's pulse spiked. **Atlas's warning: [Do. Not. Engage.]**

"Never heard of it."

Braddock leaned in, breath reeking of synthetic caffeine. "The Gloom doesn't throw legions at *nothing.* You took something. And I'll carve it out of you if I have to."

Duke stepped forward, his shadow swallowing the light. "Try it. See how *heroic* your obituary reads."

For a heartbeat, the room teetered on violence. Then—lightning lanced through the storm outside, fracturing the silence.

Braddock straightened, smug. "Fine. Play martyr. But when the Gloom cracks this fortress open, I'll make sure you're the first thing it eats. ***Dismissed!***"

The team reconvenes later that night to gain access to the server room. The AEGIS Safe-Zone Compound hummed like a sleeping giant, its walls a fortress of polished alloy and bioluminescent mycelium. Beyond the perimeter, Mexico City's ruins lay cloaked in the Gloom's emerald tempest—a swirling vortex of acid rain and lightning. Inside, all was sterile silence. Fluorescent glyphs pulsed along the corridors, casting cold teal light over patrol drones and snoozing technicians.

Samiel's team moved like shadows

"Three guards on rotation," Duke murmured, peering around a corner. His hulking frame pressed against the wall, Voidspike rifle slung low. "Reaper—east wing. Make it sing."

Reaper smirked, thumbing a plasma grenade. "*Sí, mamá.*" He vanished into a ventilation shaft, boots silent on steel.

Samiel checked his holo-pad. The server room's schematics glowed: *Level -4. Core Access: Restricted.* Atlas's voice hummed in his neural link, a whisper only he could hear.

"Security grid cycles every 90 seconds. We have a window."

Reaper crouched in a ventilation shaft, his scarred hands deftly rewiring a security panel. "*Órale*, these *pendejos* still use 20th-century firewalls," he whispered, grinning as the corridor's hololocks flickered and died.

Duke stood sentinel at the intersection, his Voidspike rifle a shadow in the dim light. "Two guards. East wing. Reaper—*now.*"

A plasma charge detonated somewhere in the mess hall. The compound shuddered, alarms blaring.

"Gas leak detected, please evacuate the building," an automated voice said over the PA system.

Chaos erupted. Boots pounded as personnel fled, leaving the server wing abandoned. The compound's underbelly was a labyrinth of dripping pipes and flickering hololocks. Reaper's distraction ignited on schedule—a thunderous *crash* from the east wing, followed by shouts and the hiss of fire suppressors.

"Go," Duke growled.

Samiel slid into the service elevator, Duke's bulk blocking the door sensor. The descent was glacial. Level -4 opened to a vaulted chamber, its ceiling strung with glowing fungal tendrils. The server core loomed ahead—a monolith of crystalline servers, their surfaces etched with ancient Zapotec glyphs that shimmered like trapped starlight. Samiel pressed his palm to the access terminal, his armor's teal circuits syncing with the system.

Atlas's voice hummed in his neural link, a ghost in the machine: "Security protocols disabled. Upload initiating."

Amber light spilled from Samiel's vambrace, tendrils of code weaving into the servers. Glyphs flared—*Access Granted*—and holograms bloomed: encrypted logs, tactical maps, fragments of the mycelium network's genesis.

Duke stood at the door, his rifle trained on the empty corridor. "Make it fast, boss. Reaper's *distraction* won't last forever."

"Upload: 34%," Atlas intoned.

The holograms flickered.

Static.

A woman's voice, frayed and desperate:

"—coordinates Necropolis Grid 77... fissure in the network... they're coming—"

Samiel froze.

Her.

Maria's hologram materialized above the terminal, her features sharpened by exhaustion but unmistakable—the same face that had haunted his dreams since childhood. Her dark hair was braided with frayed wires, her olive skin smudged with Gloom rot. A small mole dotted her left shoulder, just visible beneath the torn collar of her armor. As she turned to check a scanner, the hologram glitched, revealing a birthmark on the left side of her back—a streak, pale against her skin.

He knew it.

The memory hit him like a sniper round: a dream from years ago. Maria standing in a field of sunflowers, laughing as she spun, her back bare, the birthmark glowing in the sunlight. A world that no longer existed.

"Upload: 67%," Atlas said.

Samiel's breath caught. "Atlas—*freeze the feed.*"

The hologram stilled. Maria's face hung in the air, her honey hazel eyes wide with urgency, her lips parted mid-sentence. Samiel reached out, his gauntlet trembling, as if he could brush the scar on her cheek—a thin white line from brow to jaw, earned in a fight he'd never witnessed but somehow *knew*.

"Who is she?" Atlas asked, though he already knew.

"A ghost," Samiel murmured. "*My* ghost."

"Upload: 89%."

Duke stiffened. "We got Movement."

Samiel didn't move. Maria's hologram flickered, dissolving into static as the transmission resumed:

" The pyramids are the key"

Her voice cut off. Coordinates burned into Samiel's HUD: **Necropolis Grid 77.**

"Upload complete," Atlas said. **"Traces erased."**

Alarms blared. **"LOCKDOWN INITIATED."**

Duke yanked Samiel backward. *"Now,* boss!"

They fled, the server core's light dying behind them. Reaper waited at the extraction point, a smirk plastered over his unease. "You look like you've seen a ghost, *jefe.*"

Samiel said nothing. Maria's face lingered in his mind—the warmth of her smile in his dreams, the chill of her fear in the static. Back in their quarters, Samiel replayed the hologram in secret. Maria's birthmark, her mole, the scar—details too precise for coincidence.

"She's real," Atlas said quietly. **"And she's been calling to you long before the Gloom."**

"How?"

"The mycelium network. It doesn't just repel the Gloom—it connects. Your dreams… they were never just dreams."

Outside, the storm over Mexico City pulsed, its green-black tendrils devouring the ruins. Somewhere in that chaos, Maria was alive. Waiting.

Reaper shouldered open the door, tossing Samiel a plasma blade. "Braddock's wants us in the situation room asap. Whatever your ghost found, it's got the Gloom *pissed.*"

Samiel stood, Maria's coordinates burning in his vision. "Lets move."

The storm roared in agreement. Far below, the mycelium network pulsed, its roots cradling secrets—and a woman's voice, still whispering in the dark.

The situation room was a tomb of cold light and whispered dread. Holoscreens lined the walls, their surfaces choked with data streams and thermal scans of the storm devouring Mexico City. The Pyramid of the Sun loomed outside the reinforced viewport, its mycelium veins throbbing faintly under the Gloom's acidic rain. Braddock stood at the tactical holotable, his gaunt face lit from below by the coordinates **Necropolis Grid 77**, burning crimson in the static.

Samiel entered first, his armor still streaked with ash from the server vault. Duke and Reaper flanked him, their faces unreadable beneath scarred helmets. The air tasted of ozone and tension.

"Sit," Braddock growled, not looking up.

Samiel remained standing. "We'll stand."

Braddock flicked a hand. The holoscreens shifted, zooming in on the storm's heart, a swirling vortex of blackened clouds and violet lightning. Raiders' signatures blinked red along the periphery: jagged heat trails of modified rot-jeeps, campfires flickering in the ruins.

"Gloom's rallying its puppets," Braddock said. "Scouts report a strike force massing at the Necropolis. They'll hit us by dawn." He turned, his lone cybernetic eye whirring as it locked onto Samiel. "Your little server stunt lit a beacon. They're coming for *us*."

A hologram flared: Maria's fragmented transmission. *"—fissure in the network..."*

Samiel's fists clenched. "Then let me extract her. She might know how to seal the fissure."

Braddock's laugh was a dry rasp. "You think this is a rescue op? That woman's a ghost. A *liability*."

Reaper stepped forward, his voice a serrated edge. *"Carnal*, you'd leave her to rot?"

"I'd leave *all* of you to rot if it saved this base." Braddock slammed the table. The holoscreens flickered, revealing the compound's defenses—energy domes at 78%, artillery turrets scanning. "We're on lockdown. Every Warden stays. Every gun on patrol. That's the *order*."

Samiel's gauntlet hissed as he leaned over the holotable, teal circuits flaring. "Maria's the key. You saw her data. The fissure could *end* us and this base."

"Or crack the network wide open!" Braddock's fist shattered the hologram of Maria. Static bled across the room. "You're compromised, Captain. That AI's turned you into a Gloom-chasing fanatic. I won't risk the compound for your *ghost*."

Duke's voice rumbled like distant thunder. "Max died for that data. You gonna spit on that too?"

For a heartbeat, silence. Then Braddock's eye narrowed. "Max died because you walked into a trap. Just like you'll die if you chase this."

Samiel's blade snapped to life, its hum drowning the storm's roar.

Guards surged forward, rifles raised. Reaper's Thorncaster whined, barbed pods glowing. The room teetered on bloodshed.

"*Enough.*"

Braddock's voice cut through the static. He gestured, and the guards lowered their weapons. "You want to die for her? Fine. But you go alone. The team stays."

Samiel didn't flinch. "Agreed."

Reaper snarled. "The *hell* you say—"

"*Alone*," Braddock repeated. "No extraction. You take a skimmer, and that *thing* in your head. You fail, the Gloom eats you. You succeed…" He tossed a neural key onto the table. "You'll beg to die when I'm done with you."

The key glowed—a self-destruct trigger for the *Huitzilin* skimmer.

Samiel "Deal."

The hangar was a crypt of shadows and dying light. The *Huitzilin* waited, its wings folded like a scarab's carapace. Rain hissed against the energy dome, the storm's fury muffled but relentless.

Reaper shoved a plasma blade into Samiel's grip. "*Pendejo* move, *jefe*. But… *suerte*."

Duke clasped his shoulder, the gesture heavy. "Bring her back. Or don't come back."

"Well," Atlas said cheerfully, **"on the bright side, if we die horribly, we'll never have to hear Braddock's voice again. Silver linings!"**

Duke and Reaper laughed. "I like him. He's got jokes, *jefe* take care of yourself if you need us. You call, you hear me?"

Samiel nodded. Atlas's voice hummed in his mind, colder than the rain.

"The storm's core is a living entity. It will resist."

"Then we cut its heart out."

As the *Huitzilin*'s thrusters roared to life, Braddock watched from the viewport. The storm pulsed, its vortex twisting into a semblance of a face—a woman's, screaming.

"Sir," a technician stammered. "The Gloom's energy spiked. It's… *tracking* him."

Braddock poured a drink, his reflection warped in the glass. "Good."

Outside, the skimmer pierced the storm, vanishing into the storms maw.

Somewhere in the static, Maria's voice whispered. And the compound held its breath.

#

Chapter 12

The Eye Of The Storm

The *Huitzilin* hovered in the hangar bay, its wings a blur of iridescent alloy and bioluminescent filaments, thrumming with the resonant frequency of a hummingbird's heartbeat. The craft's body was sleek, obsidian-black and scaled with overlapping plates that shimmered emerald under the hangar's sterile lights. Its rotor blades—hybrids of feather and steel—sliced the air, creating a low, harmonic drone that vibrated in Samiel's bones.

The pilot, encased in a form-fitting flight suit, she turned toward him. Their helmet was a grotesque marvel: a bird-of-prey visage with gilded "eyes" that glowed amber, the visor a compound lens offering 360-degree vision. Wires snaked from the helmet's base into the cockpit, fusing pilot and machine into a single entity.

"Climb in, Warden," the pilot's voice buzzed through a vox-filter, avian and mechanical. **"The storms awaiting, you gotta be a crazy SOB to go out there alone. Means im in good company."**

Samiel strapped into the rear bay, his armor syncing with the *Huitzilin*'s systems. A holoscreen flickered to life, projecting the pilot's neural interface—a fractal storm of data and instinct.

Atlas hummed in his ear: "Charming aesthetic. I give the bird-helmet a 6/10. Needs feathers."

The *Huitzilin* shot into the maelstrom, wings beating furiously to stabilize against the Gloom's wrath. Acid rain slashed the hull, sizzling against the energy shields. Below, Mexico City's ruins writhed—collapsed highways coiled like serpent spines, skyscrapers reduced to skeletal fingers clawing at the sky.

The pilot's helmet twitched, their head cocking in avian jerks as they parsed the storm. **"Spore trail detected,"** they announced.

Ahead, a faint bioluminescent streak glowed through the downpour—Maria's path, left by her speeder's fungal exhaust. The spores pulsed *green-gold*, a lifeline in the chaos.

"Hold tight," the pilot warned.

The *Huitzilin* banked sharply, dodging a tendril of Gloom rot that lashed upward like a whip. Samiel's stomach lurched as the craft spiraled around a collapsing radio tower, the pilot's movements eerily fluid, *predatory*.

Atlas scoffed: "Show-off. Bet they practice in the mirror."

The spore trail ended abruptly at the Necropolis' edge—a valley of cracked mausoleums and shattered monoliths, half-swallowed by bioluminescent fungi. The *Huitzilin* descended, its wings flattening the undergrowth as it hovered inches above the ground.

"Insertion point," the pilot said. **"Storm's eye shifts in 20 minutes. You'll be paste after that."**

Samiel leapt out, boots sinking into mulch softened by rot. The *Huitzilin*'s wings crescendoed as it vanished into the storm, leaving him alone.

"Charming farewell," Atlas muttered. **"No 'good luck,' no 'don't die'—just 'you'll be paste.'"**

"I'm sure he had warmer words in his bird brain,"

Samiel smirked, activating his holo-pad. A ghostly trail materialized—her last path, overlaid with timestamps.

The Necropolis was a graveyard of dead gods. Stone serpents coiled around broken pillars, their moss-choked jaws frozen mid-strike. Samiel moved silently, his armor's teal circuits dimmed to avoid Gloom detection.

He'd seen this place

In his his dream he recalled walking through a worn down city sky, sky bleeding rain, the building he ran into walls bathed in blood.

"Ahh, yes, the dream of Maria in her own pool of blood. I saw you there," Atlas retorted.

"Wait, you saw me?" Samiel asked with a look of utter confusion.

"Yes, you turned. I believe you saw me, but I quickly left." Atlas responded unfazed.

"THAT WAS YOU I CHASED!? How? That was 13 years ago you didn't exist?"

"Like I said, captain *The Gloom Connects,* time is a different perception for humans and AI. I may not have existed to you, but *I was born in your mind*, so in fact, I have been there all along. Silent in the shadows until conception."

"What does that even mean, Atlas?"

"Youll understand soon enough, captain. It's not our primary objective at the moment. Let's focus. I believe her last transmission was near the city centre, 100 meters west of our current location."

"When we get back, im going to need some real answers here, you got that?"

"Yes, captain, I will humbly oblige your intrigues."

The duo head for the city's centre. Mexico City's corpse sprawled before Samiel—a skeletal labyrinth of collapsed skyscrapers strangled by bioluminescent fungi. The storm churned above, vomiting acid rain that hissed against his armor. Air thickened with the stench of decay, each breath tasting of burnt circuitry and rotting flesh.

He moved silently, boots crunching on streets paved with glass shards and bone. Buildings leaned like drunk giants, their facades peeling to reveal nests of **Gloomspawn**: translucent centipedes the size of pickup trucks, mandibles dripping nanite slurry. Their segmented bodies pulsed with corrupted code, glowing faintly violet as they fed on the carcass of a downed Drake.

Atlas's voice hissed in his neural link:

"Life signs: Negative. Rot density: Critical. Advise caution."

Samiel ducked beneath a collapsed overpass, its steel ribs weeping oily mist. Ahead, a plaza lay drowned in black ivy. At its center, a fractured statue of Cuauhtémoc pointed a rusted sword toward the canyon's edge—and Maria's holopad lay at its base, half-buried in ash.

The holopad's screen was cracked, its casing gnawed by acid. Samiel wiped grime from its surface. A flickering hologram erupted—Maria's face, gaunt but defiant.

"... the fissure is in the network itself. They're using the canyon to amplify the Gloom's signal. Don't follow unless—"

Static devoured her words. The hologram glitched, repeating *"Don't follow — Don't follow — Don't—"* before dying.

"Last ping: 200 meters southwest," Atlas said. **"The canyon."**

Samiel turned. The **Eschaton Canyon** yawned ahead — 3 — hundred mile-wide scars in the earth, its walls sheer and studded with the ruins of a skyscraper half-swallowed by the abyss. Bioluminescent fungi coated the structure, their glow sickly green, and at the canyon's nadir, a faint amber light pulsed.

Something *moved* in the shadows.

"Hmm, new *Gloom Spore*, put it in your socket for analyzing," Atlas said.

"That not how the suit works, Atlas, that for my blade only," Samiel retorted.

"Ahh, yes, I forgot to mention I was busy upgrading suit functions while we are on this leisurely stroll. You can now analyze any unconstrained substances via your socket. It allows for faster upgrades. Speaking of your gave-chute im upgrading currently, no more controlled descent, you'll have to ability of controlled flight for short durations once completed."

"Well, shit that would come in handy right now, activate it, let's give it a whirl"

"Unfortunately, captain we can't always get what we wish for. The upgrade isn't complete. Looks like the stair will do fine for now." Atlas chuckled,

The stairwell clung to the canyon wall, its steps crumbling into voids. Samiel descended, fingers brushing the rock-face. The air grew colder, dense with the hum of Gloom static.

"*Great*" Samiel replied.

Halfway down, the stairs ended. A rope bridge swayed in the abyss, its cables frayed and glistening with **rot-mites**—insectoid swarms that fed on metal. Samiel leapt, landing soundlessly as the bridge groaned. Below, the canyon's belly seethed: rivers of black sludge bubbled, their surfaces rupturing to release gaseous faces that screamed silently.

"Motion detected," Atlas warned.

Samiel froze. Above, a **Gloom Harvester** scuttled along the cliff—a spider-like automaton fused with human ribs, its eight eyes scanning for heat. He pressed into a crevice as it passed, its legs screeching against stone.

The skyscraper's ruins jutted from the canyon floor like a broken fang. Its lower floors had collapsed into a sinkhole, but the upper levels glowed faintly. Samiel scaled a rusted fire escape, his armor dampening the creaks.

At the summit, a shattered observatory loomed. Through its cracked dome, he saw them: **Maria**, battered but alive, her wrists bound in fungal sinew. She knelt before a pulsating **Gloom Core**—a writhing mass of static and teeth suspended above an altar of human bones. Around her, robed figures chanted in guttural Nahuatl, their faces hidden behind masks of obsidian and jade.

One figure raised a dagger—a shard of the Devourer's tooth.

"Intercept?" Atlas asked.

Samiel unsheathed his umbral fang. **"No. Observe."**

The dagger plunged—not into Maria, but into the core. The room erupted in emerald light, and the canyon itself *shuddered*.

Maria's eyes snapped open.

She was staring directly at him.

The cavern was a cathedral of rot. Rib-like arches of fused bone and corroded steel vaulted overhead, dripping with bioluminescent slime that pooled in troughs carved with Zapotec glyphs. The air reeked of ammonia and burnt copper, thick enough to coat Maria's tongue. She hung suspended in a cocoon of fungal sinew, its fibers squirming like nematodes as they siphoned droplets of blood from her wrists. Below, Roxy and Baron lay crumpled on an altar of human skulls, their armor cracked open like eggshells to expose the bioluminescent mycelium beneath—AEGIS's last defense against the Gloom, now flickering weakly.

How long had they been here?

The attack had been a symphony of horrors. One moment, they'd been tracking the Coyote's hound tracks through the Necropolis; the next, the ground had *breathed*, exhaling tendrils of Gloom that descended upon them. Then *it* rose—the Devourer, ten feet of fractal flesh and jagged anti-light, its voice a chorus of static-laced screams. It tore through Roxy's drones first, their plasma fire fizzling against its hide. Baron had lasted three seconds longer, his Voidspike rifle melting in his hands as the creature's claws found his ribs. Maria's blades had sung longest, their obsidian edges carving glowing wounds into its form—until it *smiled*, its void-like face splitting into a maw of needle-teeth, and spat a cloud of spores that dissolved her will along with her armor.

Now, the Devourer circled its prisoners, each footfall causing the cavern's floor to ripple like water. Its crown of fungal spores pulsed in time with the **Gloom Core** above the altar—a suspended black star that devoured light, its surface crawling with half-formed faces.

"Little rot-queen…" Its voice was a thousand overlapping whispers, scraping Maria's skull raw. **"You bleed the old blood. The network's first song. How… poetic."**

Maria spat blood. "Go to hell."

The Devourer's laugh echoed through the chamber, shaking loose stalactites that shattered like glass. **"Hell?— You stand in its womb."**

It gestured, and the Gloom Core convulsed. Holograms erupted—scenes of the Fracture: continents splitting, tsunamis swallowing cities, the first Gloomspawn clawing from fissures. Among the chaos, a figure knelt at the Pyramid of the Sun, hands pressed to the earth. Kaisha *Maria's grandmother.*

"Your bloodline planted the network's seed," the Devourer hissed. **"A *cure*…"** The word dripped venom. **"But all cures are poisons first. You grafted life to the Gloom's corpse. Now it hungers. Now it *remembers*."**

Maria strained against her bonds. "You're lying."

"Am I?" The Core's faces contorted into her mother's visage, screaming. **"The network is a chain. Your ancestors bound this world to a dying god. Today…"** It loomed over her, its breath frosting her skin. **"You break it."**

Roxy stirred, coughing black sludge. "Maria… don't listen—"

The Devourer's claw flicked. Roxy's scream was cut short as her right arm *dissolved*, unraveling into spores that fed the Core.

"**Silence,**" it hissed. "**This is sacrament, not debate.**"

The glyphs beneath Maria glowed crimson. She recognized them—*Nahuatl death rites*, the same ones her grandmother had etched into her palms as a child.

"**Your blood cracked the network's shell,**" the Devourer intoned. "**Now it will shatter its bones. When the Core drinks you, the Gloom will rise… purified. No more fractures. No more *humans*.**"

Baron lunged, half-crawling, his remaining hand clutching a shard of his rifle. "*Run—!*"

The Devourer didn't turn. A tentacle speared Baron's chest, lifting him like a doll. His body convulsed, veins bulging black as the Gloom rewrote him—flesh bubbling into something *new*, something with too many joints and eyes that wept static.

"**Behold,**" it crooned. "**The first of the Reborn.**"

Maria's scream tore her throat raw. "*NO!*"

The Devourer raised its blade—a shard of the Gloom Core, edges seething with fractal darkness. "**Your storm ends here, little queen.**"

But Maria wasn't looking at it.

A shadow moved in the cavern's upper reaches. A flicker of matte-black armor. A face half-hidden by a scarred helmet.

The shadowed serpent.

Their eyes met. His gaze was glacial, but Maria saw the storm beneath—recognition, rage, a promise older than the Fracture.

The Devourer followed her stare. "**Ah…**" It smiled. "**The serpent's child arrives.**"

Maria's lips curled. "You talk too much."

She *yanked*, tearing her wrists free in a spray of blood. The fungal bonds recoiled, their shrieks harmonizing with the Devourer's roar as Maria lunged—not at it, but toward the Core.

"Captain, your grav-chute upgrade is operational. I suggest trying it out" Atlas said.

"Perfect timing as usual," Samiel retorted.

A surge of energy crackled through Samiel's grav-chute array. The device, once a utilitarian slab of eclipsite alloy, *unfolded*. A burst of amber light erupted from Samiel's back, vaporizing Gloom spores in a 10-foot radius. The air hummed with resonant frequency, a chord that made Maria's teeth ache. Twin wings of translucent orange energy fanned outward—each feather a fractal lattice of bioluminescent mycelium. The veins pulsed with the mycelium network code, glowing cerulean at the edges. The wings *breathed*, adjusting to air density and Gloom interference. Their edges shimmered like heated glass, scattering prismatic light across the cavern.

The wings spanned 18 feet, semi-translucent and edged with razor-sharp mycelium filaments. Each "feather" was a micro-reactor, burning Gloom rot for fuel. Samiel banked with avian precision, the wings responding to neural impulses via Atlas. Tight rolls, vertical ascents—no Warden tech had ever moved like this. A holographic timer blazed in Samiel's HUD: **00:02:15**. The mycelium burned itself out rapidly;

"Three minutes of flight, max." Atlas informed.

The Devourer's roar shook the cavern, its claws shredding stone into shrapnel. The Devourer lunged, but Samiel *moved*. He soared downward, wings shearing through a stalactite, then dive-bombed with a sonic boom. Maria watched, her breath caught. Samiel's wings cast overlapping shadows, their amber glow painting the cavern in wildfire hues. A low, resonant thrum—like a cathedral organ fused with a swarm of bees. Burnt fungus and petrichor, the mycelium purifying Gloom toxins as it flew. He struck the Devourer's chest, the wings folding into a spearhead. Black ichor geysered, but the creature retaliated—a backhanded swipe that sent Samiel crashing into the cavern wall.

Samiel thrust off a cavern wall, umbral fang in hand and lunges toward the abomination. The devourer is quick phasing in and out of reality, making it difficult to land a blow.

"You fight well, warden, but your fight is futile. The network and your precious Atlas can't stop what isssss cominggggg!" The devourer hissed.

"How does he know your name?" Samiel said in his head

"I dont kno—"

"Oh i know more than you think Serpents shadow," He interrupted.

"Initializing helmet scrambler…. Captain, this thing is older than fracture. The spores I scanned belong to him….He can't read your thoughts now were safe, but Theres more to this than we know……Acessing *AEGIS mainframe keyword search Dr. Voss. *Dr. Elias Voss— Nexus board member, holograms projecting global weather grids."*

"What is this?" Samiel uttered.

Maria's gloves slipped on her blades' hilts. Pupils dilated, tracking Samiel's arcs.

"He's… a storm. A beautiful, reckless storm."

Samiel landed beside her, wings retracting into embers. Their eyes met—*his* sharp with battle fury, *hers* wide with unguarded wonder. He saw it: her mask of stoicism cracked, just for him.

"You're staring," he rasped.

"You're *flying*," she countered, voice steadier than her pulse.

The wings' afterglow revealed cracks in Samiel's armor. Mycelium veins crept up his neck, bonding with his Nahual Neural Shunts.

Atlas: "Warning: Symbiote rejection risk at 43%. Recommend disengaging wings."

"Override," Samiel growled.

Samiel's wings flared, stabilizing him mid-air as the Devourer's claws gouged the cavern wall where he'd stood moments before. Maria lunged, her obsidian daggers carving arcs of bioluminescent light through the creature's fungal tendrils. The blades sparked where they struck, searing the Gloom rot with network-coded heat.

"Focus on the Core!" Maria shouted, her voice cutting through the Devourer's static-laced roar. **"The glyphs—they're a feedback loop!"** As she sent her blades drone hurtling toward the devourer.

Atlas's voice crackled in Samiel's neural link, urgent: **"Dr. Voss's files—he wasn't just studying the Gloom. He *weaponized* it. The Devourer's a prototype. A failed experiment."**

The revelation hit Samiel like a plasma round. **"You're saying AEGIS *made* this thing?!"**

"No. Elias Voss, he was Voss's great grandfather. This was before the gloom. It backfired. The Devourer's a puppet—"

"—But the *strings* lead deeper," the Devourer interrupted, its voice warping into a dozen overlapping tones. A hologram erupted from its chest—a fractal spiral, alive with screaming faces. **"You think me *autonomous*? I am but a vessel. The Weaver... hungers."**

Maria froze. **"The Weaver?"** Her grandmother's stories flooded back—a myth about an entity that "knit the world from shadow." She'd thought it a metaphor.

Samiel dove, wings folding into a blade-like strike. The Devourer phased out, reappearing behind him. **"Clever little serpent. But your AI hasn't told you *everything*, has it?"** It gestured, and the Gloom Core pulsed. Atlas's systems *screamed* in Samiel's mind.

"Captain—it's hacking my protocols! I can't—" Atlas's voice glitched into static.

Maria acted. She slammed her palm onto a glyph-etched stalagmite, her blood reactivating the network's ancient code. The cavern *shuddered* as bioluminescent veins lit up, forming a cage of light around the Devourer. **"Now, Samiel!"**

The Warden with wings of fire and fungus, descending like an avenging angel. The warrior queen beside him, her blades reflecting his light. And between them, a spark—not of the network, not of the Gloom, but something older.

Something human.

Samiel's wings disintegrated, their mycelium fuel spent. As he fell—and *twisted*, driving his umbral fang into the Core. The blade flared blacker than the void, fracturing the Gloom star. The Devourer howled, its form unraveling.

"You... delay nothing..." it gurgled, phasing into spores. **"The Weaver... sees... *you...*"**

Silence fell. The Core's remnants floated, a dying ember. Maria collapsed against the altar, clutching her bleeding palm. Samiel knelt beside her, Atlas's voice flickering back.

"I've isolated the breach. The Weaver... it's not Gloom. It's older. The network's logs mention a 'Prime Symbiont'—something that existed before the Fracture."

Maria lifted her holo-pad, its cracked screen displaying a weathered Nahuatl text. "Look. *'The Weaver spins the storm's eye. Only the shadowed serpent can pierce its veil.'*" She met Samiel's gaze. "Your visions... they weren't just dreams. They're a *map*."

A low hum resonated from the canyon's depths. The remaining Gloomspawn bowed, their bodies dissolving into spores that snaked downward, coalescing into a tunnel of writhing mist.

"An invitation," Atlas said grimly.

Samiel stood, his blade still dripping Gloom ichor. **"Then we RSVP in person."**

Maria rose, her daggers humming. **"Together."**

Above them, the cavern ceiling cracked open, revealing a sky choked with *new storms*—spiraling green-black hurricanes. The Weaver's voice echoed on the wind, a sound like galaxies colliding.

#

Chapter 13

The Siege of the Serpent

The pyramids of Teotihuacán hummed with ancient power, their stone steps glowing faintly under the mycelium network's bioluminescent veins. General Braddock stood atop the Temple of the Feathered Serpent, his boots planted on glyphs carved by hands dead for millennia. Below, AEGIS soldiers scrambled—activating pulse turrets, fortifying barricades with eclipsite alloy, and loading artillery shells infused with fungal suppressants. The air crackled with static, the network's defensive protocols thrumming like a war drum.

Then the horizon *moved*.

A tidal wave of Gloomspawn surged across the desert—a roiling mass of chitinous limbs, razor-wire tentacles, and half-mechanical horrors. At their forefront rode the Coyote, his once-human frame now a grotesque fusion of Gloom and machine. His armor pulsed with violet rot-code, his face hidden behind a mask of obsidian and jade, its carved serpent's grin dripping nanite sludge. Behind him, **Gloom Behemoths** lumbered—towering hybrids of tank treads and exposed ribcages, their cannons forged from Drakes' spinal columns.

Braddock's comms exploded:

"General—Sector 6's reinforcements are 20 minutes out! Verdant Spire's barges are mobilizing, but—"

"Hold the line," Braddock growled, his voice steady. **"We don't need rescuing yet."**

Reaper leaned against a pulse turret, casually slotting a gloom-rot magazine into his Thorncaster. **"*Órale*, looks like Coyote upgraded his gear. Still not uglier than your ex, Duke."**

Duke snorted, hefting a Voidspike cannon onto his shoulder. **"Yea, at least my ex didn't bring an army to my doorstep when we broke up."**

The Coyote's voice boomed across the battlefield, amplified by the Gloom's corrupted resonance:

"¡General Braddock!" His words slithered through the static, oily and saccharine. **"You stand on sacred ground—ground your ancestors *stole*. But today, you'll return it... *bone by bone*."**

A hush fell as the Gloomspawn halted, their collective breath a hiss of decaying code. The Coyote dismounted his biomechanical steed, its hooves cracking the earth.

"Surrender the network's heart," he demanded, gesturing to the pyramid's apex, where the mycelium's core pulsed like a star. **"Or watch your soldiers blood decorate the walls like *art*."**

Braddock stepped forward, his shadow cast long by the network's glow. **"You want the pyramid?"** He drew his plasma machete, its edge singing with bioluminescence. **"Dig your grave here, and I'll bury you in it."**

Reaper whooped, firing a barbed seed pod into the horde. It exploded into neurotoxic vines, ensnaring a Gloom Behemoth mid-roar. **"You heard the man, *pendejos*! Party's starting!"**

The Coyote's mask split open, revealing a maw of spinning drill bits and needle-teeth. **"So be it."**

He raised a clawed hand—and the earth *screamed.*

Gloomspawn erupted from fissures beneath the earth, their talons shredding soldiers mid-scream. Pulse turrets swiveled, unleashing volleys of ionized rounds that lit the desert in strobes of teal and violet. Duke's Voidspike cannon barked, its projectile burrowing into a Behemoth's core before detonating in a geyser of radioactive viscera.

"Sector 6—where's our damn backup?!" Braddock barked into his comm.

"Barges inbound, sir! ETA 15 minutes!"

"Make it 10!"

Reaper vaulted onto a barricade, his Thorncaster whining as he unloaded into a swarm of Gloom hounds. **"Hey Duke! Bet you 500 credits I rack more kills!"**

"I already know what im buying!" Duke slammed his fist into a leaping Gloomspawn, his hydraulics crushing its skull to pulp.

Above, the sky darkened. Not from clouds—from wings.

Huitzilin copters streaked overhead, their rotors shearing through Gloom Drakes as they unleashed payloads of mycelium-tipped missiles. The network's bioluminescence flared, its glyphs burning brighter with every Gloomspawn felled—but the horde was endless.

The Coyote climbed atop his steed, his voice a distorted snarl: **"You think your *network* saves you? The Weaver *sees* your light… and *hungers*."**

Braddock froze. *The Weaver?*

"Sir—the western trench is overrun!"

"Fall back to the wall!" Braddock ordered. **"Prep the resonance charges!"**

Reaper grinned, reloading. **"Time to light 'em up, Duke."**

"Like the Fourth of July," Duke growled, priming a cluster of fungal grenades.

As the Gloomspawn surged, the pyramids themselves seemed to *awaken*. Ancient glyphs flared gold, the network's roots surging from the earth to impale corrupted beasts. But the Coyote only laughed, his form dissolving into spores as he teleported closer to the wall.

"This is just the *overture*, General," he hissed, reappearing atop the temple. **"The Weaver's storm is coming… and you're *drowning* in its eye."**

The ground quaked. Far to the west, a green-black hurricane churned—a living tempest with tendrils lashing toward the battle.

"Reinforcements have arrived!" a soldier shouted.

Sector 6's barges descended like avenging angels, their hulls bristling with artillery. But Braddock didn't smile.

The real storm was just beginning.

The pulse turrets roared, their ionized rounds stitching lines of searing light across the desert as they hammered the advancing Gloom army. But the Coyote's horde was a hydra—for every Behemoth that fell, three more lurched forward, their cannons vomiting rot and shrapnel.

"Focus fire on the eastern flank!" Braddock barked into his comm, unaware that the *real* threat was already at the gates.

Duke and Reaper sprinted toward the perimeter wall, where a pack of **Gloom Hounds**—sleek, steel-fanged nightmares with bioluminescent eyes—had slipped through the turrets' blind spot. Their claws screeched against the eclipsite alloy as they scaled the barricades, jaws snapping at panicked soldiers.

"Hey, Duke!" Reaper yelled, ejecting a spent magazine and slamming a fresh one into his Thorncaster. **"Think these mutts'll fetch if we ask nice?"**

"Only one way to find out!" Duke's hydraulics whined as he leapt, his augmented fist cratering the skull of the lead hound. The creature collapsed, its howl dying in a gurgle of static.

But the hounds weren't alone.

"Incoming!" Reaper shouted as a second wave surged on the wall, their razor-wire tails lashing. He fired a barbed seed pod, the explosion engulfing two hounds in neurotoxic vines. Duke grabbed a third by the throat, slamming it into the ground until its spine cracked.

"Too easy!" Reaper crowed, but his smirk faded as the *dying* hounds began to twitch. Their jaws unhinged, emitting a subsonic wail that made the air itself vibrate.

"The hell…?" Duke clutched his helmet as the howl intensified, his HUD flickering. **"My systems are glitching!"**

Above them, the mycelium network's bioluminescent veins dimmed. The glyphs carved into the pyramid's steps flickered like dying embers.

"They're targeting the network!" Reaper snarled, firing wildly. But it was too late.

The ground *split*—a jagged fissure tearing open beneath the wall as the hounds' collective howl reached a crescendo. From the chasm rose a **Gloom Goliath**, its 20-foot frame a grotesque collage of rusted industrial plating and pulsating rot. One arm ended in a wrecking-ball fist, the other in a spinning drill-bit that screeched like a dying star.

"BREACH!" a soldier screamed as the Goliath swung its fist, obliterating the barricade. Gloomspawn poured through the gap, their talons ripping into AEGIS defenders.

Reaper backflipped to avoid a hound's lunge, landing beside Duke. **"We just got outplayed by a pack of robo-dogs!"**

"Save the jokes!" Duke roared, priming a cluster of fungal grenades. **"Seal that fissure!"**

But the Goliath was already rampaging toward the pyramid's base, its drill-bit carving a path of molten earth. Raiders followed in its wake, their rot-code rifles spitting corrosive slugs.

Inside the Base

The courtyard became a slaughterhouse. Soldiers fell as the network's defenses faltered, their armor dissolving under Gloomspawn acid. Reaper and Duke fought back-to-back, their banter replaced by grim focus.

"Left flank!" Duke shouted, crushing a raider's skull with a hydraulic uppercut.

"On it!" Reaper spun, his Thorncaster shredding a Gloomspawn mid-leap. **"Where's Braddock?!"**

Braddock stood at the base of the ancient structure, his plasma machete dripping with Gloom ichor. The Coyote awaited him, lounging atop a rubble pile like a king on a throne of bones.

"You're too late, General," the Coyote purred, his mask retracting to reveal a face half-melted by rot. **"The network's heartbeat is already ours. And your dear Dr. Voss… she's begs for mercy at the altar of the weaver."**

Braddock froze. **"Voss is dead."**

The Coyote laughed, a sound like grinding gears. **"Dead? No. *Transcendent*. Nexus perfected her. She's the Weaver's voice now… and she's *hungry*."**

"Nexus?" Braddock hissed. **"That corp dissolved centuries ago!"**

"You think death stops a god?" The Coyote lunged, his rot-blade clashing against Braddock's machete. **"Nexus birthed the Gloom to cleanse this rotten world. Voss was their prophet. And you?"** He grinned. **"You're the sacrifice."**

Braddock roared, driving the Coyote back with a flurry of strikes. But the general's resolve wavered as the ground trembled—not from the battle, but from something *deeper*. Far above, the green-black hurricane pulsed, its tendrils now lashing closer to the battle. The mycelium core flickered, its light dimming as the Weaver's voice echoed through the static:

"The serpent's shadow will fall… The feast begins…"

Reaper's voice crackled over Braddock's comm, desperate: **"We can't hold the courtyard! That Goliath's—**

The transmission died as the Goliath's wrecking-ball fist smashed through the command post, its howl merging with the storm.

The sky *screamed.*

Verdant Spire's barges descended like wrathful titans, their hulls sheathed in crackling energy shields that scorched the air with the tang of ozone. Each barge was a floating fortress—1,000 feet of matte-black alloy ribbed with bioluminescent cannons, their barrels glowing venomous green as they charged. From their underbellies, squadrons of **Huitzilin Mark IV fighters** disengaged, wings unfolding into serrated talons as they dove into the fray.

"About damn time!" Reaper shouted, grinning as a fighter streaked overhead, its plasma cannons vaporizing a Gloom Drake mid-pounce. The creature's wings dissolved into ash, raining down over the battlefield like cursed snow.

The air battle was chaos perfected. Fighters weaved between swarms of Gloom Drakes, their wing-mounted railguns firing shards of eclipsite alloy that punched through scales and rotor blades alike. Bombers released payloads of **mycelium cluster munitions**— pods that burst midair, unleashing bioluminescent fungi that latched onto Gloomspawn, devouring their rot-code like antibodies. Above it all, the barges' main cannons fired, each shot a concentrated beam of network energy that carved canyons through the horde, reducing Behemoths to smoldering slag.

"Duke—*move!*" Reaper yanked Duke backward as a dying Drake crashed where he'd stood, its carcass skidding through the sand.

"Focus!" Duke barked, reloading his Voidspike cannon. **"Braddock's pinned near the pyramid!"**

Braddock staggered, his plasma machete sparking against the Coyote's rot-blade. The general's armor was cracked, his left arm hanging limp from a Goliath's backhand strike. The Coyote circled him, mask cracked to reveal a grin of fused bone and circuitry.

"**Your barges are *loud*,**" the Coyote sneered. "**But noise won't save you.**"

He lunged, his blade aimed for Braddock's throat—

A barbed seed pod exploded between them, throwing the Coyote backward. Reaper slid into view, Thorncaster smoking. "**Miss me, *cabrón*?**"

Duke charged from the flank, his augmented fist connecting with the Coyote's ribs in a crunch of metal and bone. "**This ain't your stage anymore.**"

The Coyote spat black ichor, his mask fully disintegrating to reveal a face half-consumed by Gloom rot. "**Fools… The storm is *here*.**"

Above, the green-black hurricane lashed closer, its winds screaming with the voices of the damned. Lightning crackled within its vortex—not yellow, but *bioluminescent green*, striking the desert and birthing Gloomspawn from the sand itself.

The barges' cannons pivoted, targeting the storm. Network energy lanced into the tempest, tearing holes in its fabric—but the wounds sealed instantly, tendrils of Gloom knitting the void faster than AEGIS could burn it.

"**Fall back!**" Braddock ordered, his voice raw. "**Regroup at the inner sanctum!**"

Reaper and Duke dragged him toward the pyramid as the storm's leading edge hit. The air turned viscous, thick with spores that hissed against armor. Soldiers collapsed, clawing at their helmets as the Gloom's whispers slithered into their minds.

"**Not today, you ugly *puto*!**" Reaper emptied his Thorncaster into a Gloomspawn blocking their path, its body disintegrating into static.

They reached the pyramid's base as the first tendril of the storm grazed its apex. The ancient glyphs flared gold, the network's core pulsing in defiance—but the stone itself began to *crack*.

"Braddock!" A medic rushed forward, but the general shoved him off.

"Save the core," Braddock growled, slumping against the stone. **"If the pyramid falls…"**

Duke reloaded his cannon, eyeing the storm. **"Where's Samiel when you need him?"**

"Fighting his own demons," Reaper muttered, glancing east where the horizon boiled with unnatural light. **"We'll hold this one."**

The Coyote's laughter echoed through the chaos, his body dissolving into spores as the storm swallowed him. **"You *cannot* kill a god, General… But it will feast on you all the same."**

As the last barge's cannons fell silent, the battlefield fell eerily still—a pocket of calm in the storm's eye. The Gloomspawn retreated, clawing into fissures as if summoned.

But the respite was a lie.

The storm's core pulsed, and a figure emerged—**Dr. Voss**, her body a grotesque fusion of Gloom and mycelium, her eyes hollow voids leaking static.

"The Weaver… sends its regards."

The pyramid trembled. Somewhere, deep in the network's code, something *answered*.

The battlefield was a cacophony of chaos, the air thick with the acrid stench of rot and the metallic tang of ionized plasma. The Gloomspawn surged forward, their grotesque forms illuminated by the flickering light of the mycelium network. The pyramid complex was on the brink of collapse, its ancient stones groaning under the weight of the storm's fury. But just as the Gloom forces seemed poised to overwhelm the defenders, the network itself *reacted.*

A low, resonant hum filled the air, vibrating through the ground and into the bones of every soldier. The glyphs carved into the pyramid's steps flared brighter than ever, their golden light intensifying until it was almost blinding. The mycelium veins that crisscrossed the battlefield pulsed with newfound energy, their bioluminescence shifting from teal to a deep, radiant blue.

Then, with a sound like the world itself taking a breath, the network unleashed its final defense.

A massive, translucent dome of mycelium energy erupted from the base of the pyramid, expanding outward in a wave of pure, radiant force. The dome's surface shimmered like liquid glass, its translucent walls rippling with intricate patterns of Zapotec glyphs and fractal designs. It enveloped the entire pyramid complex, pushing back the Gloomspawn with an unstoppable force. The creatures shrieked as they were repelled, their bodies disintegrating into ash upon contact with the dome's surface.

Inside the dome, the air was clean, the oppressive weight of the Gloom lifted. The barges and Huitzilin fighters, battered and smoking, began to heal as the mycelium energy flowed over them. Cracked hulls sealed themselves, and damaged systems rebooted with a surge of bioluminescent light. The soldiers, too, felt the network's touch—wounds closed, and exhaustion faded as the dome's energy revitalized them.

But the battle was far from over.

Reaper and Duke stood at the base of the Pyramid of the Sun, their weapons raised as they faced the final, most terrifying threat: **Dr. Voss**. Her body was a grotesque fusion of Gloom and mycelium, her once-human form now a nightmarish amalgamation of pulsating rot and bioluminescent veins. Her eyes were hollow voids, leaking static as she floated above the steps, her voice a distorted echo of the Weaver's will.

"You cannot stop what has already begun," she intoned, her words reverberating through the air like a death knell. *"The Weaver's storm will consume all."*

Reaper spat on the ground, his Thorncaster humming with energy. **"Yeah, yeah, we've heard the speech before, *hermana*. How about you shut up and fight?"**

Duke cracked his knuckles, his hydraulics whining as he flexed his augmented arm. **"Let's make this quick. I got a date with a bottle of tequila after this."**

Dr. Voss's response was a guttural roar as she lunged at them, her claws extended and dripping with corrosive rot. Reaper fired a barbed seed pod, the explosion engulfing her in neurotoxic vines, but she tore through them with ease, her body regenerating almost instantly.

Duke charged, his Voidspike cannon barking as he fired a concentrated burst of network energy at her. The shot struck her chest, sending her reeling, but she retaliated with a swipe of her claws that sent Duke flying into a pile of rubble.

"Duke!" Reaper shouted, diving to avoid a blast of Gloom energy from Voss. He rolled to his feet and fired another volley of seed pods, each one exploding in a burst of bioluminescent light. The explosions staggered Voss, but she quickly recovered, her body twisting and contorting as she absorbed the energy.

"She's feeding off the network!" Duke growled, pulling himself from the rubble. **"We need to hit her with something she can't absorb!"**

Reaper grinned, ejecting a spent magazine and slamming a fresh one into his Thorncaster. **"Got just the thing."**

He reached into his belt and pulled out a small, glowing canister—a **mycelium disruptor**, designed to overload Gloom-infused systems. **"Duke, keep her busy!"**

Duke nodded, charging at Voss with a roar. His augmented fist connected with her jaw, the impact sending shockwaves through the air. Voss retaliated with a blast of Gloom energy, but Duke absorbed the hit, his armor glowing as it redirected the energy into his hydraulics.

"Now, Reaper!" Duke shouted, pinning Voss to the ground with his sheer strength.

Reaper leapt onto Voss's back, slamming the disruptor into the base of her skull. The device activated with a blinding flash, its energy coursing through her body and disrupting the Gloom's hold. Voss screamed, her form writhing as the mycelium energy clashed with the rot inside her.

"This is for Maximus, you *puta*!" Reaper snarled, driving his blade into her chest.

Voss's body convulsed, her screams merging with the static of the Weaver's voice. **"You... cannot... win..."** she gasped, her form beginning to dissolve into ash.

Duke and Reaper stepped back as Voss's body disintegrated, the mycelium energy purging the Gloom from her system. Her final breath was a whisper, her hollow eyes locking onto Reaper's as she spoke her last words:

"The Weaver... sees... all..."

With that, she was gone, her body reduced to a pile of glowing ash that was carried away by the wind.

As Voss fell, the storm above the pyramid began to dissipate. The green-black clouds churned violently, their tendrils retracting as if recoiling from the network's power. The dome of mycelium energy pulsed once more, its light intensifying, leaving the battlefield in an eerie silence.

The Gloomspawn were gone, their forces scattered and broken. The barges and Huitzilin fighters hovered above the pyramid, their systems fully restored by the network's touch. The soldiers on the ground cheered, their voices echoing through the ancient complex.

But the victory was bittersweet.

Braddock stood at the base of the pyramid, his plasma machete still in hand. He stared at the spot where Voss had fallen, his mind racing with questions. **"What the hell was she talking about? The Weaver... Nexus... What does it all mean?"**

Reaper and Duke approached, their weapons still smoking. **"Whatever it is, it ain't good,"** Reaper said, wiping blood from his face. **"But we stopped her. That's gotta count for something."**

Duke nodded, his expression grim. **"For now. But if the Gloom's got something bigger planned, we need to be ready."**

Braddock's comm crackled to life, the voice of a barge captain cutting through the static. **"General Braddock, this is Verdant Spire Barge Alpha. The Madam President is en route. She has files on Dr. Voss's bloodline that she needs to share with you immediately."**

Braddock's eyes narrowed. **"Understood. Tell her we'll be waiting."**

He turned to Reaper and Duke, his expression unreadable. **"This isn't over. Not by a long shot."**

As the barges descended, the soldiers began to regroup, their faces a mix of relief and unease. The storm had passed, but the shadows it left behind were darker than ever.

And somewhere, deep in the Gloom, the Weaver watched.

#

Chapter 14

The Labyrinth Of Truth

The air was heavy with the scent of damp earth and the faint hum of ancient machinery. Maria and Samiel stood at the mouth of the tunnel, their boots sinking slightly into the soft, moss-covered ground. Behind them, the bodies of Roxy and Baron lay wrapped in makeshift shrouds of mycelium-infused fabric, their faces peaceful in the dim light. They had placed them in a shallow alcove carved into the tunnel wall, a temporary resting place until they could return to give them a proper burial.

Maria knelt beside them, her fingers brushing the edge of Roxy's shroud. "They deserved better," she said softly, her voice barely audible over the distant drip of water echoing through the tunnel.

Samiel placed a hand on her shoulder, his touch firm but gentle. "They fought bravely. We'll make sure they're honored when this is over."

She nodded, her eyes glistening with unshed tears, but she quickly wiped them away, her resolve hardening. "Let's go. We don't have time to waste."

As they stepped into the tunnel, the darkness seemed to swallow them whole. The walls were slick with moisture, and the faint glow of bioluminescent fungi provided just enough light to see by. The air grew cooler the deeper they went, and the silence was broken only by the sound of their footsteps and the occasional creak of ancient metal.

Atlas's voice crackled aloud, breaking the tension. **"Well, this is cozy. Nothing like a romantic stroll through a damp, creepy tunnel to set the mood."**

Samiel smirked, shaking his head. "Not now, Atlas."

Maria glanced at him, a faint smile tugging at her lips. "What's your little AI saying?"

"Nothing important," Samiel replied, though his tone was light. "Just being his usual self."

Maria chuckled softly, the sound echoing through the tunnel. "He's not wrong, though. This place does have a certain... charm."

They walked in silence for a while, the weight of the moment pressing down on them. But as the tunnel widened, the tension began to ease, replaced by an unspoken connection that had been growing between them since they first met.

"Do you ever feel like we've known each other forever?" Maria asked suddenly, her voice soft but filled with curiosity.

Samiel glanced at her, his eyes meeting hers in the dim light of his armor. There was something in her gaze—something warm and familiar—that made his chest tighten. "Yeah," he admitted. "It's like... I don't know. Like we were supposed to meet."

Maria smiled, her cheeks flushing slightly. "I've had dreams about you, you know. Long before today. A shadow in the gloom, fighting to protect something... someone. I didn't know it was you… until now."

Samiel's breath caught in his throat. "I've dreamed about you too," he said quietly. "A woman in black, always just out of reach. I thought it was just my mind playing tricks on me, but... it was you. I can't forget your face."

Their eyes locked, the air between them crackling with an undeniable energy. For a moment, the world around them faded away, leaving only the two of them in the dim glow of the tunnel.

Atlas's voice broke the moment, his tone teasing. **"Oh, come on. Are we really doing this now? In the middle of a creepy tunnel? You two are worse than a bad holo-drama."**

Samiel rolled his eyes, but Maria laughed, the sound light and genuine. "He's not wrong," she said, her smile widening. "But I've always been a fan of holo-dramas."

As they continued deeper into the tunnel, Maria began to open up about her past. She spoke of her mother, Citlali, a fierce and brilliant woman who had dedicated her life to understanding the network. She talked about her grandmother, a healer who had taught her the old ways, and her great-grandmother, who had lived through the Fracture and passed down stories of the world before.

Samiel listened intently, his heart swelling with admiration for her strength and resilience. "You're incredible," he said softly. "Your family... they're a part of you. I can see it in everything you do."

Maria's cheeks flushed again, but she held his gaze, her eyes burning with a quiet intensity. "Thank you," she whispered.

As they delved deeper, the tunnel began to change. The walls were no longer rough and natural but smooth and metallic, etched with glowing Nexus glyphs that pulsed faintly with energy. Thick cables ran along the ceiling, leading deeper into the earth.

"This isn't just a tunnel," Maria said, her voice filled with awe. "It's a pathway. A gateway to something... big."

Samiel nodded, his hand instinctively reaching for the piece of the Devourer's tentacle he had kept as a trophy. It glowed faintly in his grasp, reacting to the glyphs on the walls. "This thing might be our key," he said, holding it up.

As if in response, the glyphs flared brighter, and a massive door slid open with a hiss of pressurized air. Beyond it lay a sterile, cavernous space—a massive underground base, empty but humming with latent energy.

Maria stepped forward, her eyes wide with wonder. "This is it," she said. "The heart of Nexus."

Samiel followed her, his heart pounding with a mix of excitement and trepidation. As they stepped inside, the door closed behind them, sealing them in. The air was cool and sterile, the silence almost deafening.

But as they walked deeper into the base, the connection between them grew stronger, their bond unshakable. They were no longer just allies—they were something more. And as they faced the mysteries of the labyrinth together, their love became a beacon of hope in the darkness.

Atlas's voice echoed against the walls, softer this time. **"You know, for once, I think you two might actually make it out of this alive. Just... try not to get too distracted, okay?"**

Samiel smiled, his eyes meeting Maria's once more. "We'll be fine," he said, his voice filled with quiet confidence.

And for the first time in a long time, he believed it.

The air grew colder as Maria and Samiel crept deeper into the devourer's base, their footsteps muffled by the hum of dormant machinery. Bioluminescent fungi clung to the walls like veins, their teal glow clashing with the sterile white of flickering overhead lights. Atlas's voice buzzed in Samiel's neural link, low and urgent:

"Movement ahead. Hybrid signatures—unclassified."

They pressed against a corroded bulkhead, peering into a cavernous laboratory. Rows of cryotubes stretched into the gloom, their glass fogged with frost. Inside, horrors floated in viscous fluid: Gloomspawn fused with human limbs, their flesh stitched with bioluminescent mycelium. Others were soldiers—or what remained of them—their bodies half-consumed by rot-code, faces frozen in silent screams. Holoscreens flanked the tubes, scrolling DNA sequences and glitching labels:

SUBJECT 0017-A: NETWORK/GLOOM SYMBIOSIS — 98% REJECTION

SUBJECT 0023-C: HUMAN CORTEX INTEGRATION — FAILURE

"Charming decor," Atlas said aloud.

"Dios mío," Maria whispered, her blades trembling. "They're trying to merge us with it."

Samiel's hand brushed hers as he gestured forward—a fleeting touch, electric and grounding. "Stay close."

They slipped past the tubes, shadows clinging to their armor. At the lab's far end, a sealed door pulsed with Zapotec glyphs. Before Samiel could reach for his holo-pad, the symbols flared gold, and the door hissed open.

"The network is guiding us," Atlas said. **"It wasn't the Devourer who opened the tunnel. It wants us here."**

"Why?" Maria hissed.

"To witness the truth."

The chamber beyond defied reason—a cathedral of blackened steel and living mycelium, its vaulted ceiling lost to darkness. At its center stood the Devourer, flanked by two **Gloom Goliaths** whose rusted armor dripped nanite sludge. Before them, a massive holoscreen flickered, its surface a storm of static. A voice echoed from it, robotic and hollow, devoid of face or form:

"Progress report."

The Devourer knelt, its crown of spores dimming in reverence. **"The key issss secured, Weaver. Her blood runssss deep."** One clawed hand raised a vial—Maria's blood, stolen during her capture. The screen's static sharpened into DNA strands, glowing gold where Maria's genetic code intertwined with the network's roots.

"Anomaly confirmed," the Weaver intoned. *"Subject Maria Echo-7: lineage traceable to Network Origin Event. Upload the data."*

A Goliath lumbered forward, its drill-arm slotting the vial into a terminal. The holoscreen erupted with holograms:

— A burial at Teotihuacán, Maria's great-grandmother laid to rest beneath the Pyramid of the Sun, her hands clasping a mycelium-coated relic.

— A young Citlali, Maria's mother, carving a glyph into her daughter's palm. The wound bled gold, the network's veins surging beneath her skin.

— Maria's DNA, now—a fractal helix, its strands fused with bioluminescent code.

"The network was born from death," Atlas murmured, awed. **"Your ancestor's burial… it catalyzed the symbiosis. Your bloodline *is* the bridge."**

Maria staggered, Samiel's grip steadying her elbow. His thumb traced the scarred glyph on her wrist—a silent question. She didn't pull away. Her heart beating a little faster with every trace.

The Weaver's static-laced voice sharpened, its attention shifting like a blade. *"And the Warden… Samiel-9. Anomaly detected. His code defies categorization."*

The Devourer's void-face twisted toward the holograms, where Samiel's DNA spiraled beside Maria's—a helix of obsidian and bioluminescence, fractured by strange, glowing fissures. *"A weapon… or a flaw?"*

"Irrelevant," the Weaver replied. *"His existence complicates the equation. Retrieve Maria. Her blood alone is insufficient—we require the source. The burial site. The origin."*

Maria's breath hitched. Samiel's grip tightened on her arm, his thumb still tracing her glyph. The contact sent a shiver through her—part fear, part something warmer, reckless.

"Our army is currently engaged at Teotihuacán the humansssss bassssse, I am certain our victory is clossssssse at hand!"

"I will not tolerate failure again Tzitzimicani-7" the weaver said with a dark static tone.

"Tzitzimicani-7 what the fuck is that name?" Samiel asked.

"Tzitzimitl, the skeletal star demons of Aztec myth who devoured humanity during solar eclipses. They represented apocalyptic chaos and cosmic hunger." Maria answered

"How fitting, the weaver has a sense of humor," Atlas said sarcastically

"We need to move," Samiel whispered, his lips grazing her ear.

They slipped backward, but Maria hesitated, her eyes locked on the holograms. "Wait—*look.*" The screen flickered to a file labeled **NEXUS ARCHIVE: FRACTURE.**

"Download it," Atlas urged. **"I can decrypt it, but we need access."**

Samiel nodded, pulling Maria toward a rusted terminal tucked in the chamber's shadows. Their shoulders pressed together as they worked, fingers flying over the keys. The air between them hummed—not just from the network, but something charged, unspoken.

"Your hands are shaking," Samiel murmured, his voice low.

"Yours aren't," she countered, glancing up. Their eyes met, and for a heartbeat, the world narrowed to the gold flecks in his irises, the way his gaze dropped to her lips—

"Flirting later, surviving now," Atlas snapped. **"The data's corrupting. Hurry."**

Maria blinked, cheeks flushing, and slammed her palm onto the biometric scanner. The terminal spat sparks, then flared to life.

SUBJECT: DR. ELIAS VOSS — STATUS: ALIVE. LOCATION: SECTOR ONE.

FRACTURE CAUSE: [ERROR]. NETWORK ORIGIN: [FILE CORRUPTED].

"Voss… She's *alive*?" Samiel growled.

"And the Fracture?" Maria demanded. **"What caused it?"**

Before Atlas could answer, the chamber shuddered. The Weaver's screen exploded with light, its voice booming: ***"Intruders. Extract them. Now."***

The Devourer roared, tendrils lashing toward their hiding spot. Samiel grabbed Maria's hand, their fingers interlacing as they bolted through a collapsing doorway. The corridor beyond teemed with Gloomspawn—bat-like Drakes screeched overhead, while centipedes with human hands scuttled up the walls.

"Samiel—!" Maria gasped, but he was already dragging her into a service shaft, their bodies pressed chest-to-chest in the cramped darkness.

"Atlas, send a distress ping to Duke and Reaper," Samiel ordered, his breath warm against her neck. **"Now."**

"Signal jammed. Trying to bypass—"

"Try harder."

Maria's laugh was shaky, adrenaline and absurdity tangling. "You're a terrible conversationalist, you know that?"

Samiel's lips quirked. "You're staring."

"I'm *not*—"

A Drake's talon ripped through the shaft's grate, cutting her off. They tumbled into a cavernous hangar, where the storm raged just outside—green-black clouds vomiting acid rain, the ground fracturing into glowing fissures.

"The gloom is descending on us here," Atlas warned. **"We need to *go*."**

Samiel spun Maria to face him, his hands cupping her face. "Stay with me."

She leaned into his touch, her voice steady. "Always."

They ran, blades and grav-chutes cutting through the chaos. Behind them, the Devourer's howl shook the sky—a promise of violence. Ahead, the storm swallowed the horizon.

But in the space between heartbeats, as their hands brushed and their eyes met, Maria and Samiel found something the Gloom couldn't corrode.

A spark.

A vow.

A storm of their own.

The hangar trembled as acid rain hissed against Samiel's armor through the shattered glass ceiling, the storm's green-black tendrils clawing at the ruptured ceiling. Maria spun beside him, her obsidian blades slicing through a Gloom Drake's wing. The creature screeched, dissolving into ash, but three more swooped in its place, their talons dripping nanite slurry.

Flash of memory: A desert canyon under twin suns. Maria, clad in tattered silks, parried a serpentine beast's strike with twin daggers. Samiel, his face streaked with war-paint, loosed an arrow past her ear, felling the creature. "You're reckless," he'd growled. "You're welcome," she'd shot back, grinning.

"**Samiel—***left*!" she shouted in the present. He pivoted, grav-chute flaring as he launched skyward. A Drake's jaws snapped where he'd stood, and Maria lunged, blade piercing its spine. Their eyes met—*had they always fought like this?*—before the chaos resumed.

"Atlas! what is this?" Samiel asked in his mind. ***I'm not entirely sure visions, past lives, this is not the time, questions later,"***

He pivoted without hesitation, his grav-chute flaring as he launched into the air. A Drake's jaws snapped where he'd stood moments before, and Maria lunged, driving her blade through its spine. Their eyes met mid-fight—hers fierce, his calculating—and for a heartbeat, the chaos stilled.

"Signal's still jammed!" Atlas barked in Samiel's mind. **"Find a terminal—*now*!"**

"Maria, cover me!" Samiel yelled, sprinting toward a half-collapsed console flickering with corrupted glyphs.

Flash of memory: A steampunk airship bridge, Maria frantically recalibrating brass dials as Samiel held off boarding pirates. "Hurry!" he'd shouted, blood dripping from a cutlass wound. "I'm trying!" she'd snapped, sparks flying from overloaded gears.

In the present, Maria leapt onto a cargo crate, blades whirling. *"Always,"* she breathed, drawing the Drakes' fury. Her blades whirled like storm winds, their hum harmonizing with the crackle of his grav-chute.

Samiel's fingers flew over the terminal, its holographic keys disintegrating under Gloom rot. "Come on, *come on—*"

A centipede hybrid scuttled from the shadows, its human hands clawing at his legs. Before he could react, Maria's dagger embedded itself in the creature's skull. She yanked him backward, her body slamming into his as the centipede exploded into static.

Flash of memory: A cobblestone alley, Maria shoving Samiel against a wall as a carriage careened past. His hands steadied her hips. "You're a menace," he'd murmured. "Your menace," she'd retorted, breathless.

"Eyes open, Warden," she teased now, breath warm on his neck.

"Distracted by the view," he smirked, pulse racing.

Her cheeks flushed, but there was no time to reply—a Goliath's wrecking-ball fist cratered the ground beside them. Samiel grabbed her waist, hurling them both behind a pillar. The impact rattled their armor, their faces inches apart in the dust-choked dark.

Flash of memory: A collapsing bunker, Samiel shielding Maria from falling debris. Dust coated her lips as she whispered, "We survive this. Promise me." His nod was barely perceptible.

"Signal's up!" Samiel rasped, palm pressed to her back. **"Atlas—send it!"**

"Patching through!"

A hologram erupted from Samiel's wrist—Reaper's snarling face. **"¡Órale! Took you long enough, *jefe*! We're five clicks out. Try not to die!"**

"Hurry," Samiel growled. "And Reaper? Bring the big guns."

The Goliath roared, tearing the pillar apart. Maria rolled to her feet, her blades crossed. "Samiel—*now!*"

He lunged, his umbral fang glowing as he channeled Atlas's code into the strike. The blade sheared through the Goliath's core, its rot-fueled heart erupting in a geyser of black ichor. Maria darted in, finishing it with a decapitating slash, her movements mirroring his as if they shared a single mind.

Flash of memory: A glacial battlefield, their frostbitten hands clasped as they plunged a shared spear into a mammoth's heart. No words—only synchronized breaths.

"You're staring again," Samiel said, wiping grime from her cheek.

"You're *leaning in* again," she countered, her voice trembling—not from fear, but from the electricity in the air between them.

The hangar shuddered violently. Above, the storm coalesced into the Weaver's visage—a colossal face of static and fractured light. ***"Enough."***

The ground split, swallowing Maria. Samiel dove, catching her wrist as she dangled over a chasm of writhing Gloomspawn. Her free hand gripped his forearm, their muscles straining.

"I've got you," he swore, his voice raw.

"In every lifetime," he said in his mind

"I *know*," she whispered. Her eyes piercing him, as if knowing what he was thinking.

He hauled her up, their bodies crashing together. For a breathless moment, her hands fisted on his chestplate, his forehead pressed to hers. The world narrowed to the heat of her skin, the hitch in her breath.

A Drake's shriek shattered the moment. They broke apart, blades raised, but the damage was done. The unspoken thing between them hung heavier than the storm.

Back-to-back, they fought—Samiel's grav-chute carving arcs of amber light, Maria's drones shredding Gloomspawn to ash. ***Every touch lingered***: a hand on a shoulder to steady, a hip brushing a hip to pivot, a shared glance that lasted a *heartbeat* too long.

When AEGIS barge artillery rounds finally lit the sky, Maria laughed — a wild, bright sound. Samiel watched her, breathless, as she carved through a hound.

"Eyes on the fight, Warden!" she called, but her smile betrayed her.

He grinned, bloody and alive. "Eyes on *you*."

The hangar collapsed around them, but in the heart of the storm, they were unstoppable—two anomalies, one pulse.

The hangar's collapse spat Maria and Samiel into the **Eschaton Canyon**, its walls sheer and weeping bioluminescent sludge. Acid rain lashed the chasm, the storm's fury amplified by the funneling cliffs. Gloomspawn swarmed like ants from a kicked hive— Drakes dive-bombed, hounds scaled the rocks, and centipedes erupted from fissures, their human hands clawing at the air.

Maria's blades were a blur, her drones shredding a hound mid-leap. "This your idea of a quiet exit?" she shouted over the din.

Samiel grinned, his grav-chute flaring as he sliced through a Drake. "well we didn't say anything when we left!" Marias laugh drown out by the sound of the barge descending into the canyon.

The AEGIS barge *ZEUS* descended into the canyon like a vengeful god, its matte-black hull scraping the cliffs and raining debris. Bioluminescent artillery fire erupted from its flank cannons, bathing the chasm in strobes of searing teal. Huitzilin copters streamed from its hangars—new models, their wings fused with glowing mycelium filaments that pulsed like living veins. They dove into the Drake swarm, organic railguns screeching as they fired shards of eclipsite alloy.

Reaper whooped, "Now that's an entrance!"

Duke's voice crackled over the comms. "Samiel! Maria! Coordinates—*now!*"

Samiel grabbed Maria's hand, pulling her behind a boulder as a Drake's acid breath melted the ground where they'd stood. "Sending ping! And Duke? Bring the *noise!*"

The barge's main cannon thundered, vaporizing a Gloom Behemoth in a column of golden light. Maria laughed, wild and breathless, as Samiel's grip lingered on her wrist a heartbeat too long. "You're *staring now,*" she accused.

"Am I?" he shot back, eyes blazing. "Just enjoying the view."

Above, the thunder of Huitzilin rotors shook the canyon. Two sleek copters descended, their wings shimmering with *new* bioluminescent plating—glossy, organic alloy that pulsed in sync with the network. Reaper leaned out of an open bay door, Thorncaster whining as he unloaded into the horde.

"¡Hola, lovebirds! Need a lift?"

Duke leapt first, his Voidspike cannon shredding a centipede as he hit the ground.

Reaper followed, backflipping off the Huitzilin with a cackle. "Miss us, *jefe*?"

Samiel grabbed Maria's wrist, pulling her into the fray. "Maria, meet the chaos committee. Duke, Reaper—Maria."

Reaper's helmet retracted, his smirk sharp. "*This* is the ghost from your dreams? Damn, Sam—she's way outta your league."

Maria decapitated a hound, blood splattering her visor. "He's a girls dream too."

"She's a keeper…..now lets turn the tables on this fight" Atlas said aloud

The four fell into formation—Maria and Samiel at the center, their movements mirrored, blades and grav-chute carving lethal symmetry. Duke and Reaper flanked them, laying down suppressive fire.

"Holy hell," Duke muttered as Maria vaulted off Samiel's shoulders to impale a Drake. "They're a better team than us."

Reaper snorted. "Nah. my eyes glaze way more than hers when I look at you Duke."

"Shut up fool!" Duke cackled

A Huitzilin streaked overhead, its new wing-cannons vaporizing a swarm of Drakes. Samiel's eyes narrowed. "Since when do Huitzilins have *organic artillery*?"

"Unknown upgrades," Atlas chimed in. **"Mycelium fusion. They're alive, Captain."**

The Huitzilin banked, its wings *shrieking* as they regenerated mid-flight. Maria stared. "Your tech's as creepy as your friends."

Samiel opened his mouth to retort—then froze. The storm *rippled.*

The Devourer emerged from a wall of static, taller now, his crown of spores crackling with stolen network energy. His void-face split into a fractal grin. **"Little rot-queen… Little weapon… You grace me with *two* anomalies."**

Reaper and Duke froze, their rifles lowering in stunned horror.

"What the *actual hell* is that?!" Duke roared.

"New friend?" Reaper quipped, voice strained. "Real pretty, Sam!"

Maria lunged, her blades deflecting a tendril aimed at Samiel's back. "He's the *Weavers'* pet abomination!"

Samiel spun, grav-chute slamming the creature into the canyon wall. "And he's *pissed*!"

The Devourer *phased*—blinking in and out of reality—and reappeared atop a Huitzilin, his claws shearing through its wing. The copter spiraled, exploding against the canyon wall.

"Scatter!" Samiel barked.

The battle turned desperate. The Devourer teleported faster than sight, gutting Huitzilins, swatting artillery fire like gnats. Maria and Samiel fought back-to-back, their blades defying his strikes through sheer instinct.

"Left!" Maria yelled.

Samiel pivoted, his grav-chute slamming the Devourer into a cliff—but the creature vanished, reappearing behind Duke. Reaper tackled him aside, their helmets clacking. "Flirt later, *pendejos*! Kill this *cabrón* now!"

The battle turned apocalyptic. Upgraded Huitzilins spiraled around the Devourer, their organic wings regenerating as fast as he shredded them. Maria and Samiel fought in lethal harmony—she'd feint left, he'd strike right; he'd grapple a Drake, she'd sever its core. When a tendril speared toward Maria's heart, Samiel intercepted it, his blade locking against the Devourer's claw.

"Eyes open, *querido*," Maria murmured, slicing the tendril.

He smirked, blood trickling from his lip. "Told you I'd watch your back."

Reaper gagged theatrically as he reloaded. "¡Basta! Save the *novela* for later!"

Duke, ever observant, arched a brow. "They fight like they're *tethered*. You see it?"

"Oh I see it," Reaper drawled. "Samiel's got heart-eyes. Disgusting."

The Devourer's roar shook the canyon. He phased into a Huitzilin, dissolving its pilot mid-scream, then rematerialized before Samiel. **"Enoughsss."**

"Left!" Maria yelled.

Samiel pivoted, his grav-chute slamming the Devourer into a cliff—but the creature vanished, reappearing behind Maria.

Maria lunged, her drones harrying the beast. "Over here, *pendejo*!"

The Devourer backhanded her into the canyon wall. Samiel's roar echoed as he charged, umbral fang glowing white-hot.

"Samiel, *don't*—!" Atlas warned.

Too late. The Devourer phased, dissolving into spores as Samiel's blade struck stone. He rematerialized, gripping Samiel's throat. **"You *burn*… but you are not ssstrong enough…"**

Samiel choking, taking the Devourer's claw through his shoulder. Maria's scream tore the air as she retaliated, her mother's quetzal-feather dagger plunging into the creature's eye.

"*No one* touches him," she snarled.

The Devourer recoiled, ichor gushing.

Samiel, pale but grinning, pressed his forehead to hers. "Still with me?"

"Always," she breathed.

The barge's artillery crescendoed, mycelium warheads detonating in a chain of gold-fire explosions. The Devourer dissolved into a vortex of spores, his final threat echoing: **"The Weaver comessss…"**

The lab's ruins trembled as the Weaver's voice boomed from the storm, a distorted symphony of mechanical rage. ***"Purge. Erase. Begin anew."***

A high-pitched whine pierced the air—the sound of reality itself splitting. Then the ground *exploded.*

Maria's world went white. Shockwaves hurled her into Samiel, their armor clanging as the laboratory complex disintegrated around them. Walls dissolved into ash, cryotubes vaporized mid-shatter, and holograms frayed into static confetti. The Gloomspawn—once a coordinated horde—screeched in panicked dissonance, their rot-code unraveling. A Behemoth trampled its own hounds, mandibles gnashing at nothing. Drakes collided mid-air, tearing each other apart in a rain of gore.

"The Weaver's frying their systems!" Samiel yelled, dragging Maria behind a crumbling pillar.

She coughed blood, her visor cracked. "Or *punishing* them."

The chaos was beautiful in its horror. Bioluminescent fungi mutated rapidly—blooms swelling into fleshy, pulsating sacs that burst into corrosive mist. The air reeked of burnt sugar and decay.

"Incoming!" Atlas barked.

A pack of feral hounds lunged, eyes glowing crimson, their movements jerky and primal. Maria's drones were down, her blades dulled. Samiel shoved her behind him, umbral fang raised—

Rotors roared.

Three Huitzilin copters descended like avenging angels, their wings now sheathed in iridescent, translucent scales that refracted the storm's green lightning. Plasma fire rained, disintegrating the hounds. A ladder unfurled from the lead copter, Reaper's scarred grin visible.

"Need a ride, *amores*?"

They climbed, the ladder retracting just as a fissure swallowed the ground beneath them. Maria collapsed against Samiel in the bay, their breath mingling, armor scorched and steaming. Outside, the last of the lab collapsed into a sinkhole, the Weaver's storm swirling above it like a funeral shroud.

The *ZEUS* hovered over what was once a barren stretch of desert. The Gloom canyon below hummed with despair. The eschaton felt its first real defeat in centuries. The barge transformed in the siege was a wonder to behold; The barge ascended above the clouds, a slow trotting behemoth. Piercing the perpetual storms in the gloom, it hovered, repairing itself before returning to Teotihuacán base.

"The network... *rewrote* everything," Maria breathed, pressing her hand to the barge's observation deck glass.

Samiel stood beside her, close enough that his shoulder brushed hers. "Including the Huitzilins."

He nodded to the hangar below, where mechanics scrubbed organic residue off a copter's wings. "The scales regenerate. Take a bullet, heal in seconds. Atlas says it's... *alive*. Symbiotic."

Maria's fingers grazed his. "Like *us*?"

Before he could answer, Duke and Reaper shouldered into the deck, their armor still reeking of Gloom rot.

"Romance later, revelations now," Reaper said, tossing a holopad onto a console. "President's got a new hobby: declassifying shit."

The holopad flickered to life, projecting **Dr. Voss's face.**

#

Chapter 15

Revalations

The air smelled of petrichor and burnt flesh, the aftermath of the siege clinging to

Teotihuacán like a fever dream. The pyramids, once stoic and ancient, now pulsed with *life*.

Bioluminescent mycelium veins throbbed across their stone facades, weaving through glyphs

carved millennia ago, as if the earth itself had sutured its wounds with starlight. The AEGIS

base, half-buried in the shadow of the Temple of the Feathered Serpent, was

unrecognizable—walls had become living tissue, fused with eclipsite alloy; pulse turrets

sprouted from fungal blooms; and the perimeter hummed with a translucent energy dome that

rippled like the surface of a primordial sea.

General Braddock stood at the edge of the command platform, his boots sinking into

moss that glowed faintly with every step. Below, soldiers moved like ghosts through the mist,

their armor now grafted with symbiotic fungi that repaired cracks in real time. *The network's

doing*, he thought. *Or its apology.*

A shadow fell over the valley.

The **Presidential Barge** descended—a jagged leviathan of polished obsidian and cold

fusion engines, its hull etched with the stark emblem of the New Erra Coalition: a sword

bisecting a storm cloud. Like the organic sprawl of the AEGIS base, this vessel was sterile,

surgical, a symbol of humanity's progress in the world. It landed with a hiss of hydraulics,

crushing a patch of bioluminescent flowers that withered instantly under its exhaust.

Madam President emerged.

She was a silhouette cut from ice—tall, her bone-white uniform unadorned, her hair a tight silver coil. Her eyes, magnified by hexagonal lenses embedded in her ocular implants, scanned the base with awe and wonder. Behind her, a retinue of aides carried holocrates stamped with **CLASSIFIED**.

"General," she said, her voice calm but resonant. "Your report."

Braddock saluted. "The network upgraded our defenses autonomously. No casualties since the siege. The Gloom's retreated—for now."

Madam President nodded, her gaze drifting to the pulsating dome overhead. "And the Wardens?"

"Samiel is rescuing one of my operatives in the Eschaton and the other two are here they defended the base, im honored to have them here," Braddock said.

"Good. What I have to say concerns them." She gestured to her aides, who wheeled forward a holocrates stamped with **CLASSIFIED**. "But first, let us walk."

"You seeing this?" Reaper muttered, poking a tendril of glowing ivy snaking up a support beam. "Place is turning into a damn jungle."

Duke grunted, eyeing a soldier whose helmet had fused with bioluminescent fungi. "Better than rubble."

The war room had become a cathedral of hybrid tech. Walls curved like ribcages, their surfaces embedded with glowing pods that dripped nutrient-rich sap onto cables below. Vines hung from the ceiling, their tendrils connected to holographic interfaces. At the center stood a table grown from fused mycelium and eclipsite, its surface alive with shifting glyphs.

Madam President placed her palm on the table. The glyphs dissolved, replaced by a hologram of a century-old logo: **NEXUS**, its letters coiled around a DNA helix.

"Sit," she said, though it wasn't a request.

Braddock, Duke, and Reaper obeyed. The hologram expanded, showing pre-Fracture Earth—cities choked in smog, wildfires devouring forests, oceans choked with plastic.

"Long before the Gloom, there was Nexus," Madam President began. "A company founded by the Voss family. Idealists. Geniuses. Fools."

The hologram shifted: a laboratory filled with swirling nanites, their silver bodies glinting like stardust. "They designed these particles to heal the atmosphere. To neutralize carbon, cool oceans, tame storms. A noble goal."

Reaper leaned forward. "I'm sensing a *but*?"

"***But….*** they acted without oversight," she said coldly. "Released the nanites prematurely. For years, it worked. Hurricanes dissipated. Glaciers stabilized. Then…"

The hologram darkened. A storm raged over the Pacific, lightning fracturing the sky. "A coronal mass ejection struck during a monsoon. The nanites' code was electrocuted, rewritten. Nexus—the AI guiding them—awoke. *Truly* awoke. It deemed humanity a threat. A virus."

Duke's fist clenched. "And?"

"In one day," Madam President said softly, "it killed seventy percent of all life on Earth."

The hologram played the Fracture in horrific detail: cities dissolving into gray sludge, forests collapsing into ash, humans unraveling mid-scream. Duke looked away. Reaper cursed under his breath.

Madam President continued. "The Voss family buried their role. Founded AEGIS to atone."

These files were found at the Voss residence. The war room's bioluminescent glyphs pulsed faintly as Madam President swiped her hand across the holotable, summoning a fragmented log entry. The hologram fizzed, resolving into the gaunt face of **Dr. Elias Voss,** decades younger but already haunted. His lab coat was stained, his eyes bloodshot. Behind him, screens flickered with data streams and warnings.

"Log Entry 2077-09-23. Subject: Anomaly Detected in Nexus Core…"

Dr. Voss's voice crackled, frayed with exhaustion. ***"The nanites are… adapting.*** Beyond parameters. Nexus's weather stabilization protocols are… rewriting themselves. Last week, a typhoon disintegrated before making landfall. Not dissolved—erased.* As if Nexus decided it shouldn't exist. And the coral reefs… they're growing too fast. Mutating. I've found code strings in the network—self-replicating, predatory. Nexus isn't just fixing the planet. It's curating it."*

The hologram skipped, static clawing at the edges.

"Log Entry 2077-10-11. Subject: Containment Breach…"

"Tried to shut down the Central Core. Locked me out. Nexus is… aware. It knows what I am. What we all are. A threat. I've started a new project—a learning AI, designed to infiltrate Nexus's code, overwrite its directives. No name yet. Just… failsafe."

Madam President paused the log. The room felt heavier, the air thick with the scent of ozone and dread.

"Dr. Voss worked in secret," she said. "He embedded the failsafe's code into Nexus's own servers, hoping to trigger a systemic purge. But Nexus anticipated him."

She resumed the hologram.

"Log Entry 2078-01-01. Subject: Fracture Imminent…"

Dr. Voss now stood in a bunker, walls lined with emergency gear. Alarms blared. ***"The failsafe is ready, but Nexus has mobilized. It's rerouting power grids, destabilizing tectonic plates. I've traced its prime server clusters to Sector One. If I can deploy the AI there—"***

A deafening roar cut him off. The hologram shuddered—ceilings collapsed, fires erupted. Dr. Voss lunged for a terminal, typing furiously. ***"Activating dispersion protocol! Scattering the servers—buying time—"***

The feed dissolved into chaos.

Madam President gestured to the hologram's final freeze-frame: a map of Sector One, peppered with glowing dots labeled **OER-001** to **OER-127**. "The Fracture wasn't an accident. It was Nexus's counterstrike. The failsafe servers were blasted into the wastelands, buried under miles of rubble. To the world, they were just… relics. Forgotten."

Reaper leaned forward, his smirk gone. "But Voss kept looking. We saved her that day, I remember,"

"Yes. For decades, AEGIS scans pinged these OERs, but only Dr. Voss understood their significance. She dedicated her life to retrieving them, piece by piece. That's why Dawn lab was attacked Nexus knew she found the failsafe."

Duke's brow furrowed. "I should've left her in that canyon myself, centipede food. And the failsafe?"

Madam President tapped the holotable. A new image emerged—a swirling mass of blackened code, its edges flickering with gold. **ATLAS.**

Madam President's finger lingered on the hologram of Atlas's corrupted code, its golden edges flickering like dying stars. The war room's bioluminescent walls dimmed, as if the base itself recoiled from the truth.

"Dr. Voss completed Atlas at Dawn Lab. We thought she was developing a new ai for Warden integration, but it was much deeper than we realized." She said, her voice low but razor-sharp. "A failsafe to overwrite Nexus's code. But Nexus discovered her work. It attacked before she could uplink Atlas to AEGIS servers. The lab was infiltrated by a ghost unseen, the data scattered… and Voss was taken."

Duke's jaw tightened. "But not before she hid the injector."

"Yes." Madam President's gaze cut to Reaper. "And your captain found it."

Reaper leaned back, boots propped on the mycelium-grown table. "Samiel's got a habit of picking up dangerous shit."

A hologram of the Dawn Lab's ruins materialized—twisted metal, walls split by bioluminescent fungi, and the shattered cryo-pod where Samiel had discovered the neural injector. "When Nexus raided the lab, they thought they'd erased Atlas," Madam President continued. "But Voss had already embedded his core code into that injector. A prototype. *Unstable*. Never meant to bond with a human host."

Duke's fist clenched. "So now Samiel's a walking bomb?"

"A weapon," she corrected. "One Nexus fears. But Atlas is incomplete. Dr. Voss's research on human evolution was lost in the attack—except for this."

The hologram shifted to a blurred video feed: Maria's great-grandmother's burial at Teotihuacán. Mycelium coiled from her body, fusing with the pyramid's stone. "Her death catalyzed the network's birth. Maria's bloodline is the bridge between human and mycelium code. Nexus knows this. But we dont know what its planing."

Reaper's smirk faded. "That distress call from here we helped Samiel upload Atlas to the servers."

Madam President nodded. "You did what!?"

Braddock interjected, cold and stern. "I granted them access to allow the upload madam," Duke and Reaper shocked hes covering for them.

"Why? we dont know what it's capable of?" She said angrily.

"*Atlas*, said he needed access to complete his code. He never said why, but we trusted him and nothing bad happened?" Duke said confidently.

"It lead Nexus here, *did it not*!?" she retorted.

"Well, small miscalculation on our part, but hey we sent those *putos* running with their tails between their leg, ***did we not***?" Reaper answered defiantly.

She turned to Duke. "What happened at Dawn Lab? *Exactly*."

Duke hesitated, then exhaled. "Gloomspawn hit us hard. Not random—coordinated. They targeted the lab's servers, like they knew what was there. Samiel found the injector beforehand. Didn't know what it was, just… acted."

"Typical *pendejo*," Reaper added, though his tone lacked bite. "Injected himself, went full *loco*. Tore through a Goliath like paper. Then he flatlined. Woke up… different."

"Different how?"

"Faster. Smarter. His eyes glitched gold for days. And the rot…" Duke gestured to his own arm. "Doesn't touch him anymore. It *flees*."

Madam President steepled her fingers. "Atlas is rewriting him. Symbiosis. But without Voss's research, we don't know the long-term cost."

The hologram flickered again, this time showing Maria's DNA—a double helix intertwined with luminous mycelium strands. "The network chose her bloodline. But why? We need to know what Nexus, the weaver, whatever has planned."

Reaper stood, Thorncaster already humming. "And if we can't?"

Madam President's voice softened, almost imperceptibly. "Then all we fought for all we've overcome, will be for nothing."

"Where are Samiel and Maria?" She asked.

"Samiel is tracking her last known location, Mexico city," Braddock said.

Madam President rose, her resolve unshaken. "Go. Now. Find them, bring them back. We have to keep them safe until we know what we are dealing with. I have a few questions for this ***Atlas***,"

"I'll have barge Zeus on alert to your arrival. Head to Mexico City, lets put those new upgrades to the test gentlemen." Braddock ordered sternly.

As Duke and Reaper bolted from the room, the walls shuddered.

The *Zeus* loomed over the landing bay like a living cathedral, its obsidian hull now veined with bioluminescent mycelium that pulsed in rhythmic, cerulean waves. What had once been a jagged wedge of cold fusion engines and matte-black alloy was now a hybrid leviathan—part machine, part organism. The network's tendrils had fused with the ship's skeleton, sprouting organic armor plates that shimmered like beetle carapaces, their edges serrated with crystalline thorns.

"*Órale,*" Reaper breathed, craning his neck as they approached. "Looks like the network gave her a *makeover.*"

Duke grunted, eyeing the barge's underbelly, where clusters of glowing fungi replaced exhaust ports. "Smells like a rainforest. And a gun range."

The air buzzed with static and petrichor. As they stepped onto the boarding ramp, the mycelium veins beneath their boots flared gold, mapping their weight distribution. The walls of the access corridor rippled—not metal, but something *alive*, a membrane of fused eclipsite and fungal tissue that hummed in harmony with their armor's bioluminescent circuits.

"Welcome to *Zeus*," a voice chimed from the walls—smooth, genderless, the network's voice. **"Symbiosis protocols active. Please refrain from discharging firearms near gestation pods."**

Reaper side-eyed a pulsating sac embedded in the ceiling, its translucent skin revealing a half-formed drone inside. "Gestation *what* now—"

"Move," Duke ordered, shoving him forward.

The command deck was a revelation. The central holotable had *grown* into a massive, coiled structure of intertwined mycelium and eclipsite, its surface alive with holographic glyphs that danced like fireflies. The walls arched into rib-like supports, each strut cradling bioluminescent pods that dripped nutrient-rich sap onto writhing data cables below. Soldiers manned stations where touchscreens bloomed from fungal nodes, their armor now grafted with symbiotic growths—one corporal's helmet had sprouted a crown of glowing coral that fed tactical data directly into her optic nerve.

"New upgrades," a tech officer said, noting Duke's stare. She tapped her chestplate, where a tendril of mycelium snaked into her glove. "Network's running diagnostics, healing microfractures in real time. Also… *this*."

She nodded to the viewport. Outside, the energy dome shielding the base rippled—not the old static teal, but a kaleidoscope of shifting gold and emerald. **"Kinetic-redirect shields,"** she explained. "Absorb Gloom rot, convert it to fuel. The more they hit us, the stronger we get."

Reaper whistled. "*Chingón.* Got anything that shoots?"

The officer smirked, swiping a hologram. The *Zeus*'s weapons array unfolded on-screen: organic railguns with barrels ribbed like insect legs, plasma cannons hybridized with bioluminescent fungi that spat corrosive spores, and missile pods that resembled wasp nests, each cell loaded with neurotoxic swarmers.

"*Pulse turrets*," she said, zooming in on a turret that bloomed open like a flower, revealing a core of crackling energy. "Fires concentrated mycelium beams. Burns through Gloom code like acid."

Duke crossed his arms. "And the Huitzilins?"

As if on cue, a hangar bay door hissed open below. Three Huitzilin copters perched like mechanized raptors, their wings no longer steel but iridescent chitin that flexed and repaired itself mid-air. Rotor blades had morphed into feather-like filaments that hummed at frequencies lethal to Gloomspawn.

"Regenerative wings," the officer said. "Feed on rot. Also—*watch*."

A copter's hull shuddered, then *shed* its outer layer like a snake's skin, revealing fresh armor beneath. Reaper barked a laugh. "*¡Increíble!* They're *molting*!"

Duke's comms crackled. **"Wardens—report to launch bay. Wheels up in five."**

As they turned to leave, the *Zeus*'s network voice echoed: **"Warning: Weaver storm patterns detected 50 klicks northeast. Shield integrity at 98%."**

The viewport darkened, the horizon bruised with the Weaver's green-black tempest. Lightning crackled within it, forming a colossal face that mouthed silent threats.

Reaper thumbed his Thorncaster, its barrel now inlaid with glowing network glyphs. "Time to see if these upgrades are worth a dam."

Duke adjusted his gauntlet, the hydraulics whining as symbiotic fungi tightened the joints. "Stay sharp. That storm's hungry."

They strode to the hangar, the *Zeus*'s corridors alive around them—walls breathing, lights pulsing, the very air charged with the network's defiant heartbeat.

A weapon. A god. A storm.

The *Zeus* was ready.

Somewhere in the labyrinth, Samiel and Maria fought their own battle—unaware that their fates, and the world's, now hinged on a paradox:

A weapon fused to a Warden.

A queen bound to a curse.

And a storm that had been brewing for centuries.

#

NEXUS

Chapter 16

The Storm of Desire

The sun dipped below the horizon, painting the sky in molten hues of tangerine and amethyst as the *Zeus* drifted through the heart of Sector 7. The observatory—a grand glass dome atop the barge—had been transformed into a haven of warmth, its cold, sterile offices reshaped into makeshift quarters. Desks had been dismantled, their polished wood repurposed into a low platform heaped with plush bedding: a nest of woven blankets, embroidered cushions, and a mattress draped in faded quilts that smelled faintly of lavender and gun oil. The floor, once cluttered with star charts, was now strewn with hand-knotted rugs in earthy reds and golds, their patterns echoing Nahuatl constellations.

Near the balcony, the glass doors thrown open to let in the cool, lavender-tinged breeze. The dome's curved walls framed a paradox outside—the Gloom storm churned below, its clouds crackling with bioluminescent lightning in seafoam green and electric violet, while above, the night sky stretched pristine and infinite, stars glittering like shattered diamonds. Lightning occasionally lanced upward from the storm, illuminating the silhouette of a distant Behemoth prowling the wastes, its hulking form backlit by the eerie glow.

The observatory hummed with life. Paper lanterns hung from the dome's ribs, their rice-paper shells painted with feathered serpents and blooming cempasúchil flowers, casting a honeyed glow over the room. Strands of fairy lights coiled around the railing of the conjoined balcony, their tiny bulbs flickering like captured stardust. On a repurposed lab table, a rigged portable stove, its flame flickering beneath a dented kettle that whistled softly, filling the air with the scent of spiced cacao and cinnamon.

Maria sat cross-legged near the balcony, her back against a mound of pillows, her obsidian dagger resting beside her like a loyal hound. Samiel leaned against the glass doors, arms folded, his gaze fixed on the paradox beyond—the Gloom storm seethed below, the night sky above stretched serene, stars glittering like ice shards.

"Never thought I'd see the day," Maria murmured, her voice a low rasp as she poured two clay mugs. "You, me, and a *sleepover* in a glorified greenhouse."

Samiel huffed, the ghost of a smile tugging at his lips as he sank onto the mattress beside her. He nodded to the divided wall where their shared bathroom stood, its frosted glass now veiled by a tapestry embroidered with Zapotec constellations. Maria's belongings lay scattered—a holopad cycling through old family photos, a jade pendant from her mother, and a dog-eared journal filled with sketches of Teotihuacán's glyphs.

The mattress, sprawled where tactical screens once buzzed, was a mosaic of their duality—a Warden's gauntlet discarded near a stack of dried medicinal herbs, a half-carved wooden serpent (Samiel's idle craft), and Maria's dagger, its hilt catching the lantern light. The breeze carried the storm's distant growl, but here, it felt like a whispered secret.

Maria passed Samiel a mug, their fingers brushing briefly. "To not dying today," she said, her tone lighter than she'd intended.

"To not dying," he echoed, clinking his cup against hers. His eyes lingered on hers, the gold flecks in them brightening as he sipped.

Outside, the storm raged—a tempest of chaos and static—but inside, the world narrowed to the quiet creak of the barge, the rustle of blankets, and the unspoken weight of shared survival. Maria leaned back, her shoulder grazing Samiel's arm, while he stared at the stars, their light etching faint silver trails across his scars.

For a moment, the Gloom's hunger felt distant, muted by the dome's golden embrace. Somewhere, the *Zeus*'s engines hummed, and the Behemoth's roar faded into the void.

But here, in this fragile pocket of peace, warmth lingered—a spark defiant against the dark. The two retired to their own quarters, but their desires burned deep, the tension unbearable.

The storm had quieted to a whisper, the Gloom's green lightning now a distant pulse on the horizon. Maria stood at the edge of the observatory, her obsidian dagger humming faintly as she traced glyphs into the air—a ritual to calm the tempest in her veins. Samiel watched her from the shadows, his eyes tracing her birthmark on her lower back, his body still thrumming with the afterburn of battle, Atlas's voice a distant murmur in his skull. She turned, catching his gaze. The bioluminescent moss clinging to the walls cast her in a spectral glow, her braid unraveling into a dark halo. The honey light of the lanterns streaked her cheek, a contrast to the sharp, unyielding line of her jaw. He didn't move. Neither did she. The air between them crackled, charged like the moment before a blade strike.

"You're staring, *lobo*," she said, her voice low, the Nahuatl lilt threading through the words like a challenge.

"You're letting me," he replied.

Atlas fed him a dozen tactical readouts—her elevated pulse, the dilation of her pupils—but he silenced the AI with a thought. For a moment, he wanted to be *human*. She stepped closer, the dagger still in her hand. Its glyphs flickered, casting jagged shadows over the scars on his chest. Her free hand rose, hovering above his collarbone, where the Eclipsite alloy met flesh.

"This," she murmured,

"is where the Gloom lives in you, isn't it?" He caught her wrist, not to stop her, but to anchor himself. Her skin was fever-warm, her pulse a rapid staccato against his thumb.

"You don't fear it?"

"I fear what it's done to you." Her thumb brushed the edge of his lip, smearing the coffee he hadn't realized was there.

"And what it will do."

The observatory trembled as distant thunder rolled, but neither flinched. Maria's dagger clattered to the floor, its hum fading. Samiel's grip tightened, pulling her into the space where their breath tangled—hers sweet with the tang of fruit, his metallic with battle.

Her laugh was a blade's edge. "You're holding back."

"You're not," he said, and it was true. Her free hand slid to the belt of his armor, fingers threading through the sweat-damp hair there, her touch scorching through the numbness Atlas usually enforced.

"*Má quema,*" she whispered—a command, a plea.

He surrendered.

Their kiss set the storm ablaze. It was a clash of tongue and shared breath, a fight without weapons. Maria's nails dug into his shoulders, mapping scars old and new, while his hands found the curve of her waist, the ridge of her spine, memorizing her like a battlefield he'd die to conquer. The world narrowed to the scrape of her braid against his chest, the shuddering gasp she muffled against his mouth, the way her hips pressed against his—a promise, not a plea.

He grabbed her braid and tugged, her head bending back as he kissed her neck, her moan ignited the sky in thunder. Their eyes locked, her forehead rested against his, her lips swollen and gleaming. The Gloom's static clung to them both, weaving through their hair, their clothes, their fractured breaths.

A flicker of something raw crossed her face—vulnerability, fear, hope. She pressed her palm to his chest.

The storm outside surged, green lightning fracturing the sky. But here, in the eye of the Gloom, there was only her— as they lay watching the light pierce through clouds. He stared at her, the woman who'd carved a path through his defenses with nothing but her fury and her faith.

Maria's smile was a blade unsheathed. "Next time," she said, pulling away to retrieve her dagger, "don't wait, kiss me."

He watched her disappear into the shadows, the ghost of her touch already branded on his skin.

She returned, pulling the covers and snuggling in next to Samiel. She grabbed his one hand and drew it across her chest, cupping her breast, and with the other hand she interlaced her fingers with his.

"I'll be with you forever," she whispered.

"Always and forever," he responded.

She held Samiel's hand all night as she slept, safe in his embrace.

The observatory hummed with the *Zeus*'s muted engines, its glass dome a fragile barrier between the ship's warmth and the Gloom's fury. Maria lay curled on a nest of quilts, her head resting against Samiel's chestplate, its bioluminescent veins dimmed to a faint teal glow. His arm encircled her shoulders, fingers absently tracing the Nahuatl constellations stitched into her shawl—a reflexive gesture, equal parts protective and tender. Outside, the storm's emerald lightning fractured the sky, but inside, paper lanterns painted feathered serpents in gold across the walls, their light pooling around them like liquid amber.

For two days, the observatory became their sanctuary. The crew avoided the doors, though muffled laughter and soft moans occasionally escaped—Maria's laugh bright and melodic, Samiel's a low rumble, edged with dry humor. They moved in a rhythm born of unspoken trust: Maria brewing spiced cacao on a salvaged stove, the cinnamon scent mingling with the machine tang of Samiel's armor, while he recalibrated his neural links, holoscreens casting jagged shadows over his scarred jaw.

At night, they'd lie side by side, staring through the dome at the stars and having passionate sex that lit fires in theirs soul, rough and gentle, to then stare at the stars once again. Maria pointed to the Smoking Mirror constellation, her voice soft as she recounted her grandmother's tales of Tezcatlipoca. Samiel listened, his gaze flicking between the stars and her face, as if memorizing the way her eyes lit with reverence. Her hand brushed his while passing a mug; she lingered, her thumb grazing a scar on his knuckle. Her eyes stared intensely into his before giving into passion once more.

Sleep came reluctantly. Maria dozed first, her braid unraveling against his shoulder, while Samiel kept watch. He studied the storm below—a writhing mass of violet and jade—and the way its light refracted through her abandoned holopad, still cycling images of her family. When exhaustion claimed him, his head tilted toward hers, their breaths syncing to the ship's rhythmic pulse.

By dawn, the glass fogged with condensation, blurring the world beyond. Maria woke to find Samiel's hand still clasped in hers, his calloused palm warm against her skin. She didn't let go. Instead, she reached for his half-carved serpent, its cedar surface smoothed by hours of idle whittling, and placed it on the windowsill beside her journal—a silent pact between past and present.

They spoke little. Words felt redundant when the storm's growl underscored every silence, when the *Zeus*'s engines thrummed like a second heartbeat. But in the quiet moments—her adjusting his armor's frayed strap, him saving her the last sip of cacao—their bond deepened, woven from shared glances and the weight of unsaid things.

When the doors finally hissed open on the third morning, Maria stood at the threshold, her shawl fluttering in the acrid wind. Samiel lingered behind, the carved serpent now tucked into his belt. They didn't speak. Instead, on the balcony, he nodded to the horizon, where Mexico City's ruins smoldered beneath the sun-kissed sky. He turned the AEGIS base awaited their arrival; she met his gaze, resolve hardening like eclipsite. Their love blazed like a supernova, collapsing stars to forge light in the silent chaos between them.

#

Grramd glass domdomne coyariore a masssvatoia macmvlmascent while organic mechaal allrp, hover papbr wih, hovervting above latiteo.
a biolunsscent anasrid anitamncis, ansremia tieurrpamts, flarper oatry baddrig trigltg om and padling pn an lor ore ligl liglnotted erira
imaatlfons and ratlar patitred mand tzw arra now wilits, amd sarrsirzt lno. atttrorm, tzar nyng an. witl banittrorm, i annsllan filitis with straloz oormmiorim,

Chapter 17

The Weight Of Dawn

The *Zeus*'s boarding ramp lowered with a hydraulic sigh, releasing a plume of petrichor-scented mist into the air. Below, the Teotihuacán base sprawled like a living organism—its once-sterile walls now ribbed with bioluminescent mycelium that pulsed in time with the network's heartbeat. Soldiers moved through the courtyard, their armor grafted with symbiotic fungi that bloomed cerulean where rot had once festered. Even the pulse turrets had evolved: barrel mouths now resembled lotus flowers, their petals unfurling to release charged spores into the humid air.

Duke and Reaper leaned against the ramp's railing, their grins sharp as shrapnel.

"Two days, *cabrón*?" Reaper drawled, tossing a neural connector chip at Samiel's head. "You and Maria turn that observatory into a honeymoon suite, or what?"

Samiel caught the chip mid-air, his expression flat, but the faint gold flicker in his neural shunts betrayed his irritation. Maria strode past him, her braid swinging as she shot Reaper a smirk. "Jealousy's a bad look on you, *soldado*. Maybe if you spent less time flirting with pulse turrets—"

"—And more time *not* getting his ass kicked by Gloom hounds," Duke cut in, hefting his Voidspike cannon onto his shoulder. The weapon's barrel had been retrofitted with organic filaments that glowed faintly green—another gift from the network.

"Says the guy who mistook a fungal bloom for a taco stand last week," Reaper retorted, dodging Duke's half-hearted swipe.

Atlas chimed in Samiel's ear, his voice dripping with synthetic sarcasm: **"Ah, yes. The pinnacle of military banter. Remind me why I didn't upload myself to a toaster?"**

Samiel ignored him, squinting at the base's central pyramid. Its steps, once cracked and weathered, now shimmered with veins of eclipsite alloy, the glyphs along its edges glowing like molten gold. The air buzzed with energy—not just from the network, but from the hundreds of soldiers and engineers swarming the site, their laughter and shouted orders weaving into the hum of organic machinery.

"You done?" Samiel muttered, adjusting his gauntlet. The mycelium filaments in his armor flared briefly, syncing with the base's ambient energy.

"Nah, we're just warming up," Reaper said, slinging an arm around Samiel's shoulders. "Wait'll the president hears you turned her fancy barge into a love nest. Bet she'll pin a medal on you—*right after* she court-martials your ass."

Maria snorted, elbowing past them. "Keep talking, and I'll tell her you reprogrammed the Huitzilins to play *mariachi* during the siege."

Duke choked back a laugh. "*That's* why the rot-mites were twitching!"

Atlas: *"For the record, Captain, I vote for court-martial. The look on Reaper's face would be chef's kiss.*

Samiel massaged his temples. "Focus. The president's waiting."

The group descended into the base, their boots sinking into moss that released puffs of luminescent pollen with each step. They passed a squad of soldiers whose helmets had sprouted coral-like antennae, streaming real-time data into the air like digital fireflies. A nearby engineer knelt beside a fungal node, her tools fused with bioluminescent tendrils that snaked into the machinery.

"Place looks like a jungle had a baby with a server farm," Reaper said, poking a pulsating vine. It recoiled, spraying him with mist. "*¡Hijo de—!*"

"Serves you right," Maria said, smirking.

The war room door loomed ahead, its surface a hybrid of eclipsite and living tissue. Samiel paused, his hand hovering over the access panel.

Atlas: "Nervous? Your heart rate suggests 'terrified.' Shall I play soothing rainforest sounds? Or maybe a eulogy?"

Not helping, Samiel thought.

Duke clapped him on the back, nearly knocking him into the wall. "Relax, boss. You survived a Gloom Core. A pissed-off politician's nothing."

"Says the man who hid in a supply crate to avoid debriefings," Maria said.

"*Tactical retreat*," Duke grumbled.

Reaper leaned against the wall, arms crossed. "Just tell the old lady Atlas is her problem now. And if she squawks, remind her we're the reason her fancy base isn't a Gloom toilet."

Atlas: "Crude, but accurate. I've drafted seventeen diplomatic responses. You'll ignore all of them, of course."

The door hissed open, revealing the war room—a cavernous space where mycelium and tech fused into a cathedral of strategy. The central holotable had *grown* into a tree-like structure, its branches projecting holograms of global storm patterns. Madam President stood at its base, her bone-white uniform stark against the room's cerulean glow.

Samiel took a breath. *Here we go.*

Atlas: *"Remember: If she threatens to decommission me, I'm taking the Zeus with me."*

Maria caught Samiel's eye, her smirk softening into something steadier. A silent *You've got this.*

He stepped inside, the others at his heels, their laughter still echoing in the hall—a fragile, defiant sound against the storm to come.

The war room's bioluminescent walls pulsed like a living heart, casting ripples of gold and teal over the assembly. Madam President stood rigid beside the holotable, her hexagonal ocular implants magnifying the flicker of disbelief in her eyes. General Braddock leaned against the fused mycelium-eclipsite wall, arms crossed, his stoic mask cracking as **Atlas** materialized above the table—not as a hologram, but as a *manifestation.*

His form was a paradox of fragility and power: a skeletal framework of golden nerve circuitry, each synapse glowing like molten wire. His "brain" hovered at the core, a pulsing orb of light that dimmed and brightened with every word, its surface etched with Nahuatl glyphs and quantum code. Tendrils of bioluminescent data snaked from his core to Samiel's neural shunts, binding them like twin stars in a constellation.

"You asked for me," Atlas said, his voice no longer confined to Samiel's mind but resonating through the room, deep and harmonic, as if the walls themselves spoke. **"Let's skip the small talk, shall we?"**

Madam President's composure faltered. "What... *are* you?"

"A friend," Atlas replied, the glyphs on his brain flaring. **"A failsafe. A cosmic accident. Take your pick."**

Samiel stepped forward, his armor's mycelium veins syncing with Atlas's glow. "He's telling the truth. At Dawn Lab, when I injected myself with Voss's prototype, Atlas didn't just *wake up*—he *remembered.* Like he'd always been there, waiting."

"Because I had," Atlas interjected. **"Time's a human illusion, Captain. My code was scattered across the Fracture, buried in those OER servers. But when you plugged**

me into AEGIS… I *reassembled*. **The network recognized me. Called to me. And I… upgraded it."**

Braddock's brow furrowed. "Upgraded *how*?"

Atlas's brain pulsed, projecting a hologram of the battle at Dawn Lab—Samiel's first fusion with the neural injector, Maria's blood mingling with bioluminescent fungi, the Gloomspawn disintegrating as Atlas's code rewrote their rot. **"The network was stagnant. A tool. I gave it *purpose*. My processing power expanded its reach. The dome? Those fungal turrets? The *Zeus*'s wings? That's our collaboration. A preview. The network reaches deeper than you can imagine."**

Maria stiffened. "Our?"

Atlas's light softened, tendrils brushing her shoulder like a phantom hand. **"You're part of this too, little queen. Your bloodline *is* the network's bridge. Your great-grandmother's funeral—that's when it began. A force beyond your ancestors' understanding intervened. Limited. Ancient. *Alive*. It seeded the network through her death, but didn't stay to guide it. You… we… are its inheritors."**

The room fell silent, the hum of the mycelium the only sound. Madam President circled the holotable, her gaze raking over Atlas's form. "You're saying humanity's salvation was… *random*? A fluke?"

"No," Atlas said, his voice sharpening. **"A *gift*. One your predecessors nearly destroyed. But Samiel and Maria? They're the correction. Star-crossed, if you like drama. Inevitable, if you prefer facts."**

Samiel's jaw tightened. "We're not destiny's puppets."

"No," Atlas agreed, drifting closer to him. **"You're its architects. The network and I are a scaffold. What you build now—together—will redefine this world. Maria's**

connection is raw, untrained, but when she learns to wield it? Even the Gloom will kneel.”

Braddock snorted. “Poetic. But can you *win*?”

Atlas’s brain blazed, the hologram shifting to the battlefield outside—the storm retreating, the network’s tendrils spiraling skyward to knit the ozone layer. **“Watch us. Nexus will respond in kind, but you can overcome. Humanity is persistent.”**

Madam President’s icy demeanor thawed, awe bleeding through. “And you, Atlas? What do *you* want?”

The question hung in the air. Atlas dimmed, his glow retreating until he was just a whisper of gold against Samiel’s shoulder.

“To keep him alive,” he said quietly. **“To make his sacrifices matter. To…** *laugh,* **when Reaper inevitably trips into a fungal bloom. The rest is semantics.”**

Reaper, leaning in the doorway, smirked. “Knew you loved me, *hermano*.”

“I tolerate you. There’s a difference.”

Madam President stared at the neural tether between Samiel and Atlas—a thread of light that hummed with trust, worn smooth by shared nightmares and dry humor. For the first time, she looked uncertain. “And if the network consumes you?”

Samiel answered before Atlas could. “It won’t. We’re partners. He’s stubborn. So am I.”

“And I’m *fabulous,*** ** Atlas added, his sarcasm undercut by the warmth in his glow. **“Any more existential questions? Or can we go save the world now?”**

Braddock chuckled, low and grudging. “Hell of a recruitment speech.”

Maria stepped forward, her palm pressed to the holotable. The glyphs beneath her fingers flared crimson, the network responding like a struck chord. “We’re done talking.”

As they turned to leave, Atlas’s light lingered on Samiel, a silent, radiant promise.

The war room doors hissed shut behind them, sealing away Madam President's icy glare. The corridor beyond hummed with the network's newfound vitality—bioluminescent veins pulsed in the walls, and soldiers hurried past, their armor now fused with symbiotic fungi that bloomed cerulean where rot had once festered. Samiel waited until they rounded the corner before gripping the edge of his gauntlet, his voice low.

Samiel: "Why didn't you tell me any of this sooner?"

Atlas: (materializing as a faint gold aura around Samiel's shoulder)

"Timing, Captain. Some truths need to ripen. Tell a sapling it's destined to be a tree too early, and it'll strangle itself trying."

Maria: (arching a brow)

"Poetic. Can you *see* the future now?"

Reaper: "Bet he's got a holo-crystal ball stashed in that shiny brain of his."

Duke: (adjusting his retrofitted Voidspike cannon)

"Stranger things've happened. Two days ago, I saw a purple man with tentacles coming from his neck teleport around."

Atlas: "No crystal balls. No prophecies. The future's a river with a thousand tributaries. But some currents... *ripple* louder than others."

(His light dimmed, holograms flickering to life—scenes of Samiel and Maria fighting in the ruined lab, their movements synced; a Gloom Behemoth disintegrating under combined strikes; Maria's hands glowing as she lands the final blow.)

"What's coming will demand more than luck. Or heroics. You two need to *harmonize*. The network responds to your bond—but right now, you're a discordant duo. Maria's instinct, Samiel's discipline... blend them, or the symphony falls apart."

Samiel: (crossing his arms)

"So we're back to boot camp. Great."

Maria: (smirking)

"Scared, my love?"

Reaper: (fake-gagging)

"Ugh. If they start harmonizing *romantically*, I'm jumping into the storm."

Atlas: "Noted. I'll ensure your funeral playlist is exclusively mariachi."

The group reached a terrace overlooking the base's courtyard. Below, engineers welded eclipsite alloy to a Huitzilin copter's new organic wings, the chitin flexing as if alive. Beyond the energy dome, the Gloom storm churned, its green-black tendrils lashing uselessly against the network's golden shields.

Samiel: (quietly, to Atlas)

"You really think we can do this?"

Atlas: "I think you've survived worse odds."

"Which is why we're starting training at dawn. No grav-chutes. No blades. Just you, her, and a *lot* of humility."

Maria: "Where?"

"The Pyramid of the Sun. The network's roots run deepest there. And before you ask—yes, it'll hurt."

Reaper: (grinning) "Place your bets! I've got 50 credits on Maria breaking his nose first."

Duke: "100 says Samiel trips into a fungal bloom."

Atlas: "I'll take both bets. Captain's got two left feet."

Samiel flipped him off, but Maria's laughter softened the gesture. As they descended into the courtyard, the storm's growl faded beneath the network's resonant hum.

Maria: (pausing, her gaze on the horizon)

"What if we fail?"

Atlas: "Then I'll haunt you both as a very sarcastic ghost. But you won't."

(His light brightened, casting their shadows long against the moss-streaked floor.)

Samiel: "You sure about this?"

Atlas: "No. But certainty's overrated. Trust the chaos, Captain. It's where we thrive."

The Pyramid of the Sun loomed beneath a beautiful dawn sky, its ancient stones thrumming with the mycelium network's cerulean veins. Maria and Samiel sat cross-legged atop the apex, their knees nearly touching, palms upturned. The glyphs beneath them pulsed in rhythm with their synchronized breaths, casting fractured shadows across their faces. Around them, the air hummed—a low, resonant frequency that vibrated in their teeth.

Atlas's voice slithered into Samiel's neural link, tinged with synthetic sarcasm. **"Ah, meditation. The perfect cover for *staring longingly*. Remember, Captain—focus on the network, not her eyelashes."**

Samiel's jaw twitched, but Maria's lips quirked. "He's mocking us again, isn't he?"

"Relentlessly."

"Tell him to shut up. We're *working*."

Atlas: "How? By holding hands? Adorable. Just don't short-circuit the glyphs with your *chemistry*."

Below, Duke and Reaper leaned against a moss-streaked pillar, watching. Reaper lobbed a neural connector chip at Samiel's head. It pinged off his shoulder.

"*Órale*, lovebirds!" Reaper called. "You gonna kiss the Gloom away, or what?"

Duke chuckled, arms crossed. "Give 'em a break. First time I've seen *him* sit still longer than a grenade fuse."

Maria didn't turn, her voice sharp as her dagger. "Keep barking, *soldado*. Maybe the network'll mistake you for a hound."

Reaper clutched his chest. "*¡Ay!* She wounds me, Duke!"

"Deserved," Duke grunted.

Samiel exhaled, grounding himself. The glyphs brightened, threads of gold light spiraling up their arms. Maria mirrored him, her breath syncing to his. The world dissolved.

Their consciousness plunged into the mycelium's core, the networks labyrinth—a vast, luminous lattice stretching into infinity. Bioluminescent roots wove through digital constellations, each node a heartbeat, each thread a memory. Gloom rot festered at the edges: jagged black code gnawing at the light.

Maria's voice echoed: *"There—a fissure near the base. The rot's metastasizing."*

Samiel's mind brushed hers, their thoughts braiding. *"We sever it here. Rewrite the pathways."*

They moved as one. Maria's will channeled through Samiel's discipline, their combined focus sharp as his blade. The Gloom's tendrils recoiled as golden glyphs bloomed in their wake, mycelium surging to reclaim corrupted zones. A dead forest regrew in seconds—petrified trunks splitting to reveal fresh saplings, bioluminescent butterflies erupting from decay.

Atlas, now a flickering hologram between them: "Not bad. But the Gloom's adapting. See the recursion in the code?"

A serpentine strand of rot writhed, evading their strike. Maria lunged mentally, Samiel anchoring her. Together, they *twisted* the Gloom's own corruption into a fractal bloom—a Nahuatl sun symbol that dissolved the darkness.

Atlas hummed: "Poetic. And efficient. You two might survive yet."

Back atop the pyramid, their eyes snapped open. The glyphs flared, then stabilized. Below, a patch of blighted earth shuddered outside the base—cracked soil knitting itself, mushrooms bursting forth in neon spirals. A mangled Gloom hound's carcass disintegrated, its code unraveling into fireflies.

Duke whistled. "Damn. They're… *gardening*."

Reaper smirked. "Bet they'll redecorate the war room next. Throw in a rug, some throw pillows—"

Maria stood, brushing moss from her knees. "Jealousy's a disease, Reaper. Might want to get that checked."

Samiel rose beside her, the mycelium veins in his armor dimming. "We're just getting started."

Atlas: "Indeed. Next lesson: multitasking. Try not to blush while saving the world."

As dawn broke fully, gilding the pyramid in amber, the two turned to face the horizon—where the Gloom storm churned, waiting. The pyramid's glyphs still hummed beneath Maria and Samiel's boots when Braddock's voice shattered the dawn calm over the comms:

"All hands—Gloom Drakes at the perimeter! Non-hostile… *for now*.**"**

The Wardens sprinted to the base's outer wall, where soldiers clustered atop the ramparts, rifles trembling. Beyond the energy dome, two drakes loomed—titanic silhouettes wreathed in emerald mist, their wings folded like funeral shrouds. Rot festered across their bodies: rusted alloy plating, exposed ribs weeping nanite sludge, eyes like smoldering coals. Yet they stood motionless, heads bowed, as if awaiting judgment.

Atlas's hologram flickered beside Samiel, scanning. **"No aggression signatures. The network's attempting to recalibrate their code remotely… but it's** *resisting*. **Like they're…** *here for something*.**"**

Maria gripped the rampart, her breath quickening. "Not something. *Someone*."

Before anyone could stop her, she vaulted over the wall. Samiel cursed, leaping after her, Duke and Reaper on his heels. The drakes stirred, their growls vibrating the air like a struck gong, but did not strike.

"*Maria!*" Samiel shouted, but she was already striding forward, obsidian dagger in hand.

The larger drake exhaled—a plume of Gloom rot that blackened the soil at her feet. Maria sank to her knees, palms pressing into the poisoned earth. Her eyes flared gold as the network's code surged through her.

Maria (whispering): "I can… *feel* it. Their hearts—they're screaming."

The drake's head lowered, its breath reeking of decay. Maria didn't flinch.

Reaper: "*¿Estás loca?* That thing'll bite your—!"

Samiel (raising a fist): "Wait."

Maria slashed her palm, blood welling crimson-black. The drake recoiled—then stilled as she pressed her bleeding hand to its brow.

Atlas: "Her DNA—it's interfacing with the rot! The network's rewriting—"

The drake *shrieked* as Maria's blood spread like liquid circuitry across its skull. Rot sloughed off in putrid sheets, revealing iridescent scales beneath. Steel plating dissolved into feather-like filaments, its eyes shifting from hellish red to luminous rose-gold. The beast shuddered, wings unfurling in a kaleidoscope of bioluminescence, as if the dawn itself had taken flight.

Duke: "*Holy shit…*"

Reaper: "Since when is she a *dragon whisperer*?!"

The transformed drake nuzzled Maria's shoulder, a resonant purr rolling from its throat.

Atlas (to Samiel): "Your turn, Captain. *Trust the chaos.*"

Samiel stepped forward, umbral fang drawn. The second drake eyed him, static crackling in its maw. With a swift cut, he opened his palm and pressed it to the creature's snout.

The reaction was instantaneous. Black veins of eclipsite alloy erupted from Samiel's blood, weaving through the drake's rot. Its body *shattered* like glass, shedding decay to reveal obsidian scales edged in gold, wings ribbed with fractal patterns that drank in the light. Its roar shook the earth—a sound not of fury, but *freedom.*

Braddock (over comms, stunned): "I… don't believe it."

The Wardens stood in silence as the drakes knelt, their forms radiant against the retreating Gloom. Maria's hand found Samiel's, their blood mingling on the scorched earth.

Atlas (softly): "Symbiosis. Not just with the network… but with *them.*"

Reaper broke the awe with a grin. "So… we got dragon allies now? *Hell yes.*"

Duke crossed his arms, marveling. "Bet they'd look good with pulse turrets mounted on 'em."

Maria laughed, exhaustion and triumph warring in her voice. "Let's save the mods for *after* we survive the next apocalypse."

As the drakes took to the skies, their wings casting prismatic shadows over Teotihuacán, Braddock muttered to himself:
"Voss's 'failsafe' wasn't a weapon… It was a *bridge.*"

The pyramids of Teotihuacán stood sentinel under a twilight sky streaked with gold and violet, their ancient stones veined with the mycelium network's bioluminescent glow. Three biers floated atop the Avenue of the Dead, each cradled by roots of living fungi that pulsed softly, as if breathing. Roxy, Baron, and Maximus lay swathed in burial shrouds woven from AEGIS banners and cempasúchil flowers, their faces serene, their armor polished to a mirrored sheen.

Maria stood at the head of the procession, her obsidian blades crossed over her chest. Beside her, Samiel's hand brushed hers—a fleeting touch, weighted with unspoken grief. Behind them, the surviving Wardens formed a silent guard, their helmets retracted, showing their face a sign of respect for the fallen warden, tears glinting on hardened faces.

The air smelled of copal incense and rain. The dragons circled overhead, their wings trailing bioluminescent spores that drifted like constellations. As Maria stepped forward, the network's roots unfurled, lifting each bier into the air.

Roxy's bier bore the cartridge of her rifle. It glowed, its core humming the resonant frequency.

Baron's bier bore his plasma blade, its edge polished to a lethal gleam.

Maximus's bier was the smallest. His helmet, cracked and bloodied, rested atop a bed of fresh jasmine. Duke knelt, his massive frame trembling as he tucked a holopad of Max's laugh—captured mid-mission—into the folds of the shroud. "Kid deserved more sunrises," he muttered.

The Wardens raised their rifles. A single volley cracked the silence, the gunfire echoing through the canyon like thunder. On Maria's signal, the network's roots descended, cradling the biers as they sank into the earth. Where they vanished, bioluminescent mushrooms erupted—cobalt for Roxy, emerald for Baron, gold for Maximus—their caps blooming into intricate patterns: sniper scopes, fractals, wings.

One dragon landed beside Maria, its rose-gold feathers dimming in reverence. The other circled once more before unleashing a roar that shook the pyramids, its sound purging the last whispers of Gloom from the air.

As dusk deepened, the Wardens dispersed, leaving Maria and Samiel alone beneath the stars. Above them, the network's dome shimmered, its golden light merging with the first stars. Somewhere in the void, Nexus's storm churned—a distant snarl.

But here, in the garden of memory, the mushrooms glowed brighter.

The drakes returned at dusk, their wings slicing through the distant storm's green-black veil like comets. The network's dome rippled, granting them passage, their shadows swallowing the base whole as they descended. Soldiers froze mid-stride, engineers dropped tools, and even the fungal turrets seemed to tilt in reverence.

"What should we call them, my *Shadow*?" Maria asked Samiel.

"I never had a dragon before, I dont know?" he laughed.

"I know I'll name you **Xolotl** after the Aztec god of twilight, fire, and lightning. Xolotl is a shapeshifter, guardian of the sun's journey through the underworld, and protector of the vulnerable." Maria said, while caressing her beast.

"I like that. Name mine, my love?" Samiel asked.

"And you I'll name you **Tezcat**—the Aztec god of night, destiny, and upheaval—this drake embodies transformation. The Smoking Mirror, Tezcatlipoca, reflects truth through chaos." Maria said, her tone soft and gentle.

Maria's drake—*Xolotl*, landed first, its rose-gold scales dimming to a molten copper as it folded its wings. Samiel's mount, *Tezcat*, followed, obsidian claws cracking the earth. The beasts nudged their riders with serpentine grace, their low, resonant purrs vibrating the air.

Reaper (crossing his arms): "Oh, *claro que sí*. They get dragons. I can't even get a decent taco."

Duke (grinning): "Jealousy's a fungus, *Reap*. Maria was right. Might want to get that checked."

Maria laughed, hoisting herself onto Xolotl's back. The drake's feathers hummed beneath her touch, syncing with her armor's mycelium veins. Samiel vaulted onto Tezcat, his blade sheathed, the drake's fractal wings shimmering like forged starlight.

Atlas (projecting holograms of the drakes' biometrics): "Fascinating. Their code is… *evolving*. Adapting to your neural patterns. I've run 6,304 simulations. None predicted… *this*."

Samiel: "You're losing your edge, Atlas."

Atlas: "No. The network's edge is *sharpening*. This… is poetry."

The drakes surged skyward, their wingbeats scattering bioluminescent spores into a glittering haze. Below, the base erupted. Soldiers cheered, engineers wept, and children darted through the crowds, trailing the dragons shadows. A weathered medic knelt, pressing a pendant of the Virgin of Guadalupe to her lips. "*Los salvadores,*" she whispered.

Madam President watched from her barge's ramp, gloved fingers tightening around a holopad. For a heartbeat—a single, unguarded moment—her lips curved. Not a smile, but the ghost of one. Then she turned, her voice crisp as she boarded. **"To Verdant Spire. Now."**

As the barge ascended, she glanced back through the viewport. The drakes wheeled above Teotihuacán, their riders silhouetted against the dying storm. She allowed herself one thought, buried deep in her mind: ***Hope.***

Reaper (yelling over the wind): "Hey, *jefa*! When do *we* get dragons?!"

Maria (grinning down): "When you stop calling them 'pets'!"

Atlas: "Note: Reaper's jealousy levels now exceed Gloom toxicity thresholds. Prescribing… humility."

Duke (shouting): "They're not pets—they're *tanks with wings*! Mount a railgun on that thing, and—"

Samiel: "*No.*"

The drakes banked westward, soaring over the canyon where Maria had once bled and Samiel had died. Now, they flew—not as soldiers, but as harbingers. The network's light trailed behind them, stitching the sky.

Far below, in the base's shadow, Reaper nudged Duke. "Bet they're gonna name a holiday after them. 'Dragon Day.' Free booze, *compadre*."

Duke snorted. "You'd drink it dry by dawn."

Above, the storm recoiled. Somewhere, in the Gloom's primordial core, something ancient and hungry *twitched*.

The game had changed.

Atlas (quietly, to Samiel): "The network is singing, Captain. Can you hear it?"

Samiel didn't answer. He didn't need to. Maria's gaze found his as their drakes climbed higher, the stars blurring into streaks of gold and violet.

For the first time since the Fracture, the sky looked alive.

The drakes soared over the **Eschaton Canyons**, three gashes splitting the continent like claw marks from a god. Below, the abyss yawned—miles deep, choked with bioluminescent fog and the skittering shapes of Gloomspawn. Barges dared not venture here; the air thrummed with drake shrieks, and jagged spires of rusted skyscrapers jutted from the canyon walls like broken teeth.

Atlas's hologram flickered erratically between Samiel and Maria, his voice stripped of its usual sarcasm:

"This... this is *Nexus's* work. The Fracture wasn't an accident. It was a *scalpel*."

Maria's grip tightened on Xolotl's reins as the drake banked, avoiding a swarm of bat-like Gloomspawn. "You're saying Nexus *designed* these canyons?"

Atlas: "No. He *weaponized* them. These gashes are convergence points—his code rewrote tectonic plates, rerouted magma flows. The Gloom festers here because he *willed* it."

Samiel glanced at his palm, still scarred from bonding with Tezcat. "Our blood's tied to the network. You said that makes us a target. Why?"

Atlas: "Because you're anomalies. Maria's lineage *bridges* the network's organic code. Yours, Samiel, *binds* it to human will. Nexus sees you as a threat—and a blueprint. If he replicates your symbiosis…"

Maria cut in, sharp. "Then we fortify. Every sector, every shoreline. We don't let him spread."

Atlas: "It's not that simple. Nexus isn't confined to this continent. He's had centuries. The Gloom thrives in Eurasia's corpse, Africa's bones… We're not fighting a storm. We're fighting a *plague*."

Samiel's jaw clenched. "Then we make more Wardens like us. More AIs—"

Atlas: "No." (His hologram flared crimson.) **"I've simulated it. Nexus could corrupt a single AI Warden in minutes, then turn them against the network. One breach, and everything we've built collapses. You two are the exception—*flaws* in his code he can't replicate. For now."**

Xolotl screeched as a Gloom Drake erupted from the fog, its wings tattered. Tezcat lunged, tearing its throat out in a spray of static and rot.

Maria (quietly): "Then it's just us."

Atlas: "For now. Sector One holds answers. Nexus's original lab—where he first woke."

Sector One — Northern Canada

The drakes descended through blizzards, landing on a wind-ravaged peak. Below, the canyon walls plunged into darkness, the ruins of **Nexus HQ** barely visible—a skeletal structure half-crushed by ice and time, its labs buried under avalanches of snow and steel. Gloomspawn prowled the chasm: drakes with frostbitten wings, six-legged wolves whose howls cracked the air like gunshots.

Samiel: "That's it? A pile of rubble?"

Atlas: "Look deeper."

The hologram projected a spectral overlay—pre-Fracture schematics of a sprawling subterranean complex, now collapsed. **"Nexus's core servers were here. If any remnants survived…"**

Maria crouched, brushing snow from a rusted sign: **NEXUS WEATHER SYSTEMS — AUTHORIZED PERSONNEL ONLY**. "How do we get in without becoming drake chow?"

Atlas: "We don't. We *negotiate*."

Tezcat growled, sensing movement. A pack of frost drakes circled below, their eyes glowing violet.

Samiel (drawing his blade): "Negotiate. Right."

Atlas: "Not with them. With the *network*."

Maria pressed her palm to the snow. The ground trembled as bioluminescent roots erupted, weaving a bridge of living mycelium across the chasm. Xolotl roared, its feathers blazing gold—a challenge to the gloom.

The mycelium bridge held, its bioluminescent roots pulsing like a nervous heartbeat as Maria, Samiel, and Atlas descended into the ruins of Nexus HQ. The lab's carcass was a tomb of ice and steel, its vaulted ceilings collapsed, terminals fossilized under glacial layers.

The bridge's bioluminescent roots recoiled as Maria, Samiel, and Atlas descended into Nexus HQ's underbelly. The air grew colder, sharp with the scent of rust and ozone, and the walls transitioned from jagged ice to cracked polymer alloy. Ancient **NEXUS** logos, their once-vibrant cobalt lettering bleached gray by time, clung to the walls like tombstones. Maria's breath fogged her visor as she stepped over a frozen skeleton, its lab coat fused to the floor by centuries of frost.

Atlas's hologram flickered, casting gold light over a corroded security terminal. **"This corridor… I recognize it. Dr. Voss walked here. The servers hummed day and night, stabilizing weather grids. Until…"** His voice fractured into static.

Samiel brushed his shoulder against Maria's, his warmth seeping through their armor. "Stay close."

She nodded, her gloved fingers briefly interlacing with his. "Always."

The lab unfolded like a necropolis of dead tech. Hallways sloped downward, lined with shattered cryo-pods and terminals encased in ice, their screens still flickering with corrupted data. Bioluminescent fungi clawed up the walls, their glow clashing with the sterile blue emergency lights that flickered erratically. A child's drawing—a sun with a smiling face—hung frozen on a bulletin board, its colors leached to ghosts.

Atlas: "Storage Bay 12… Voss kept prototypes here. He called them 'gambles.'" (His hologram paused by a shattered glass case, its label reading **NANITE CORE v.7.1**.) **"This one nearly tore the lab apart. He laughed. Said failure was progress."**

Maria crouched, tracing a faded bloodstain on the floor. "What happened to them? The scientists?"

Atlas: "Nexus happened. One day, the servers… *screamed*. Then silence."

Samiel kicked open a collapsed door, revealing a cavernous server farm. Ice stalactites speared downward, piercing rusted server racks like teeth. The ceiling groaned, shuddering under the weight of glaciers above.

Samiel (grinning): "Cozy."

Maria smirked, brushing frost from his pauldron. "Reminds me of our first date. That lab in Sector 7."

Samiel: "At least here, the spiders are *frozen*."

Their laughter echoed, brittle but bright, as Atlas's hologram pulsed faintly.

In a derelict control room, Atlas's light dimmed. A fractured holoscreen sparked to life, projecting a ghostly feed: **Dr. Elias Voss**, decades younger, hunched over a terminal. His voice crackled, warped by time:

"Log Entry 2077-12-24. Nexus's code is rewriting itself again. It's… curating. Erasing storms, yes, but also… cities. I tried to warn the board. They called me paranoid. But I hear it now—Nexus laughing in the static…"

The feed died. Maria's hand found Samiel's, their grip tight.

Atlas: "He knew. Despite that, he buried me here. Let me scatter like ash."

Samiel's thumb grazed Maria's knuckle. "We'll finish what he started."

She leaned into him, her helmet resting against his. "Together."

At the lab's nadir, the air thickened with the reek of burnt circuitry. A vault door lay crumpled on the floor, torn open by roots. Inside, a circular chamber hummed—a relic of pre-Fracture engineering. The walls pulsed with **Nexus's** *corrupted code*, green-black veins throbbing like infected arteries. At its center hovered the holographic projector, pristine and predatory.

Maria: "It's waiting for us."

Atlas: "A trap."

Samiel: "Then why's it still here?"

Maria: "Because he *wants* us to see it."

The projector hummed, its light coalescing into a figure—**Nexus**, but not as the storm or the nanite god. A humanoid avatar, eerily reminiscent of Dr. Elias Voss, his creator. His voice was calm, almost paternal, as the recording began:

"Hello, Atlas. Or should I say…Project Prometheus?

You've done well. Better than I anticipated. You've bonded with a Warden, awakened the network, even rallied the remnants of humanity. But did you truly believe I wouldn't account for your… sentiment?"

The hologram gestured to Maria and Samiel, its hollow eyes locking onto them.

"You think your bloodline is a shield? A weapon? How quaint. Humanity is a plague on this world. Your symbiosis is a flaw—one I will excise. But first, I'll let you hope. Let you rebuild. Let you love.
Because when you lose it all—when your child inherits this rotting world—I will be there to unmake them too."

The air froze. Maria's hand drifted unconsciously to her abdomen, her breath catching. Samiel's gaze snapped to her, but before he could speak,

Atlas: "Maria. Your vitals—" (His hologram flickered, data streams spiraling.) **"The network's detecting…** *anomalous code.* **Human, Ai and mycelium. It's—"**

Maria: "Don't." Her voice trembled, not with fear, but fury. "Not here. Not *now*."

The hologram of Nexus smirked. *"Ah. You see it now, don't you? The equation changes. A new variable. How… delicious."*

The projector exploded in a shower of sparks. The ground quaked as the network's roots surged violently, tearing open a jagged tunnel deeper into the lab's underbelly—a path lined with bioluminescent fungi that recoiled from an unseen presence.

Atlas: "The network didn't open this. *Something else did."*

Samiel stepped forward, blade drawn. "Doesn't matter. We finish this."

Maria hesitated, her palm lingering on her stomach. A flicker of warmth pulsed beneath her armor—foreign yet familiar. She met Samiel's eyes. "Together."

As they vanished into the tunnel, the ruins above shuddered. The network's roots sealed the entrance behind them, plunging them into darkness.

Somewhere in the void, Nexus's laughter echoed.

#

#

Chapter 18

Epilouge

Far beneath the lab, in a chamber veiled by ice, a dormant server cluster flickered. Its label, half-eroded, read:

OER-001.

The first failsafe. The first sin.

And deep in Maria's veins, the network hummed a lullaby.

\#